WHATEVER YOU WANT

S. JONES

Whatever You Want
The Protective Series Book 3
Copyright by S. Jones 2021

Editor: Marla Selkow Esposito
Proofreader: Virginia Tesi Carey

PROLOGUE

The priest recited, "I am the resurrection and the life," as my husband's body was lowered into the ground. I stared straight ahead, as if I were witnessing my life flash slowly before my eyes.

I could hear the cries from my mother-in-law as she sobbed uncontrollably next to me, clinging to a pair of rosary beads as if they could somehow bring her son back from the dead.

For some reason, every little thing was getting to me. I barely even recognized myself. It was as if all the light in the world had faded into the background, and I just wanted to run away to a place where I could escape this insufferable pain.

A week ago, Drew, my college sweetheart, built our daughter a playhouse in our backyard. Now, his dead body was resting in a closed casket surrounded by dirt and overpriced flowers. He hated flowers. He said they were a giant waste of money, but I couldn't tell people not to send them. After all, they were a tradition, an expression of sympathy, but no matter how beautiful they were, they did nothing to comfort me.

My heart pounded in my chest with each passing second. I wasn't ready to say goodbye to him forever. I wasn't ready to let him go. He should be at home, in his recliner, watching a Phillies game on the TV while Madison played on her iPad next to him. Not at this mythical place that the priest was preaching about. He talked about heaven as if he'd been there. How do any of us know what is waiting for us on the other side? We can believe whatever we want, but no one knows what it's like until we get there. And for the first time in my life, I wondered if it even existed because the only thing I felt as I looked around was pure hell.

"Ava." My best friend Amelia's hand landed on my shoulder. "Are you okay?"

No, I was not okay, and I wasn't sure if I would ever be again.

This cemetery was filled with people who loved my husband. Over the past hour, I've listened as his close friends talked about what a great guy he was and told stories that I've heard a dozen times. But this heartbreak hurt so damn much that no words could lessen my pain, no matter how beautiful or humorous. Nothing could bring him back.

Amelia leaned forward and whispered in my ear, "Say something. Let me know that you're okay."

What was I supposed to say? At that moment, I hated the universe and everyone in it. The man I spent the last ten years of my life with was dead, and my daughter would never see her father again. Nothing would ever be the same.

"This is so unfair," I said, feeling a sob unleash from my throat. "He shouldn't be here."

My mother-in-law sensed that I was about ready to lose it and slid Madison onto her lap. Amelia wrapped her arms around me from behind, holding me in place. The emotions I've kept bottled up started to spill out of me. I've tried to stay strong and hold it together, but that dam in my chest holding these feelings back was about to burst.

Pressure! I felt it everywhere, and I was sick of feeling it. I was over it all. I've spent the last five days having people tell me how sorry they were. I was so sick of the hugs, the hovering, the food. I just wanted to go somewhere and suffer in silence. I didn't want to plaster on another fake smile. I didn't want to reassure my family and friends that I was okay.

Something inside me snapped. Everyone turned while I stood on shaky legs, and I did my best to block out the noise. I tried not to think about how messed up this was or how out of control I felt.

"Mommy," Madison cried while my mother-in-law held her against her chest. I moved around the folding chairs and made it to the back, where I tripped on the green outdoor carpet. I blamed it on the damn shoes. I hated the heels. I hated my dress. I hated everything about this day.

A set of muscular arms reached out and grabbed me, stopping my fall.

I looked up, and my gaze locked on a pair of hazel-green eyes. They were the same somber eyes that knocked on my door less than five days ago and told me that my husband was killed in a car crash. I clutched my stomach at the reminder, feeling that pain slice through me all over again.

"Please back up and get out of my way." I wiped at the tears streaming down my face. All I could smell was his scent, and it was wrong. It smelled like soap and sandalwood, not the clean citrus smell I was used to. And his touch wasn't the one I wanted. The only person who could bring me comfort at that moment was lying in a wooden box.

His jaw ticked, and something that I didn't understand flashed in his eyes. Was it pity? Of course it was. Shame washed over me as I frantically looked around the cemetery. I couldn't decide which way to go. All I knew was that I had to get away.

Logan stared down at me as if he wasn't sure how to handle me, and for some strange reason, that only angered me even more. I pushed against his chest with as much strength as I had. "Did you not hear me? You need to get away from me. Can't you see I'm breaking into a million fucking pieces here?"

"Ava, calm down." His voice was soft, but all I could focus on was that storm raging inside me. "Take a deep breath." He stepped closer, trying to calm me down, but that only agitated me even more.

"Don't tell me what to do. You barely know me. Don't act like you care. You're only here because you're friends with Marco," I spat out, feeling completely unhinged. I just needed to get to a place where I could breathe.

Amelia rushed over and pulled me out of his arms. "Ava. I know you're in pain, but it's going to be okay." She held me close, but I could feel myself breaking apart.

That's when I realized I had caused a scene. Everyone watched in stunned silence. Their stares and whispers were a mixture of sympathy and disbelief.

Drew's friend Jeremy lifted Madison in his arms, her little hands wrapped around his neck. Tears flowed relentlessly down my cheeks as I watched him console her. That was my job, so why couldn't I get my feet to move?

"What the hell is wrong with me?" I asked my best friend as if she held all the answers. "Why am I doing this? I don't understand."

I was going from one extreme to another, and all I could do was squeeze my eyes shut and pray that this nightmare would pass.

"Ava, you've suffered an unbearable loss. I think it's finally catching up to you." She squeezed my arm gently. "Let's get you somewhere away from prying eyes where you can process this in peace and quiet."

"Madison." I took a step forward; her cries grew quieter, but she still clung to Jeremy as if her life depended on it. "I can't leave her."

Amelia's hands ran up and down my back. "She's fine," she whispered as her husband, Marco, placed his arm along my shoulder.

"How am I going to do this alone? I don't know how I'm going to live in this world without him." I fell to my knees and begged God to take my pain away, to put me out of my misery. Logan stepped forward. His face was pinched with worry. Marco held his hand out and silently urged his friend to stay back.

My stomach dropped at the realization of what I'd done. "Oh, my God." A sob sprung from my throat.

Amelia and Marco lifted me up by my elbows and guided me over to a parked car. "Let's get you out of here," Marco whispered as Logan held the passenger door open. Amelia's lip trembled as she buckled my seat belt.

Marco whispered something in her ear and kissed the top of her forehead. As soon as the door shut and we pulled away, I felt my muscles relax. I swallowed down the burn in my throat and silently wondered how I was ever going to recover from this.

ONE

AVA

ONE YEAR LATER

"Oh, my God. She is so adorable," I said, smiling down at the little cutie in my arms. Marco sat next to Amelia on her hospital bed, watching me across the room as I buried my face in little Gia's hair. She smelled like heaven. I pulled the little pink blanket back to get a better look at her face. "You are all your daddy, you know that?"

"Hey, she has my eyes," Amelia grumbled, but there was nothing but happiness in her expression.

Marco kissed the top of her head. "Sweetheart, most babies have blue eyes when they're first born."

"Well, obviously some people keep their blue eyes, don't they?" She pointed to her face, and he kissed her again. It was such a tender moment, one that made my heart ache. It reminded me of the type of love I once had. I swallowed down that familiar pain and focused on the little bundle in my arms.

"You've got quite the Italian name for yourself, little girl." I beamed as she let out a yawn.

Gianna Sophia Rubintino was born yesterday, weighing eight pounds and five ounces, and was absolutely perfect. I trailed my fingertips along her chubby pink cheeks. It seemed like two lifetimes ago when Madison was this tiny.

"Giving her Sophia's name was the only way to get Marco's grandmother to talk to us again," Amelia said, pushing a few buttons on her remote so she could raise her bed forward.

A laugh spilled out of me. Marco's grandmother was a hoot. That little old lady said whatever was on her mind, and if you didn't like it, too bad.

"That's what you get for running off and eloping when the groom has a big Italian family." I grinned as little Gia kicked her pudgy pink legs out. "I think someone is hungry." I placed her gently in her mother's arms. Marco's brown eyes shined with adoration as he stared at his wife and daughter. I wondered if I would ever have anyone look at me like that again.

There was a knock at the door, and we all turned our heads, expecting it to be one of Marco's many family members. Instead, my heart clenched when I saw who was standing there.

"Look who's here." Marco smiled. "It's your uncle Logan."

Marco's best friend, Logan Blake, stood in the doorway with his thick arms, short-trimmed black hair, and his famous grin, which slipped from his face when he spotted me. His green T-shirt tightened around his chest as he lowered his hands into the front pockets of his jeans.

"Hey," he said, greeting Marco and Amelia and shifting his eyes over to me. Then he put his head down and started to back away. "I just wanted to come by and drop off a little something for Gia." He held out a little pink gift bag with white tissue paper, and placed it on a chair by the door. His hands moved nervously across his jaw. "But I got a call from the station just before I got here, so I'll have to come back later."

I could just ignore him like I normally did, but I didn't want to do that this time. Logan wasn't fooling anyone, and as Marco's best friend, he had just as much right to be here as I did. Ever since last year and the horrible scene I caused at the cemetery, Logan and I have steered clear of each other. If Marco and Amelia had people over, he would either show up before or after I got there. And on the few rare occasions where we ended up in the same room together, he kept his distance and avoided me at all costs.

I was grieving when I lashed out at him, but it was painfully obvious that we couldn't keep tiptoeing around each other. He was doing Marco a favor by delivering the news to me the day my husband died in a car accident.

"Logan," I called out as he was turning to leave. He stiffened and looked over his shoulder. "Can we go out into the hall and talk for a minute?"

He cleared his throat like he wasn't sure what to do. "Of course."

"I'll be right back." I patted Amelia's leg as Logan followed me out of the room.

I looked for a place that would grant us a little privacy as we walked down the long hallway, but there wasn't a spot to be found. Not with the number of people milling around. "On second thought, do you have time to join me for a cup of coffee in the cafeteria?"

He stopped and stared at me with hesitancy. It was

probably no more than a few seconds, but it seemed like hours before he finally answered, "Sure."

We headed toward the elevators, and for once, I was grateful that they didn't take forever. We moved to the side so doctors and nurses could scatter in before the doors closed. I was standing directly behind Logan when he pulled out his phone. I couldn't help but notice how his arms flexed as he texted away on his keyboard. The man had some serious muscles.

The doors pinged open, and he held his hand out so I could step out first.

"Do you want to grab a table while I get the coffees?" I asked.

He shook his head. "I don't mind waiting in line with you. Besides," he looked around, "it's not too crowded. We shouldn't have any trouble finding a place to sit."

Thankfully, the line moved quickly, and before I knew it, we found a wide-open spot right in the middle of the cafeteria.

I lifted my coffee and blew inside, taking a small sip. "I'm just going to cut to the chase." I set the cup down. "I want to apologize for how I treated you at Drew's funeral. I wasn't myself that day and you were just at the wrong place at the wrong time."

It certainly wasn't my best moment. I wasn't proud of how I behaved, but there wasn't much I could do about it other than own it and apologize.

"You were grieving, Ava. You have nothing to be sorry for."

I ran my hands along the paper cup. "Thank you for saying that, but that's no excuse for my rude behavior. Somehow, in my messed-up head, I associated you with my pain and suffering because you were the one who told me about Drew. I understand now that it was irrational to feel that way." When our eyes locked, something soft flutter in my stomach. "That day at the cemetery, I lost all sense of reality. I just wanted to get the hell out of there, and then you stopped me."

"From falling, but apparently not from running."

I ducked my head to the side, avoiding his gaze. "You're right. I'm sorry."

"Will you please stop apologizing." He gripped the back of his neck. "I've dealt with a lot of fatalities over the years and have knocked on many doors. Everyone handles grief differently. I'm just glad to see you're in a better place."

I picked at my white napkin, feeling more nervous than I wanted to admit. "It's been a long year."

I still missed Drew, and in a way, I always would, but I couldn't keep living in the past. The grief was eating me alive, and if I wanted to survive, I needed to keep moving forward, regardless of how difficult it was. I had a young daughter who needed me.

"I'm sure it hasn't been easy, but you've come a long way; I hope you realize that."

"Thank you." I swallowed, feeling awkward under his praise. "I do know that, and I'm fine now."

I gave him the same rehearsed widow response I've given everyone else.

He didn't look like he believed me. I forgot that this man interrogated people for a living.

"Okay." I held my hands up. "I'm not a complete mess like I was in the beginning. How's that?"

He smirked. "Better."

I liked that he wasn't treating me with kid gloves. That he wasn't being cautious with his words, even though he should have after the way I've behaved. He watched me intently, and I had to admit, it was nice not having to act like I had my shit together. Just sitting back and relaxing without any expectations or worrying about putting on a show was a welcome change, even if his smile was a bit disarming.

"So, how have you been? I'm sure your life has been more exciting than mine."

"I've been all right. Nothing to write home about."

"Yeah, right. If only I could get out half as much as you do," I said, adding a healthy dose of sarcasm. "Going to the bars every weekend and fighting off all those attractive women must be hard." I rolled my eyes, catching sight of those dimples.

He leaned forward, keeping his gaze fixed on mine. "The guy who used to be my wingman is sitting upstairs in the maternity ward holding his newborn daughter. In fact, all my friends seem to be settling down. Despite what you think, I don't get out as much as I used to."

"I didn't mean…" I shook my head. "I'm sorry," I said, wishing I had a shot of whiskey in front of me instead of a cup of coffee.

"Ava." He laughed and shook his head. "You did mean to say that, so don't apologize. Admit it, you just can't help yourself. You love to bust my balls. And lucky for you, I've got some pretty big balls to bust."

"And a pretty big ego too." I snorted because I couldn't help it. There was something about Logan that I found endearing. I couldn't put my finger on it, but he had a way of making me feel comfortable. He was easygoing, and I couldn't for the life of me, understand how this man was still single.

"Maybe you could be my new wingman," he said with a teasing grin.

"I don't think so."

Going to bars and helping him score dates, no thank you. For some reason, that thought left a sour taste in my mouth.

"You don't know what you're missing." His eyes sparkled, and I squirmed in my seat at the attention he was giving me.

"You just told me you don't go out that much anymore."

"For you I'd make an exception."

Such a flirt.

"Maybe we could settle on being friends," I suggested while playing with the little black straw in my cup like it was the most fascinating thing in the world.

He angled his head to the side. "Does that mean I don't have to hide from you anymore whenever I walk into a room?"

I groaned. "I'm so ashamed."

He chuckled lightly. "You should be. You haven't been very nice to me."

"Now, who can't help themself?" I smiled playfully. Then it hit me. This was the first genuine smile I've felt in a long time.

I felt oddly comfortable in a way I probably didn't want to look at too closely. Maybe starting over wouldn't be so bad after all.

TWO

AVA

MY DAUGHTER LOOKED TWO SECONDS AWAY FROM THROWING a fit.

"Where am I supposed to sit?" She folded her arms, looking around the church. I knew it wouldn't always be like this, but she could be a handful, even at age eight.

I glanced around to make sure no one was staring at us. "Emery will be here soon. You can sit with her family once they get here."

"They're not here yet and I don't want to sit alone."

"Madison, you can sit at the end of the pew and wait for them, or you can find someone to sit with. Those are your two options."

I tried hard not to raise my voice, but this little girl could trigger my nerves with just one look. It was almost impossible to reason with her when she was like this.

"I'm not sitting by myself," she whined, and I closed my eyes and counted to ten. The one thing she inherited from her father was his stubbornness. Of all the good qualities that could have been passed down to her, she had to have the one that drove me insane.

"It will only be for a few minutes, so you can suck it up." My words came out more harshly than I intended them to, but my sharp tone didn't even faze her. I don't ever remember giving my mother a hard time like this, and if I did, I owed her a big apology.

When Amelia asked me to be Gia's godmother, I never imagined finding my daughter a place to sit during the baptism would turn into such an ordeal. I thought I had it covered when I arranged for my mom to come, but she called this morning and said she wasn't feeling well. So, there went that plan.

"Can't you stay with me until they get here?"

My frustration was growing by the second, but then again, it didn't take much with her. "I already explained to you that I have to sit up front."

She glowered at me. "Then I want to go home."

I took a steadying breath and was about to respond when Logan and his daughter walked up. His eyes squinted in concern when he noticed my frown.

"Hey," I said, trying to smile through my frustration. I was usually pretty good at hiding my emotions, but having my eight-year-old act out in a church full of people, sent whatever patience I had left flying out the stained-glass windows.

He slipped his hands in the front pockets of his dress pants and tilted his head to the side. "Everything okay?"

I've seen Logan in a suit a few times, but there was something different about how he looked today. His dark brown hair was short like it was recently trimmed. I owned a salon, so I knew these things. His jaw was clean-shaven, and I was trying to decide if I liked him better with or without the scruff. If I were being honest with myself, Logan Blake was one fine-looking man. But it wasn't just his looks that pulled me in, he was charming and fun, and there was so much more to him than just his appearance.

I shook my head, reminding myself I needed to focus on settling my little "pew problem."

"Yes, someone is just having a little meltdown over seating arrangements." I smiled at his daughter, whom I've met a couple of times. She was a mini female version of her father. From her assessing eyes, thick dark hair, and crooked little smile. "Hi, Brina. Don't you look pretty today."

"Thanks, my dad took me to the nail shop and let me get my nails painted." She held out her hand for me to inspect. I grinned, noticing each fingernail painted a different color. She was absolutely adorable.

"I love all those colors, and I love your dress too." She was wearing a long pink and white sundress, and her hair was pulled back in a tight ponytail. It looked like her father had styled it in a rush, and my heart melted a little bit at the thought.

Madison lifted her dress and held out her foot. She turned so Brina could see the hair that I spent an hour on this morning. "I got new sparkly shoes and my mom did my hair in a fishnet braid at her salon today."

"So, what's the issue with seating arrangements?" Logan asked, stepping to the side so someone could pass by.

My daughter glared at me and shifted her gaze to him. "My mom has to sit up front and she wants me to sit alone with a stranger." Apparently, her attitude was back, and it was embarrassing. I dropped my hands to the side and silently prayed that they would serve actual wine during communion and not grape juice.

"She was supposed to sit with my mom, but she's sick," I tried to explain as if that would be a good enough answer to why she was acting out.

Logan ran a hand through his hair to smooth it out. I tried to ignore the flip in my belly, but that was a bit of a challenge. He was too easy on the eyes. "She's welcome to sit with us, right, Brina?" He gave her shoulder a gentle squeeze. She looked from her dad to me and back again.

"Can I, Mom? Please," Madison practically begged while pulling on my skirt. I grabbed her hand and gave her a warning look.

Logan crouched down and met Madison at eye level. "You are more than welcome to hang out with us. I can bring you back to your mom when the service is over."

"Are you sure you don't mind?" I asked, hoping that he didn't feel put on the spot. His grin stretched wide, and I felt my pulse kick up a notch.

"I wouldn't have offered if I did. I have a daughter of my own, so I know what I'm dealing with." He winked and turned the girls around so he could guide them to their seats. If I thought he looked good from the front, that was nothing compared to his back.

———

I set my coffee on the table and rushed over to help Marco's brother, who was carrying a large cooler filled with ice through the backyard.

"Thanks," Matteo said as I grabbed the handle on the other end. We walked it over and set it down on the grass under the white party tent. Marco had a large Italian family, so there was no such thing as a small gathering.

I lifted my hand to shield the sun from my eyes and

searched for Madison. She was sitting on a blanket, making friendship bracelets with Brina and a few other girls. Logan walked over and reached for a beer in the cooler. He brushed the ice off and popped it open.

"It's a hot one today, huh?" I noticed he stopped home and changed. His worn black T-shirt stretched tight across his broad chest, and every time he brought the can to his lips, the sleeves would strain against his biceps.

I looked away and closed my eyes, letting the sunshine warm my face. "I love it hot and humid."

He chuckled and tipped his chin to the sky. "I don't mind the warm weather, I'm just not a big fan of the humidity."

I studied him out of the corner of my eye. The strong lines around his face made him look even more handsome. He lifted his hand and wiped a bead of sweat off his right eyebrow.

"How did you get that scar?" I asked, pointing to the white faded mark in between his temple and his forehead.

"Got hit with a metal swing when I was younger."

"Ouch."

He laughed and took a huge sip of his beer. "Yep. My brother and I were at the playground. We were trying to wrap the swings around the top of the poll. The sucker came back and almost took out my right eye."

"Your mom must have freaked." I shivered at the thought.

He turned, and I noticed that his green eyes had a hint of blue to them. "She wasn't too happy with me. Unfortunately, it was the first of many cuts and broken bones throughout my youth."

"It's boys like you that make me glad I had a girl."

He smirked. "In case you haven't noticed, I haven't been a boy in a long time."

I bent over to retrieve a bottle of water. "Sounds like you're fishing for compliments," I teased.

"If you've got the hook, I've got the bait."

A splatter of water flew from my mouth. I was still smiling while wiping the water off my chin. "That was so bad."

"I've been known to drop a line or two."

I shook my head, trying to erase the grin on my face. "You better be careful there, Detective. Sometimes those lines can sink."

"Is that right?" His eyebrows raised in a challenge. He was about ready to drop another fishing pun when Marco's grandmother came strolling over.

"Logan Blake, I thought that was your handsome face." He leaned down and kissed Sophia on both cheeks.

"It's so good to see you. How are you, Sophia?"

"I'd be better if you stopped by and visited me once in a while."

Marco's grandmother lived in an independent living facility and always complained that she didn't get enough visitors. I got the impression that she was lonely but was too stubborn to admit it.

"I was just there with Marco a couple of weeks ago," he pointed out and took a sip of his beer.

"Yes, but my young nurse has been asking about you."

He arched an eyebrow. "Really, which one?"

"Kristina, the one that was there when you and Marco brought me that cheesecake from Stock's Bakery. And stop acting like you don't give all those young girls something to look at."

"Sophia." His eyes darted around the backyard, and

he lowered his voice. "Keep the cheesecake on the down low. That was supposed to be just between the three of us, remember? If your daughter finds out we've been sneaking you sweets, that will be the end of my leftovers. And I'm a bachelor who doesn't know how to cook. I'll have to live on fast food for the rest of my life. Capiche?"

I knew Logan was a player, and flirting came easy to him. He was in his element, and it was strangely comforting and relaxing listening to their banter, despite the mention of the young nurse.

She patted his arm gently. "Maybe it's time you found yourself a nice girl to settle down with. One that knows how to cook."

Her eyes darted to mine, but I quickly looked away. Sophia was also a meddling matchmaker. When she set her mind to something, there was no stopping her.

Logan grinned down at her while rubbing a hand over his jaw. "Well, gorgeous, anytime you want to run off with me, I'll be waiting. I've heard Italy is beautiful this time of year."

She thumped him on the shoulder. "Your flirting is going to get you in trouble one of these days."

He winked. "It's a good thing I've got you to keep me in line. Speaking of line, I was just explaining to Ava that I'm quite the catch."

I rolled my eyes. "I swear to God, if you tell one more fish joke, I'll string you up myself."

"Come on, Ava. Don't be a spoilsport. Besides, don't you have bigger fish to fry?"

Sophia shook her head. "I think you might want to quit while you're ahead."

He chuckled while I stared down at the ground. I had

to bite down on my bottom lip to hold in my laugh. I seemed to do a lot of that when he was around.

"So, Ava," Sophia said, taking a big sip from her wineglass. She loved a good Chianti. "I have a picture from a magazine I wanted to show you." She patted her short white hair. "I want to go for a new look."

Shit! There was nothing that a hairstylist hated more than hearing those words. Especially from someone like Sophia. She expected things a certain way, and she expected to get her way. While I took pride in what I did, I would never live up to her expectations.

"What are you thinking?" I asked, taking a sip of my water.

She tapped her lip with her finger. "I want something more modern. Maybe grow out my layers. A lot of these young nurses are talking about this technique called, balayage highlights. At least that's what I think it's called. It sounds French, so I wouldn't know." She shrugged.

"You know what?" Logan started to back away. I think I'm going to check on Brina."

I shot him a look that said, *traitor*.

Sophia sat down on a nearby chair and got comfortable. "Logan, before you leave, will you be a doll and refill my glass, please? Now, as I was saying about the color."

"Um…" Logan looked lost and a little scared. "You drank that one a little fast. Are you sure you're ready for another one?"

"Logan," she scolded him. "They don't allow booze at the nursing home, so I'm going to enjoy this good stuff while I can get my hands on it." He started to walk away, but she called out, "And don't be stingy, make sure my glass is filled to the top."

I couldn't help but laugh. There was something about

being around Marco's crazy family that always made me happy. My best friend was one lucky lady. And speaking of the devil, here she was now.

Marco and Amelia made their way through the backyard with matching smiles. Marco's mom rushed over to grab Gia out of his arms, and he quickly pulled Amelia in for a kiss. While I was glad they found each other, my heart felt that familiar longing for a man who was no longer alive.

I pushed a fake smile past my lips. Logan's eyes caught mine from across the yard. It was like there was an invisible magnet preventing either of us from looking away. Then overwhelming guilt hit me. How could I look at another man like that? My heart still belonged to Drew. I had nothing to offer Logan or any man, for that matter. It wouldn't be fair to start something with anyone while I was still in love with my husband. Because in my heart of hearts, I was still married. In fact, I don't know if I would ever be able to move on. And Logan didn't seem like the type to just sit and wait around for me to put my life back together.

The bigger question was, did I want him to?

THREE
LOGAN

"WHAT'S WITH THE FACE?" MY FRIEND QUINN WALKED UP, adjusting the bill of his ball cap. Quinn was a fellow officer and a mutual friend. We used to work the same shift and hung out often until he settled down. Something all my friends seemed to be doing lately.

"Just thinking about how different this scene is from the Friday night poker games and beer pong competitions Marco would throw in this backyard," I said just as his daughter Emery walked up to grab a drink out of the cooler.

"Uh..." Quinn closed the lid and pointed to the other cooler. "Kid drinks are in that one," he said, guiding her to the white cooler that was labeled "juice." Emery rolled her eyes and grabbed a couple of Capri Suns while I silently chuckled.

"In a few more years you're going to have to keep your liquor cabinet locked up." I flipped the lid on the cooler, dug through the ice, grabbed a couple of beers, and handed him one.

"Don't remind me." He tipped the beer to his lips and pointed it at me. "And you won't be too far behind me."

"Are you kidding me? My daughter is an angel." I chuckled.

He perched himself in one of the folding chairs in the shade. "You better hope she takes after you and not her mother."

My laughter stopped because it was true. My ex-wife would never win any popularity contests with my friends. She was high-maintenance on a good day and not very well-liked.

"Let's hope, although I was a little shit when I was younger, so I'm not sure that's much better," I said as Marco's mom walked by.

She smacked me on the arm. "Language, Logan. There are little ears everywhere."

I winced. "Sorry, Marietta." She gave me a look and continued over to the buffet table to fix herself a plate of food. Amelia tried to have the party catered, but Marco's mother would not allow it. Her family came right off the boat from Italy where the rule was; if it wasn't homemade, it would not get eaten. And Marco might have been a married adult, but he was still a momma's boy. It was a good thing that Amelia and Marietta got along so well. Otherwise, my friend would be in a tough spot.

Quinn leaned forward with his elbows on his knees. My eyes followed Ava as she carried her plate over to the trash can.

"Do you see something you like?" The corner of Quinn's mouth twitched.

I gave my head a slight shake and pretended to pay attention to the kids who were throwing a frisbee across the yard. "I'm going to pretend you didn't ask me that."

A slow smile spread across his face. "I see you're not denying it."

"Is there a reason why you feel the need to call me out?"

"I'm just wondering if you're ever going to pull your head out of your ass and make a move." I tossed him a glare, which only made him laugh. "I saw Ava's daughter sitting with you and Brina at church."

I pulled my aviators down over my eyes even though we were in the shade. "I was just helping her out. Madison needed a place to sit."

"I didn't realize you two had become so friendly."

I rubbed the back of my neck. It suddenly felt itchy. "I wouldn't exactly call us friends, but she doesn't hate me like she used to."

"I guess that's a step in the right direction." He eyed me carefully.

"Quinn, just because she's single now, that doesn't mean she's available."

At least that's what I convinced myself. I usually played off my attraction to Ava like it was no big deal, but lately, these feelings were getting harder to ignore.

Marco strolled over, and I clapped him on the shoulder. He was holding Gia, something he'd been doing a lot. He adjusted her little white hat to keep the sun out of her eyes. "You guys doing good?" he asked, settling Gia on his chest and gently patting her back as his niece and nephew rushed through the yard at full speed. I had to jump back to avoid getting hit with a water gun.

"You might want to consider cutting back on those juice boxes and cupcakes you've been putting out on the table."

Marco laughed. "They're kids and they're excited.

Besides, they're going home with my brother tonight, not me."

"Hey." Amelia approached the group, seeming slightly out of breath. She had a diaper bag along her shoulder, a bottle in her one hand, and a can of baby sunscreen in the other. Man, I don't miss those days. "Are you guys enjoying the party?"

I took a sip of my beer and looked around the yard. "You did a nice job putting everything together."

Watching all the young kids run around, and looking over at my friend, there was no question he was a changed man. I was happy for him.

Brina and Madison sprinted across the lawn, over-flowing goodie bags dangled from their fingertips. "Dad." Brina loaded everything into my hands, and I groaned, knowing this junk would end up all over my house. "Can you hold this so I can do the water balloon toss?"

"Sure." I noticed Madison's hands were full. "Want me to hold on to yours too?"

Ava slid over, securing her hair into a ponytail. "You mean you're not going to play?"

"I didn't realize that adults were allowed to partici-pate," I lied, reaching for Madison's party favors. I'd worked a long-ass week and was running on little sleep. The only thing I wanted to do was kick my feet up and enjoy a cold beer.

She bumped my shoulder. "Why should the kids get to have all the fun, right?" She winked at the girls. "So, who wants to be my partner?"

Madison grabbed on to my daughter's arm. "I already promised Brina."

Amelia and Marco took advantage of the distraction and snuck away before they could get guilted into playing.

I was about to suggest Quinn until Emery came up and grabbed on to his forearm.

"Dad, are you ready to play?"

He looked like he would rather have his balls tugged off than play a silly lawn game. For Emery's sake, he'd act like getting splattered with water balloons was the best time ever.

Ava blew a piece of hair out of her eyes and turned her attention to me. "I guess you're the last man standing."

"Are you going to be able to catch it without letting it pop?" I asked, setting the goody bags off to the side. If I were lucky, maybe they'd be gone by the time we were done. My daughter didn't need any more chalk, bubbles, or cheap jump ropes.

She arched an eyebrow. Her playfulness was cute. "Are you going to be able to catch it if I throw it?"

I was just about to respond that I wouldn't mind if we both ended up a little wet when Marco's brother called all the players to the back of the yard. "All right, everybody, find your partner and form two lines."

Once the lines were formed, he instructed us to face each other and take a step back. He blew a whistle, and I picked my balloon out of the bucket and tossed one to Ava nice and gently. She caught it, but her throw was a little low when she threw it back, and it almost landed at my feet.

She shook her head, and we spent the next couple of minutes laughing and tossing the balloon back and forth until it was just us and another couple left. We stood twenty-five feet apart, so this would be a tough one. Our daughters stood off to the side, cheering us on, while the rest of the party guests stood around to see who the winner would be.

Matteo blew the whistle, and Ava threw the balloon a little high. I had to step back to catch it, but thankfully I grabbed it without an issue. I looked to my left, and Marco's cousin completely missed her catch as the balloon splattered on the grass. Ava pumped her fists in the air in victory and ran over to me.

I lifted her up and spun her around. Her legs wrapped around my waist, and my hands went to the middle of her back. The hair at the end of her ponytail tickled my fingertips. I inhaled the scent of whatever lotion was on her skin. She fit perfectly in my arms like they were always meant to hold her. She reached forward and grazed the side of my temple with her palm. It was taking everything in me not to lean into her touch. Our faces were inches apart, and I wondered what she would do if I kissed her?

The sound of the people cheering off to the side was drowned out by the thickening current flowing between us. I didn't understand how I could be so calm with the way my heart felt like it was going to beat out of my chest.

But just as quickly as that moment came, it ended. Ava cleared her throat and slid back down to the ground. My hands fell to the side when she took a step away from me.

"Great job, champ." My voice was steady despite how nervous I felt.

Her shoulders relaxed now that there was some distance between us. "Thanks. We make a great team."

She walked briskly over to Amelia. Marco stood at her side, giving me a funny look.

I ran a hand through my hair and slipped my shades over my eyes. I was fucked.

FOUR

AVA

"WHAT HAPPENED TO YOUR WRIST?" I ASKED, EVEN THOUGH I already had a pretty good idea. I looked around the house, searching for any sign of that sorry excuse she called a husband.

My mother met Richard when I was in third grade. She worked for his family as their housekeeper until his first wife died of breast cancer. When I was a senior in high school, he moved us from the guesthouse to the main house. Five months later, she married him—something to this day I still didn't understand.

She sat back in her chair and placed her hand in her lap. "I slipped in the bathroom. It looks worse than it feels."

Based on the blue and purple bruising on her skin, I highly doubted that.

I took a deep breath and tried to keep my tone gentle. "Mom, are you ever going to leave him? I don't understand why you continue to put up with this."

Tears filled her eyes. "Honey, when you're older like me, you don't have a lot of options."

"Is that what he's filling your head with?" I looked at her in disbelief. "You can't possibly believe that."

My mother was in her mid-fifties, but she still took great care of herself. She walked three miles every day and ate a healthy diet. Sure, she had laugh lines, wrinkles, and a few gray hairs, but she was still beautiful, both inside and out. She would have no trouble finding someone if she decided to put herself out there again.

"I don't expect you to understand." Her eyes stayed glued to the floor as she spoke. "Just trust that I know what's best for my marriage."

"What about what's best for you?"

I wanted to reach across the table and shake her by the shoulders. Get her to stop believing his lies. Scream at her until she listened to me, but nothing I said would ever make a difference. She would always defend Richard and make excuses for his behavior, and I hated him even more for the tension he caused between us.

"Ava." She sighed. "You need to drop it, okay? I know you don't approve, and you mean well, but this isn't help-ing." My fingernails dug into the table. Sometimes, talking to her was like waiting for a ship to sail into an airport. No matter how many different ways I tried, I couldn't seem to get through to her. "Let's talk about something else, shall we? How was the baptism?"

It was clear that she was done with this discussion.

"The baptism was nice." I looked out the front window and almost fell from my chair when I noticed Richard's tall, looming frame staring daggers at me. Unease traveled up my spine. How long had he been standing there for? Did he hear us talking?

Of course he did.

I stiffened when I heard his heavy steps descend

through the doorway. He strode into the kitchen and drew to a stop. His stance was intimidating, and I held my breath, waiting to see if he would call me out.

"Ava," he said coldly. "I didn't realize you were stopping by today."

"I wanted to check on my mother," I told him, trying and failing to keep the bite out of my tone. "I heard she slipped and fell in the bathroom."

Her eyes widened with fear, and I already regretted provoking him.

A muscle ticked in his jaw. "Yes, that was unfortunate."

"You're home early." My mother quickly stood up and headed to the stove to check the chicken and biscuits. Even bruised up, she was in a Chanel sundress with high-heeled sandals. I'm not even sure she owned a pair of jeans anymore. Richard would never allow her to dress casually.

"Will you and Madison be staying for dinner?" he asked, glancing into the other room where Madison was watching something on TV. Her body was bent forward in concentration while she snacked on a bag of pretzels.

"Sorry, we have plans."

The truth was, I didn't want my daughter anywhere near him. I was ready to get the hell out of here.

His eyes narrowed. "You know, you really should try to spend more time with your mother." He spoke the words calmly, but I sensed his irritation. "It would be nice if you didn't just use her as a babysitter all the time."

While he's never been physical with me, I didn't trust him. Drew never liked him, and we both always made a point of visiting my mom when he wasn't home. If she watched Madison, it was always at my house. An arrangement she understood, but apparently, he didn't. Now I was kicking myself for bringing my daughter here today. Never again.

"I don't think you need to worry about how much time I spend with my mother. Our relationship is just fine."

"Ava," my mother began.

"Don't." He shot my mother a warning glance, and she just looked down at the floor. He glared at me with annoyance. "I'll excuse your rudeness this time, but please remember whose house this is."

"And I'd like you to remember that I'm not an idiot. Touch my mother one more time in anger and it might just be your last."

He pressed his lips into a tight line. "I don't know what you're talking about, but I don't appreciate the threat or your tone, young lady."

"And I don't appreciate you using my mother as a punching bag either."

I really needed to do something with my sharp tongue. Pissing him off wasn't going to help the situation. If anything, it would make things worse for her—something I needed to remind myself of.

"Careful, Ava. You're walking a very thin line here. I've never touched your mother in anger." His face was a mask of controlled fury. "In fact, I've given her a good life. Isn't that right, dear?"

He placed his hands along her shoulder, and she flinched. Sure, he provided for her. She no longer had to scrub toilets or work long, twelve-hour days. Instead, she had to worry about stepping out of line and doing anything that would trigger his temper, especially when he was drinking.

My anger flared, but I kept it under control. I could say more, but I didn't. Nothing would get resolved today, and

I wasn't stupid enough to fire him up more than I already have.

He stepped closer, kissing her on the side of the head. She gave him a tight smile while I sat there with my arms crossed over my chest. Somehow, someway, I would get her away from him.

"I'm going upstairs to take a shower. Make sure my dinner is still hot when I come back down." He turned on his heels and walked up the stairs without another word.

Good riddance.

I rose from my seat to bring my empty glass over to the dishwasher. I checked my phone for the umpteenth time and saw an email from my realtor. I clicked on the message, noticing he had sent three new listings. My shoulders dropped as I scrolled through the first attachment. It was way out of my price range, but I was in love by the time I got to the third one.

"Oh my gosh." My eyes lit up as I clicked on the images to make them larger.

"What's that?" My mom put the spoon down on the stove and looked over my shoulder. "Oh, that's really nice," she commented as I swiped through the photos. This property was exactly what I was looking for. It had a big eat-in kitchen that flowed into an open family room with high ceilings and the prettiest stone fireplace I've ever seen. The bedrooms were all spacious, and the best part, Madison and I would have our own bathrooms.

I immediately texted my realtor and told him I wanted to look at the property ASAP.

"I take it that's your favorite so far?"

I leaned against the counter. "Yeah, and it's not far from where we are now. Madison won't have to change schools."

When I started the search, that was one of my concerns. While I loved the townhouse that Drew and I bought when we first got married, I was ready for a change. Sure, I would miss my neighbors, but Madison and I needed a fresh start. A place where there weren't memories of Drew at every turn.

"That's wonderful. It looks really nice from the pictures."

I grabbed my keys off the table, ready to get out of there before Richard came back downstairs. "Madison, please get your shoes on. It's time to go."

My mom twisted her hands together. "I'm glad you're taking this huge step."

"Thanks." I stared at her wrist, feeling my heart pinch with sadness. "Mom, you know you can always stay with me, right?" I looked over to the stairs to make sure we were alone. "Just say the word and I'll do whatever I can to get you away from him."

She patted the side of my face gently like she used to do when I was a child. "I know you don't agree with my decision, but this is the life I chose for myself."

"Is this the life you would choose for me?" I lowered my voice and looked over my shoulder. "Would you want this life for me and your granddaughter?"

She looked away, unable to meet my eyes. "I would never want this for you or Madison, and I thank God every day that Drew gave you both a good life. My only wish is that you find that again someday. Somebody deserving because you deserve to be loved."

I felt horrible for being so hard on her. I wish there was a way to make her see that she deserved those things too.

"I'm sorry for snapping. I hope I didn't make things

worse for you. Everything I said was out of love and concern."

She pulled me into her arms. The same arms that would comfort me when I was sad and promised to make all my troubles disappear. If only she would allow me to do the same. "You are a good daughter. A little stubborn like me, but I wouldn't have it any other way." She patted my back and released me.

My lips pressed together as I looked her over. "I won't give up on you." I forced myself to take a step back. The thought of leaving her alone with him killed me. She deserved so much better, but she had to participate in her own rescue at some point. I couldn't help her if she wasn't willing to help herself.

"I know, dear. Love you."

I sighed and turned around to collect my daughter. I hated leaving her like this. If only I could convince her to come with me. Maybe someday.

FIVE

LOGAN

"Well, if it isn't my favorite detective," Freddie, the owner of the Second Chance diner, greeted my brother and me as we walked up to the hostess stand.

"Hey." I held my hand out for a shake. "How's it going, dude?" I looked around at the packed restaurant. "Looks like business is doing good."

He shook his head like he couldn't believe it. "Never thought I would see the day, and I owe it all to you."

"Stop. You did this all on your own."

Freddie was a recovering heroin addict who I met years ago. I had just transferred to narcotics and was on one of my first drug raids when I found him unconscious on a dirty floor with a needle sticking out of his arm. I stayed with Freddie at the hospital that night and sat with him until his family arrived. He was young, and something told me he didn't belong in that life. After taking his statement and meeting his mother, I could tell that he was just a good kid who found himself hanging with the wrong crowd.

"You saved my life and I can never repay you for that."

"I just pointed you in the right direction. You're the one who put in all the work."

Freddie used his short stint in prison to turn his life around. It's guys like him who deserve a second chance—hence the name of the diner.

"Let me show you guys to your table."

Luke and I followed Freddie to the back of the restaurant and slid into a small booth. After exchanging small talk, he called one of his servers over to take our order.

"So, how was the baptism?" my brother Luke asked once we were alone.

"It was all right," I said, taking a sip of my coffee and trying to keep my tone casual—no need to tell him how bad I was lusting over a woman that I could never have.

"I'm surprised the church didn't burn down the second you walked in." He smirked while adding a little cream and sugar to his cup.

I laughed. "When is the last time you went into a church?"

The waitress dropped off a few napkins as she passed our table. "I go every Sunday. I started going when I got out of the hospital."

My brows furrowed. "How did I not know that?"

He shrugged his shoulders like it was no big deal. When, in fact, it was huge. "Didn't feel the need to advertise it."

Our waitress came over to take our orders. "I'll have the Denver omelet with a side of wheat toast." I folded the menu while Luke looked over his.

"I'll have the number two and a side of corned beef hash."

I raised my eyebrow. "That's a lot of sodium."

"I just ran four miles, so I think I'm good."

Luke was born with a genetic heart issue and had a heart transplant a little over a year ago. I considered challenging him on that fact, but I knew when to shut my mouth. He was a grown adult, but that didn't stop me from worrying about him. Since his surgery, my family has been extra cautious about what he did and the things he ate. While he was doing great physically, you were never fully cured. It was like trading one medical condition for another.

"All right, big man, how did your date go last night?" I asked, pushing the condiments aside to make room on the table for when my food arrived.

"I've had better."

"What was wrong with her?"

"Well, first of all, she was a little on the young side."

"Define, young?"

"Easy there, Detective." He laughed. "She was legal, just a little immature. She spent most of the date on her phone taking selfies and posting pics of our food."

I chuckled and stretched my legs out under the table. "Maybe you should try dating someone your own age."

"It's not easy trying to find someone when you're over thirty."

I set my coffee down. "You're only two years older than me," I pointed out. My brother was a good man. He wasn't ugly either, thanks to good genetics. He had so much to offer, and I hated when he went out on these bullshit dates. If only he would find the courage and tell his friend Heather how he really felt about her. He's been in love with her for years. And if I were to guess, the feelings were mutual. But he waited too long, and now she's engaged. Every time I would bring the subject up, he would get pissed off, so I stayed silent.

Our server came by and set our plates down in front of us. He took a bite of his bacon. "So, how about you? Have you been swiping lately?"

Slicing off a piece of my omelet with the fork, I brought it to my mouth. "I don't need to go on Tinder to score a date."

"Oh yeah? I haven't heard you bragging about 'doing the nasty' lately. Are you performing solo now?"

I choked on my eggs and took a sip of my coffee. "What the fuck? What are we, fifteen?"

"Tell me again what you've been doing in your free time? Because normally, you don't shut up about your hookups."

Sitting back, I glared at him. "Maybe I'm trying to set a good example for my young daughter."

His eyes mocked me. "Or maybe you're just having one hell of a dry spell."

"You're a dick."

A grin pulled at his mouth. "At least I have one that works now."

When Luke was going through his heart issues, he had to take medicine that had the worst side-effects known to mankind—erectile disfunction. He didn't talk about it much, but then again, why would he? Now that he had his new heart, those medications were no longer needed. It was as if he was making up for the lost time.

"Just be careful where you dip that thing," I said, picking up my fork to swallow a mouthful of eggs. "The last thing you need is to pick up a disease. Who knows what it would do to your new heart?"

"Don't worry, I wrap it up tight." I watched in horror as he poured a mountain of salt over his eggs. "I'm not going to do anything stupid."

"Considering you gave me my first *Playboy* magazine and box of condoms, I'm not sure about that. I still have PTSD from Mom's shriek when she found them under my bed."

A loud, boisterous chuckle rumbled from his chest. "That's what older brothers are for."

"Yeah, some older brother." I held out my coffee cup as the waitress was walking by. Once she refilled it and was out of earshot, I said, "You knew that was a shitty hiding spot. I'm convinced you didn't tell me on purpose."

He grinned. "You were so damned stupid. It was so fucking hysterical though listening to you try to talk your way out of it."

I slumped in my seat. That was hands down one of the most embarrassing moments of my life. I lied and told my parents that it was research for my biology class. I never anticipated my mom calling the school to talk to my teacher, Mrs. Hellmes. I cringed every time that memory popped up of me sitting in the guidance office trying to explain why those magazines and condoms were really under my bed. Kids don't realize how lucky they are to have digital technology today.

"Listen, as much as I'm loving this trip down memory lane, I have a favor to ask you." He took a sip of his orange juice while I eyed him skeptically. I knew before he even asked that I was about to be guilted into doing something that I didn't want to do.

"What's up?" I asked, even though I would pretty much do anything for him.

"Kenzi is having a get-together next weekend. She asked me to bring you."

"No."

"Come on. What's the big deal? You already slept with her."

I pointed my finger at him. "Exactly. It was five months ago, and she's still texting me."

"So?"

"I haven't texted her back. Can you say stage five fucking clinger?"

He laughed. "She's not that bad. Plus, she's hot."

"Then why don't you go out with her?"

"We work together. I don't date people I have to see every day."

Luke was an eleventh-grade history teacher, and Kenzi taught English at the same school. While she was nice and attractive, she wasn't my type. She was too nice, too sweet. There wasn't anything memorable about her. There wasn't a spark or a connection, at least on my end. Sleeping with her all those months ago was a mistake. I was her date for a wedding, and we had a hotel room, so it was kind of expected. What was not expected was for her not to follow the rules when I explained it was a one-time thing. I hated when a woman said they understood and turned around and acted like they were hurt because you didn't want anything serious.

I looked around the restaurant and took a sip of my black coffee. "Sorry, but I'm busy next weekend."

"You're so full of shit. And before you use Brina as an excuse, I know for a fact that she is with Satan next weekend."

My ex-wife wasn't very popular with my family. They only put up with her for Brina's sake.

"I'm not using my daughter as an excuse to get out of seeing a woman I have no desire to see again. Like I said, I'm busy."

The waitress came over to take our plates. As she was scooping them up, Luke bent over and scraped his fork along the dish to get the last bit of hash. "Okay, so what exactly are these big plans of yours?"

I played with the straw in my water glass. "Just a few projects I've been putting off around the house that need to get done."

He stopped licking his fork and stared at me. "Alone?"

"Is there a crime against staying in on a Saturday night?"

"Well, if there was, I would hope you would know."

Leaning back in my seat, I scratched at the stubble on my chin. "Regardless of what you think, I don't need to go out and get laid every weekend."

"Maybe not, but I've known you since birth. I used to change your dirty diapers, remember? You are holding out on me, and something tells me avoiding the cute little English teacher isn't the only reason why you're saying no."

My eyes rolled so far back in my head, I was surprised they didn't get stuck. "You are two years older than me. I find it hard to believe that you would remember that."

A sly grin took over his face. "What can I say, your shit's memorable. Now tell me who you've got your eye on."

I toyed with the napkin on the table. "Do you remember when I told you about Amelia's friend? The one who lost her husband?"

He straightened up in his seat. That got his attention. "The single mother?"

"Yeah." I tried to keep my face free of any reaction. He knew I'd always had a bit of a crush on her. The problem was, the attraction was only growing, and I had no idea what to do about it. It was easier to ignore it when she was married. But now that she was single, there was no way I could put this attraction to her on simmer.

"What about her?"

I picked at the paper napkin, needing to do something with my hands. "I can't stop thinking about her. I thought as time went on that this infatuation I had with her would fade." I blew out a frustrated breath. "It's only gotten worse."

"So, you've got it bad."

"So fucking bad." I lifted my gaze to meet his. "Do you think I'm crazy?"

He pushed his utensils to the side and leaned his elbows on the table. "Of course, I don't think you're crazy. The bigger question is, how does she feel?"

I ran my finger along my bottom lip. "My gut tells me she's not ready to make that jump yet, or maybe not ever. The whole thing sucks because there is this connection between us that can't be ignored. I know she feels it too, I just don't know if she'll ever be over her husband."

"The only way you'll know for sure is if you put it all out there for her to deal with." I thought his advice was a bit ironic given his own silent feelings for Heather, but I kept my comments to myself.

I scratched the back of my neck. "I'm afraid if I pounce too soon, she'll get spooked."

Understanding dawned on his features. "Well, then maybe you could throw some feelers out there. Be subtle without taking it too far. You're the detective; you should be able to tell if you are onto something or not."

I threw my head back and folded my hands behind my neck. If only things were that easy. It didn't matter that there was always something between us that churned below the surface. I would never be anything other than a friend to her. She still wore her rings, which screamed to me that she was physically and emotionally unavailable. She might have been attracted to me, but that pain that filled her eyes was for the man she still loved. I wasn't so sure competing with a ghost would be the best thing for me because there was a chance I'd never come out the winner.

SIX

AVA

"ALL RIGHT, BIRTHDAY GIRL." AMELIA BUMPED MY SHOULDER. "What's it going to be?"

We were at a trendy tavern in downtown Philly, right off of Samson Street. It was known to draw a mostly local crowd but still close enough to all the touristy spots. The drinks were cheap, and the atmosphere was laid-back. It was the perfect place for us to unwind after a long day.

"Hmm." I tapped my chin with my finger, perusing my choices. They had a corkboard with IPAs and specialty drinks. "I can't decide. Surprise me."

Kara, my coworker, took a seat at the bar and pulled out her credit card. "I think we should start out with a round of shots." She turned to the bad boy looking bartender, who looked like he walked right off of a Harley Davidson ad. He was all defined muscles, faded jeans, and sex appeal, which was exactly her type.

He leaned sideways, putting his long tattooed arms on display as he wiped the bar down. He plucked a few cocktail napkins out of the holder and placed them in front of us. "What can I get you, ladies?"

Kara's eyes raked him over. "How about a round of orgasms," she said, her voice all silky and smooth. The girl was unfamiliar with the word subtle.

The corner of his lips lifted in a playful smirk. "Are we still talking about the ones filled with vodka or the ones filled with something else?"

I glanced at Amelia and Charlotte, who were trying to hold in their laughter. Kara was entirely on board with his sexual innuendo, and the last thing she needed was the encouragement to keep it going. There would be no stopping her.

"We'll take the one filled with vodka for now. Maybe we can discuss other options later." She licked her lips while pulling down the neckline of her top.

His eyes dipped to her chest, where it seemed to linger for a minute. "A single round of orgasms coming right up." He winked and turned around, giving us all a view of his backside.

I nudged Kara with my foot, trying to get her attention. She was too busy admiring him as he fixed our drinks. "You couldn't be more obvious if you tried."

She pulled her lipstick out and applied it to her mouth. "That's the point. How's he supposed to know I'm interested if I don't make it known?"

Charlotte stepped forward to get a closer look. "I'm tempted to take a quarter and see if it bounces off that fine ass."

"You have a husband who would cut his dick off if he heard you say that." I elbowed her in the ribs, but she was still watching him as he poured the liquor into the shaker.

"Oh, please. I still have eyes, and I can't ignore what's right in front of me." My mouth hung open in shock at her brazen comment. She saw my expression and rolled her eyes. "Quinn knows the only ass I'm interested in is his, but I can still look." She smiled mischievously and turned her attention back to the bar.

We all stared as he held the shaker with both hands and shook it vigorously over his shoulder; he was putting on quite the show. His tight black T-shirt rode up to his back, revealing the colored ink along the rest of his skin.

Kara took her phone out and snapped a picture as he bent over to retrieve a few glasses. "I'm captioning this, photo of the day."

He looked over his shoulder with a raised brow. "Would you like a front view too?"

"I'm not going to object if you want to lift up your whole shirt." She smirked, not the least bit embarrassed that he overheard us talking about him.

He chuckled while placing the chilled shot glasses in front of us. "So, what are we celebrating tonight, ladies?"

I stood back so he could see the ridiculous pink sash the girls made me wear tonight that said 'BIRTHDAY BABE' in gold letters.

"Well, happy fucking birthday." He grabbed the bottle of Maker's Mark off the top shelf and poured his own shot. He threw it back with ease and grinned. His eyes locked on my lips, and I had no clue what he was thinking, but I didn't want to be the center of his attention. I took a step back as the girls made small talk with a group of men next to us.

We placed our drink order and waited for him to finish up and cash us out.

"Why don't we see if we can find a table." I picked up my glass, searching for a place to sit. The five-inch heels I thought would look cute with my outfit were killing my feet. They were not meant to be worn for more than a few hours.

"You ladies holler if you need anything," the flirty bartender yelled out as we walked away with a freshly poured martini in each of our hands.

The girls and I found a table right smack in the center of all the action. It was the perfect spot to watch all the dumb men make fools of themselves while the women they were trying to impress acted like they were unaffected.

"God, I feel old." Amelia took a sip of her drink. "I'm so glad I'm not single anymore."

A feeling of sadness washed over me. I didn't want to be single forever, but judging by the scene in this bar, dating wasn't as much fun as it used to be. If this was what I had to look forward to, I think I'd rather be alone.

The table went quiet, despite the rowdy group of men next to us. My fingers toyed with the stem of the martini glass. I lifted my head to see my friends staring at me as if they could read my mind. Drew always told me I was transparent, and sucked at hiding my feelings.

"I'm sorry." Amelia placed her hand on my knee, her eyes were filled with concern. "That was insensitive."

"Amelia, it's fine." I ran my fingers through my hair. "Seriously, I'm okay."

"So, Karen and David leave tomorrow, right?" she asked, switching topics. My friends had no idea how on edge I've been lately.

"Yep." I picked up my drink and threw it back in one gulp.

She eyed me warily. "I'm sure dealing with Karen twenty-four seven hasn't helped."

I pushed my empty glass across the table, ready for

another refill. "No, it hasn't. I'd rather have my eyelashes plucked out with chopsticks than endure another week with my mother-in-law. Thank God they're leaving tomorrow, although David's been fine. Karen has, without a doubt, overstayed her welcome."

Their visit was nothing but stressful, and I was sick of screaming into my pillow every night. Amelia had no idea how lucky she was to have a mother-in-law like Marietta.

"I didn't realize you didn't get along." Charlotte frowned.

"It's not usually this bad." I sighed in frustration. "I've tried to be the bigger person and kill Karen with kindness, but my patience is wearing off." I filled them in on how my mother-in-law had spent the entire week telling endless stories about Drew when he was little. "When we weren't talking about my dead husband, she was commenting on my parenting skills and giving me helpful advice on how to raise my daughter." I rolled my eyes and continued. "And poor Madison would stare off into space while bouncing her legs under the dinner table each night. I almost lost it when she went through my photo albums and helped herself to pictures that she felt were hers, but I did finally put my foot down when she tried to tell me how to fold my laundry."

They all stared at me with a mixture of pity and disbelief.

"You know what?" Kara said a little too loudly and stood on shaky legs. "We are switching things up."

She strutted across the bar in a ridiculous pair of high heels. It was entertaining watching her flirt with all the guys lined up to place their drink order. Kara had no problem putting herself out there and drawing attention. I wish I had her confidence.

The bartender squinted at us from across the room when she finally made her way up to the front. The crowd was picking up, but he didn't seem in a hurry to tend to his other customers.

A few minutes later, Kara carefully maneuvered her way through the crowd, balancing a tray of tequila shots.

She set the drinks on the table and passed out the tiny glasses. "On the house, girls."

Amelia groaned while Kara lowered herself into her seat. "The last time I did shots of tequila, I ended up handcuffed to a bedpost."

The entire table erupted in laughter at that memory. I bumped my leg with hers under the table. "Yeah, but you met your husband that night so I think it all worked out for you."

Amelia glared at me while holding the liquid away from her face. She looked like she was debating on drinking it.

"At least your husband will be the one doing the handcuffing tonight," I said with a cheeky smile on my face. Teasing her was one of my favorite things to do.

Charlotte held her glass to her lips. "Maybe I can convince Quinn to do a little role play tonight too."

I looked at both of them and wondered if they realized how lucky they were. I never appreciated what I had until it was gone. I missed the simple moments that I took for granted. Words I'd never hear again and so much wasted time that I'd never get back. God, just when I convinced myself that I had a handle on things, I'd get suckerpunched in the gut with innocent memories out of the blue.

Amelia gave me a puzzled look, as if she could read

my mind. Enough time has passed where things like this shouldn't bother me, but they did.

I brought my shot glass to my lips, knowing I would probably regret this in the morning.

Two hours later, my eyes blinked at all the empty glasses scattered along the table. Whatever troubles I had earlier were long forgotten. I was happy and relaxed. I even got up a few times to dance, something I rarely did. Whenever a nineties song that I recognized would blare from the jukebox, I would grab the girls, and we would twirl, dip, and spin around like idiots. The crowd went nuts when Kara pulled me up on the bar. Jake, our friendly bartender, graciously volunteered to lie flat on the wood counter so we could do body shots off his abs. The man clearly spent a reasonable amount of time at the gym. He was fun, entertaining, and knew how to work for those tips.

I squinted my eyes, watching Amelia lick the rim of her martini glass. "Are you thirsty or are you just practicing something with your tongue?"

"Neither, I'm starving. I want pizza," she whined, "with extra cheese."

"Do you think Uber Eats would deliver here?" Charlotte asked, picking up her phone.

Kara slammed her glass down with a loud thud, causing some of the liquid from our drinks to spill on the table. "Maybe we should just hit a drive thru on the way home."

"Oh my God." Charlotte's voice was a little louder than necessary. "I could kill for some Taco Bell right now."

"Food sounds good to me. I'm going to the bathroom while you guys decide." I stood up to release my bladder when I stumbled back a bit. Thankfully, my friendly bartender was there to catch me.

"Whoa," he said, probably thinking he should have predicted this, considering he was the one who kept the endless supply coming.

"Shit. Sorry," I slurred, trying to walk around him. I was dizzy and a little unsteady on my feet. It's a good thing I wasn't driving tonight. There wasn't a chance in hell I could pass a sobriety test.

Amelia's chair scraped across the floor. "I'll go with you." Her movements weren't much better than mine, but it was better than having tattoo boy help me go to the bathroom. We bypassed the men's restroom, which, of course, had no line, and waited for ours to become available. As soon as we made it inside, I rushed to the open stall and pushed up my skirt while hovering over the toilet. Once I finished, I blew out a sigh of relief and stumbled over to the sink to wash my hands.

Amelia was leaning up against the wall, talking on the phone. "Okay, babe. See you soon."

She hung up as I searched for the paper towels to dry off my hands. "Are you leaving me?" I asked, bending over to pick up my purse that had fallen on the floor. I bumped my head on the vanity on my way up. "Ow." I slung my hand to the back of my head. "Son of a bitch that hurt."

"I'm surprised you can even feel anything at all." She laughed, handing me a clean paper towel.

"Thanks," I mumbled as she slid her phone in the back pocket of her jeans.

"Marco is having Logan drop him off so he can drive my car home."

My entire body froze. There wasn't enough alcohol in

this bar to prepare me to face him right now. I was drunk, and although it was unintentional, he unnerved me. It was like he could see everything inside that I kept hidden. Glancing in the mirror, I smoothed a hand down my shirt. Regardless of how nervous he made me feel, I was smiling like an idiot at the thought of seeing him tonight. He's all I've been able to think about lately.

Cautiously, I grabbed my lip gloss out of my purse and focused on not dropping it. "Come on. Let's go have one more drink before they get here."

I tore my sash off, crumbled it up, and threw it in the trash can.

The hall was dimly lit with dark oak paneling on either side of the wall, making it hard to see. Amelia walked ahead of me while I pulled my phone out to check my messages. I groaned when I noticed my battery was running low.

Tucking my phone into my purse, I turned around, only to bump into a wall of muscle. My head tipped back, and my eyes landed on a pair of familiar hazel green ones.

"How the hell did you get here so quickly?" I blinked, wondering if he was real or if my drunk mind was just conjuring him up as a fantasy.

His Adam's apple bobbed in his throat, and my body tightened in awareness. Being so close, I could see the flecks of gold in his green eyes. His lashes were long, and his jaw was covered with just the right amount of scruff. For a moment, I just stood there and stared, unable to look away.

"We were at the pub across the street." He finally smiled, causing his dimples to pop out of nowhere.

My body swayed to the side; it was a logical answer, I guess. I just couldn't believe they were here already. Logan brought his hand out and wrapped it around my waist. I should have been embarrassed by how heavy my chest moved up and down. You would have thought I just ran five miles with how winded I was.

"Come on, your friends are leaving. I'm going to get you home."

He slid his hand from around my waist but kept his palm at the small of my back. It felt like a flock of butterflies stormed my stomach.

"What do you mean, 'you're getting me home'?" I stumbled to a stop causing my purse to fall off my arm. Logan picked it up and tossed it over his shoulder.

"Marco drove with me, so I have my truck. I'm your designated driver."

Shit! Shit! Shit! This was not good.

He guided me across the room as we weaved our way alongside the tables filled with empty beer pitchers and half-drunken people. Marco and Amelia were already outside, waiting for Quinn to pick up Charlotte, and Kara was waiting for her Uber. I gave everyone a wave after we all said our goodbyes. When Logan reached for my hand, I tried not to read too much into it.

He didn't seem to be in much of a hurry to get me home. I might not have been thinking clearly, but I knew when I leaned into his side and gazed up at him, I didn't want this night to end. His touch felt nice, his smile was captivating, and the faint scent of his cologne floated in the breeze, sending a wave of goose bumps over my skin.

When we turned the corner, a street performer was playing an upbeat song. A small crowd gathered around. People were clapping and cheering and throwing money into his guitar case. I took a ten-dollar bill out of my wallet and tossed it in. Logan chuckled when I decided to join the crowd and move my hips to the live music.

"It's so completely unfair." I laughed, not caring if my dance moves were in sync with the beat or not. It was only a little past midnight, but there were still plenty of people out.

"What's unfair?" His twinkling eyes stared down at me.

"That I feel like I'm floating on air." I tried to spin in a circle to demonstrate my dance moves, but he caught me from completely being out of his reach.

A grin stretched across his face. "You're drunk."

"And you're hot." I stood on my tiptoes and folded my hands along his neck. His body tensed at the contact. There was something about the way he gazed at me that kept me standing there. A voice in my head reminded me that there were a million reasons why I shouldn't do this. But there was a spark lingering between us I couldn't ignore. Even if I could, I didn't want to. I wanted to give in to the undeniable need that coursed through me. I was done putting up barriers to keep us apart. I didn't want to fight this attraction or pretend it wasn't happening.

His chest rose and fell as I inched closer. I was about to cross a line, but I was past caring about the consequences. Logan and I have been skirting around each other for far too long. I wanted him. It was as simple as that. Just being this close to him made my head dizzy, which was fine with me because I didn't want to think. I just wanted to feel.

His eyes held mine, waiting for me to make the first move. I wasn't sure which part of him I wanted to touch first. All I knew was that I wanted to kiss him.

"Ava." His breath hit my ear as I leaned into him. "You don't know what you're doing."

"I know exactly what I'm doing," I assured him, waiting to see how he would react. People were making noise while getting into their cars nearby, but he didn't take his eyes off mine.

I pressed a kiss to his mouth, and he froze. My lips brushed against his, soft and slow. The feel of his faint stubble mixed with his warm, musky scent only heightened my desire.

His hand reached out and flexed on my hip. I sensed him holding back, which was ironic because all I wanted was to feel what those hands were capable of.

It's been too long since I've felt a human touch, and it caused that spark I felt earlier to turn into a flame. And I just knew it was going to change everything.

SEVEN

LOGAN

MY HEART POUNDED IN MY CHEST AT THE FEELING OF OUR LIPS moving together. They were soft and sensitive, coaxing me on as I tried to make sense of what I was feeling. I splayed my hand against her back, bringing her closer to me. I needed to know if this was real. If she was feeling the same shift in the universe that I was. I wanted to take my time and get my fill, do whatever was necessary to keep it going. Block out all common sense and just appreciate that this was finally happening. I've imagined kissing her so many times in my head, and despite how amazing it felt, something wasn't quite right with the way she kissed me.

Warning bells went off in my head. I wanted to shut off all the noise, but my heart was telling me this was a bad idea, especially under these circumstances. This kiss was nothing like I'd hoped it would be. There was no emotion in her kiss, no feeling in her touch. It felt like she was simply scratching an itch, and it sent a wave of disappointment rippling through my chest.

I pulled my mouth away from hers and took a step back, hoping it would clear my head. She was drunk, and the last thing I wanted was for her to wake up tomorrow morning and regret this.

"Logan, I'm so sorry." She averted her gaze away from me. The embarrassment in her eyes was clear. "I shouldn't have attacked you like that."

Was she insane? There was nothing about the way I kissed her that screamed "uninterested." Couldn't she see how crazy I was about her? That I practically had to force myself to stand here when all I wanted to do was pull her back in my arms.

I looked her up and down; my breaths were heavy, and I could still taste her on my lips. She had no reason to be embarrassed. She had no idea how much I wanted her. But I would not allow her to use me just to forget him.

"Ava, you didn't attack me. In case you didn't notice, I kissed you back."

She started to rub her hands up and down her arms. While temperatures had dropped slightly, this was more about nerves than the temperature.

"Where is your car?" she asked, looking around the parking lot. "I'm sure you want to get home."

My gaze narrowed at the switch she just flipped. I didn't like it. I considered calling her out and explaining that she had nothing to be ashamed of. But the tension was growing thicker by the second, and the last thing I wanted was for her to be more uncomfortable.

"My truck is this way." I held out my hand and waited for her to walk alongside me, but she intentionally kept her distance. I plowed my hand through my hair, knowing I'd royally fucked up. Stopping things from going too far was the right thing to do, so why was she making me feel like I did something wrong?

We navigated through the heavy traffic, making our

way out of the city. I felt like such a dumbass. She hadn't said a word since we left the parking lot. I wanted to punch myself for making her uneasy, for allowing my emotions to get the best of me. I glanced over at Ava a few times, noticing she did everything she could to not look at me. The car ride was tense, so I did my best to focus on the road and not on the stifling silence.

When we finally pulled onto her street, I could have sworn I heard her sigh with relief. I steered my truck into her driveway and turned the engine off.

She unclicked her seat belt and quickly glanced in my direction. "Thanks for the lift."

She reached for the handle and was ready to jump out when I leaned forward to grab on to her arm. "Wait, please don't go like this."

"It's fine." She tried to wave me off like it was no big deal. She wasn't fooling me, though. The confident woman who kissed me earlier was gone.

I glanced at her through the dim lighting of the vehicle. "Ava, you're not doing a very good job of convincing me that you're not upset about earlier."

She rested her head back against the seat. "I may be under the influence, but I still feel things. And I'm not sure how to process those thoughts. I miss feeling, Logan." She wiped a tear from her eye. "I miss feeling wanted as a woman. I miss the feeling of a human touch."

"Hey." I reached over and cupped her cheek in my palm, waiting for her to look at me. "I understand why you would feel those things. You're a beautiful woman, Ava. You're young and you have needs. No one would ever judge you for wanting or needing those things."

She swallowed hard, focusing her attention out of the

windshield of my truck. "I don't want your pity or your sympathy."

"How about compassion? Can I tell you how wonderful I think you are without you turning my words against me?" I took her hand in mine and entwined our fingers. "You lost the love of your life. I know you miss him, but it's okay to want to move on. I didn't know Drew very well, but I would guess that he wouldn't want you to feel so alone."

"I don't want to forget him." She sniffed. "I worry that I'm going to forget all these little things. Like the sound of his laugh, his crooked smile, or the way he would rub my back every time he held me. Will I ever get those things again? Will I ever feel that type of connection again?" She peered up at me, and I brushed a piece of hair off her face. I wanted to say something to make her feel better, but really, what the hell was I supposed to say to that? "I don't know what scares me more, falling in love again or never finding it at all."

"You will experience those things when the time is right. One day when you're ready to give your heart away, you'll get all of that and more."

"Do you know how many times I reach for him first thing in the morning. Only to feel his side of the bed empty. I cried myself to sleep for six months straight. I still have his voicemails and text messages on my phone. I can't bring myself to delete them. I hate this, Logan. I hate that I have to live without him. I hate that this can't be fixed."

"Shh…" I pulled her into my chest as she broke down in my arms. "Just breathe. I promise you that life will be okay again. I know normal seems so far away, and you're still hurting inside, but you don't have to go through this alone. There are a lot of people who care about you. If you need someone to hold on to, I got you."

"Oh my God." She pulled back and wiped her cheeks. "First, I try to kiss you, and now I'm crying in your arms over my dead husband."

"No judgment." I smiled weakly. "I know I'm speaking from the outside, looking in. You're in pain. That's the reality of grief. I know you carry a heavy burden, but you don't have to carry it alone."

She wiped at her cheeks and looked across the lawn. "I don't want to go home. The house will be quiet. I just…" She stopped and closed her eyes. "Never mind. Don't mind me. Clearly, I'm a hot mess."

I should have walked her to her door. I should have offered her words of encouragement about how tomorrow is a new day. But it felt like whatever I said would be wrong.

"Would you like to go for a drive?"

She turned to me with a puzzled expression. "Don't you want to get home?"

No, what I wanted was every second I could get with her.

"I'm not that tired." I shrugged like it wasn't a big deal. "I'm used to running on little sleep due to my job, and sometimes a good drive helps clear the head."

She looked at the darkened house and back at me. She toyed with her bottom lip, and I gave her the time she needed to think it over. After a few beats, she fastened her seat belt and placed her purse on her lap.

"Okay, I'll go for a drive with you as long as I can pick the music." She smiled. It was small, but it caused something to move across my chest. I would have done anything to keep her smiling.

———

"What is all this?" she asked as I handed her the plastic bag full of junk food.

I buckled my seat belt and reversed the truck out of the parking spot of the gas station. "It's all I could come up with on short notice. I wasn't sure what you liked, so I bought a little bit of everything."

"Wow." She started pulling stuff out of the bag and piling it on her lap. "Beef jerky, potato chips, Cheez-Its, Skittles, Peanut M&M's." She paused and let out a loud squeal. "Did you know these little Hostess pies are my favorite?" She tore off the wrapper and took a massive chunk off the glazed pie crust. When she let out a little moan, I had to shift myself in my seat. "Do you want anything?" she asked, pulling out a pack of Twizzlers and looking at the bottom of the bag to make sure she didn't miss anything. I wasn't even paying attention to what I bought. I just threw the first things I saw into the basket and checked out.

"I'm good for now."

"So where are we going?" She reached forward and grabbed a couple of napkins that fell on the floor.

"It's a surprise," I said, merging onto the interstate. The car ride was filled with light conversation and her teasing me about my Spotify playlist. I was glad to see that she was in a lighter mood than earlier.

"I told you," I said, turning onto the rough terrain road that led to the state park. "Shawn Mendes and Harry Styles are on there for Brina."

"Sure." Her tone was teasing, and then it stopped. "Are you planning on burying my body in the woods or something?" She looked around, unsure about where I had brought her. The truck bounced along the unpaved gravel road. There was nothing around but trees and nature for miles. It was completely dark and secluded.

"This is where I come to clear my head. It's peaceful and relaxing."

"I had no idea this place existed," she said as we pulled up along the creek. This was as far as my truck was legally permitted to go. The only vehicles that were allowed to go deeper into the woods were the park rangers.

I shifted my truck into park and turned off the ignition. "Come on." I opened my door and hopped out. "I've got a few things in the back."

"I swear to God. If you pull out a shovel, I'm running." She looked down at her feet. "I may be in heels, but I'll use them as weapons if I have to."

I laughed. "You probably shouldn't tell me that. A smart captive wouldn't tell her kidnapper her escape plan."

I walked around and pulled out the storage bin where I kept all my camping stuff. I set up the two folding chairs, the small table, the lantern, a can of bug spray, and my little radio.

"See." I smiled and held my hands out. "No shovel or spade, but I do have some duct tape and some fishing line to tie you up."

"If you tell another dumb fish joke, I will run you over with your own truck." She settled into the chair and smiled. I handed her a sweatshirt to put on and grabbed a few drinks I purchased at the store.

"I promise to be on my best behavior." I tilted my face up to the moon. There was a slight breeze, making it feel less humid. "I love the outdoors, in case you didn't know."

There were no horns, no sirens, and best of all, no

construction; just peace and quiet, clean air, and a fresh breeze.

"I can tell." She sprayed some bug spray on her legs and handed me the can.

I sprayed a little bit along my arms and the back of my neck. I took a sip from my water bottle and glanced up at the night sky. "If you like to hike, you won't find better trails than you will here. There are also a few watering holes that are great for swimming even though you're not supposed to."

"I take it you come here often."

I leaned against the flatbed of my truck. "Whenever I have the time."

"Do you ever bring Brina with you?"

I laughed. "I've tried a few times but she's not a nature girl and gets bored easily."

"Does she take after her mother?"

I crossed my legs at the ankles and stared up into the sky. "When it comes to camping, yes."

"Amelia mentioned that you and your ex-wife don't get along. That's got to make raising a child together more difficult."

I got the feeling that she was trying to take the attention off of her tonight. While I didn't like to talk about my ex, I would give her the distraction she needed.

I slid into the empty chair next to her. "Vanessa was never someone I pictured forever with, but she got pregnant shortly after we started dating." I ran a hand over my ticking jaw, scratching it at the side. "I grew up looking at my parents' marriage and thought that's what I wanted someday. I thought I was doing the right thing when I asked her to marry me. I tried to make it work but things were difficult right from the start." I let out a heavy sigh.

"As time went on, things continued to get worse. I'll spare you all the ugly details, but my ex-wife isn't the easiest person to get along with. I don't want to talk bad about her because she is the mother of my child, and I don't want to sound like an asshole, but there just wasn't enough good in our relationship to outweigh the bad. I was walking around angry and miserable all the time. I didn't want my daughter to think that was okay. I would never want that kind of marriage for her, but I didn't want to be just a weekend dad either."

She reached out and touched my hand. "You're a good dad, Logan. Brina is lucky to have you, and I would never think you're an asshole. It sounds like you tried to make the best out of a shitty situation."

I swallowed and focused on the moon. "Thanks. I do my best. If I did anything right in this life, it was her."

I was grateful she wasn't focusing on my failed marriage and relieved that she was being so understanding. There was a small part of me that feared she would think less of me after that conversation.

She shifted in her chair and crossed her legs. She seemed to be content in the moment while we both sat there listening to the leaves blowing in the soft breeze.

"I meant what I said, Logan, you're a good guy. Your ex-wife just wasn't the right one for you."

"How do you know I'm a good guy?" I asked, sliding my hands along the armrest of the chair before I did something stupid like pull her on my lap. All I could think about was that kiss, and I wanted another one. I wanted a kiss that meant something to both of us.

"Well, you could be home, resting peacefully in a nice cozy bed, instead you're out here in the middle of the woods getting eaten alive by mosquitos just because I was feeling sad. If you weren't a nice guy, we wouldn't be here right now."

"You were upset." I stared into her eyes. "I wanted to take care of you tonight. Not because I felt sorry for you, but because I didn't want you to be alone."

"See." Her smile was smug, as if I had just proven her point.

I laughed. "Okay. Point made. Let's just keep this conversation between us. I have a reputation to uphold and I need people to be afraid of me."

"Your secret is safe with me, Detective."

I looked at my phone and pulled the twin pack of Hostess CupCakes out of my pocket that I kept hidden along with a box of candles. I wasn't sure how much longer she was willing to sit out here with me. I wanted to get this part over with before we had to pack up and leave.

"What are you doing?" she asked as I set a single candle into one of the chocolate cupcakes and lit it with a lighter.

"Happy birthday, Ava."

Her eyes grew misty, and the smile that spread across her face caused one of my own to break out. She took the treat from my hand, closed her eyes, and blew out the candle.

"Thank you. This has been really nice and it beats going home to an empty bed."

I reclined back in my chair and looked up at the stars. "A bed would definitely be more comfortable than these chairs. When you're ready to head back, just say the word."

"Surprisingly, my buzz is wearing off and I'm not even tired. Must be all this sugar." She took a bite of her cupcake, closed her eyes, and sighed. "This is heaven. One of the best nights I've had in a long time."

Ava and I spent the next few hours talking about Brina and Madison. We told embarrassing stories about Marco and Amelia, and about stupid stuff we did when we were younger. We laughed until tears leaked from our eyes and our bellies hurt from all the junk food we put into our stomachs. We stayed in those cheap folding chairs until the sun started to peek from the clouds. The sky turned red, and Keith Urban's "Making Memories Of Us" played through my cheap Bluetooth speaker.

I watched her hair blow in the soft breeze. A smile touched my lips at the sight of her being swallowed in my green Eagles hoodie. By the time I pulled into her driveway and watched her walk into her house, I knew I would never forget that night for as long as I lived.

EIGHT

AVA

"Mom." Madison rubbed her eyes, still half asleep. "Grandma and Grandpa are leaving."

"Shit." I pushed the covers to the side. My eyes squinted at the sunlight peeking through the blinds. It was only nine a.m. I'd only been asleep for a little under three hours. It's been years since I've stayed out that late. I was going to be exhausted today, but it would totally be worth it. Closing my eyes, a smile formed on my lips, remembering how much fun I had last night with Logan. I leaned forward and kissed Madison on the forehead. "Let's go say goodbye."

I padded across the hardwood and rummaged through my dresser, searching for a pair of shorts and a tank top. I slipped inside my bathroom, ran a quick comb through my hair, and brushed my teeth. I was only going back to bed after they left, so there was no need to do anything else.

I made my way down the hall into the living room. There were boxes in every corner, reminding me of my upcoming move.

"Late night?" my mother-in-law quipped.

My face burned with embarrassment; I could only imagine what she was thinking. She was a light sleeper, so I was positive she heard me come in this morning. Suddenly, I felt like a sixteen-year-old girl getting caught sneaking in by her parents instead of a thirty-two-year-old who just woke up in her own damn bed.

"You only turn thirty-two once, right?" I smiled while walking past the coffee sitting on the counter. I really wanted a cup, but if I was going back to sleep after this, the last thing I needed was caffeine.

Karen's eyes were on Madison as she helped herself to a Pop-Tart and went into the living room to watch cartoons. Once she was out of earshot, my mother-in-law turned and placed her hands on her hips.

"Don't you think you should be setting a good example for your daughter?"

"Excuse me?"

I couldn't help but stare at her. Karen has always had a sharp tongue, but it had never been directed at me. Sure, we'd had our differences like every mother- and daughter-in-law, but never in all the years I'd known her had she talked to me like this.

"You were obviously with someone last night." She looked away. "I would have thought my son's memory would have meant more to you than just a cheap roll in the hay."

My jaw practically hit the floor. How the hell was I supposed to respond to that? I didn't have the desire or the energy to spar with her, but she was way out of line. Yes, I was with a man last night, but nothing happened, not that it was any of her business. I refused to apologize for going out with my friends and having a fun time.

"Not that I owe you an explanation, but I was out with

the girls. I didn't feel like coming home to an empty bed, so a friend took me for a drive," I explained, trying to keep the irritation out of my voice. My head understood this hostility was coming from pain. She missed Drew, and I get it. I was sick of grieving too, but my heart hurt from her tongue lashing.

"You were gone all night?"

I rubbed my temples; maybe I should have had the cup of coffee after all. "I didn't realize I had a curfew."

She seemed surprised by my retort. "Are you even going to give me an apology?"

"I didn't realize I owed you one," I shot back. I didn't know what her problem was; but she was pissing me off. "What exactly are you insinuating, Karen?"

"We agreed to watch our granddaughter so you could go out for drinks with your friends. If we would have known that you would…" she paused. "If we knew what was going to happen, we never would have offered."

"Please enlighten me on what you think happened?"

"You obviously had sex with another man." I cringed. "I thought you valued my son's love and your reputation more than that."

It took me a minute to get my bearings. I glanced in the other room to make sure Madison couldn't hear us.

"I can't believe you just said that to me."

"David and I fully expected you to move on someday, we just assumed it would be in a respectable manner."

My father-in-law came storming into the kitchen, his rolling suitcase behind him. "That's enough, Karen." He stood there shaking his head as if he couldn't believe the words coming out of his wife's mouth. He crossed his arms in front of his chest, not looking too happy with the conversation he just walked in on. "Drew would not want you to treat Ava this way."

"Well, Drew probably didn't expect Ava to turn into a whore either."

I gasped. My body raged with shock and fury. I've seen Karen snap at people over the years, but I've never been on the receiving end of her assaults. This was a woman I'd respected and cared about. While we were never close because she lived on the other side of the country, she was always kind to me. This woman standing in front of me might as well have been a complete stranger. I wanted to blame it on her grief and justify her actions, but that didn't give her the right to disrespect me like that.

This entire week has been a giant shitshow. I didn't want to send her back to Colorado like this, so I would take the high road and show some empathy.

"I understand that you are still hurting, but I will not allow you to insult me in my own home."

"This was my son's home too. Maybe you should remember that."

David walked over and grabbed his wife's elbow. "Karen, please stop this. You are going to say some things you can't take back."

"You know nothing about what I've gone through," I said, feeling moisture spring to my eyes. "You don't get to make assumptions about the kind of person you think I am. You are doing a dishonor to your son by flying off the handle and calling me names. You talk about setting a good example for Madison. Maybe you should take a look in the mirror."

"Ava," David's eyes filled with shame, "I'm very sorry about all this."

"Don't you dare apologize for me," she snapped. As

angry as she was, it broke my heart to see her this way. "I'm going to say goodbye to my granddaughter, and if you know what's best for you, you'll be right behind me." She swung her arm back and stormed across the room.

David pinched the bridge of his nose and blew out a heavy sigh. "I'm not making excuses for her, but she's been struggling and refuses to seek help." His shoulders shook, and his eyes filled with tears. "I don't know what to do. I don't know how to help her. Just please don't keep Madison from us. She is all we have left of our son."

"David." I stepped forward and placed a comforting hand on his shoulder. Drew's father was such a strong man, so seeing him so broken was tearing me up inside. "The last thing I would ever want to do is keep Madison from her grandparents. She needs that connection just as much as you do. I loved Drew with everything I had, but Karen needs to understand that I can't continue to live the life that Drew left behind. I'm not saying I'm ready to move on, but when I do, I would like your support."

His hand reached out and cupped my cheek. "My son loved you until his last breath. I know that you will never try to replace him, but I hope that someday you'll find someone to fill in those cracks that he left behind. You and my granddaughter deserve to be happy."

He gathered me up in his arms. I held on to him as if he were the last thread holding me together. Drew was always close with his dad, and there wasn't a doubt in my mind that his spirit wasn't in the room with us. Don't ask me how I knew that, but I felt it deep down in my soul. So, I sent up a silent prayer that he would somehow help his mother heal, so she could get back to a better place.

———

"I'm sorry, she said what?" Kara spat out her coffee in disbelief. I'm not sure how either of us was even functioning today. Thankfully, my first appointment wasn't until noon, so I was able to go back to sleep for a couple of hours after Drew's parents left for the airport.

"She's just angry and lashing out, but she needed to know that I wasn't okay with her taking it out on me."

"She should know you well enough to know that you won't just roll over and take her shit."

I took a sip of my iced coffee and set it down. "I don't think she cares at the moment."

"So what are you going to do now?"

"Nothing. I'm going to give her time to cool down and hopefully realize that she was out of line."

She shook her head and started going through her purse. "So, tell me again what happened with Logan after you kissed him?"

"I'd rather not. It's embarrassing." I ran my fingers over my lips at the memory of throwing myself at him.

She pulled out her phone, setting it down on her desk. "He really pulled away in the middle of your make-out session?"

"More like pushed me away." I sat back in my chair and tried to figure out where I went wrong with that move. There was no way I imagined that spark between us, though. Especially with all the effort he took into making my birthday so special. He could have left me at my door after that, but he didn't. He certainly didn't need to drive me to a secluded park, load me up on snacks, and stay up to watch the sunrise with me.

"I don't know." She shook her head. "Maybe he was just being a gentleman."

The compassion in her voice had me looking up from my lap. "Or maybe he just isn't interested in me."

She set her coffee cup down and folded her arms. "I don't think that's it. He could have just drove your drunk ass straight home. Instead, he took you someplace that is very special to him. I think what he did was sweet." She got a dreamy look in her eyes. "And I'm so proud of you for putting yourself out there and making the first move."

A lot of good that did me. I wanted to believe that maybe he just didn't know how to handle me, which was wishful thinking on my part. I was almost sure he felt something too.

"Making the first move was so out of character for me." I cringed, thinking about everything I said and did. The last time I was single, I was very young. I don't remember things being this complicated. It blew my mind that people actually enjoyed and chose this lifestyle.

"I think it's a sign that you're ready to start testing the waters."

"I'm not so sure about that." I laughed it off. "I've got so much change going on now with the new house and moving across town. I don't think I could handle anything else."

"When do you close?"

"I sign the paperwork next week."

I should have been happy about closing on a new home because it was perfect. Instead, I was sad. It felt like a final goodbye to my old life.

"It will be good for you and Madison in the long run."

Aside from Amelia, Kara was one of my closest friends, and I was grateful to have her. She stepped in and made sure the shop ran like a well-oiled machine while I took time off to handle everything around the house when

Drew died. It was an adjustment because he did so much —more than I ever gave him credit for. If something broke, he fixed it. Me, I had to call a professional and write a check. Sure, I could handle the cleaning and day-to-day stuff that popped up, but I couldn't fix a broken washing machine, and I didn't know how to replace a leaky pipe.

I smiled and looked down at the rings I still wore on my left finger. "It's going to be bittersweet, for sure, but I'm looking forward to starting over."

"It's been a tough year and I know you're worried about what the future holds, but it's nice to see you approaching the change with a positive attitude."

"I don't have much of a choice."

My cell started ringing in my pocket. I pulled it out and gasped. "Oh my God. It's Logan." I clutched the phone to my chest. Kara squealed, and I glared at her. "What do I say?"

She moved closer and rested her hand under her chin. "Why don't you start with hello."

I scowled, brought the phone up to my ear, and hit accept. "Hi, Logan."

"You picked up." There was relief in his voice.

"Did you think I'd send your call to voicemail?" I teased, trying to mask how excited I was about this phone call.

"I figured my chances were fifty-fifty."

Damn. He knew me well.

"Curiosity got the better of me, so your bet paid off." I cleared my throat and tried to scoot away from my nosy friend. I needed to focus on not stumbling my way through this conversation.

"I just wanted to check in and make sure you were feeling okay today." My heart fluttered at his thoughtfulness. He was sweet and charming and everything I should avoid.

"Thank you. I'm dragging a little today. Getting older sucks. I guess my glory days are behind me." I glanced up at Kara, who was still eavesdropping on my conversation. I waved my hand, telling her to go away. Instead, she rolled her eyes and shifted closer.

"Well, that's disappointing." Logan sighed dramatically. "I'm starting to wonder if all those badass stories you told me about your college days were all lies."

"Please." I could feel my smile growing bigger by the second. What the hell was wrong with me? "You wouldn't have been able to handle me back then."

"In all seriousness. It was great to see you enjoying yourself."

"Thank you for saying that." I lowered my voice and looked away. "And thank you for the snacks and for taking me to your secret spot. And for not burying me in the woods."

"You're welcome for the snacks, but I have to be honest, I'm going to have to do some extra cardio to work off all that sugar. I'm not as young as I used to be. I can't eat like that and not pay for it the next day. Maybe I could do some landscaping around my house and practice my digging."

I laughed. "I don't know, Detective, your arms seemed pretty strong and solid last night when you had to help me into your truck."

"Why, Ava Donavon, were you objectifying me when I was trying to be a gentleman by lending you a hand during your time of need? If you were, I would totally be okay with it."

Was he really flirting with me? It was hard to tell

because it was such a big part of his personality. I always felt there was a physical attraction on his end, well, until he rejected me.

"There you go again fishing for compliments."

"Did it work? Or should I float by again and…"

"I'm hanging up now."

"Wait." He laughed. "Marco called and asked if I could lend him my truck next weekend to help you move. I figured you might need some manual labor too."

"Oh." I sunk my teeth into my lower lip. My thoughts went back and forth on why this wouldn't be a good idea. As much as I didn't want to admit it, an extra pair of hands would be nice. So, whatever reasons I came up with wouldn't be very good.

"You don't have to, but I appreciate the offer. I could use all the help I can get."

"Then it's settled. I also wanted to ask if it was okay if Brina came with me. It's my weekend with her and my ex will give me shit if I'm late picking her up."

I remembered him telling me how difficult she could be.

"Absolutely. Madison will be excited to have her tag along. They could keep each other busy."

"Great. I look forward to seeing you."

I laughed. "You mean helping me move, lifting heavy boxes, and probably getting sucked into putting furniture together."

"More than you know." He ended the call before I could say anything else. What the hell did that mean? I tossed my phone on the table and looked up. Kara was smiling at me.

"Why do you look so amused with yourself?"

She swept her long blond hair over her shoulder. "You are smitten."

"You're ridiculous."

She pushed away from the counter and stalked over to me. "Listen to me. You are going to let that gorgeous hunk help you. He obviously wants to or he never would have offered."

"Marco asked him too," I pointed out, but she just ignored me.

"After he's done his part, you are going to thank him, by cooking him dinner and maybe enjoying a little dessert after too." She waggled her eyebrows, and I tipped my head back on a groan.

"I will do no such thing." I got to my feet and started to walk away from her.

"This isn't over," she hollered, and being the mature adult I was, I flipped her off as I walked to the backroom to pull myself together.

NINE

LOGAN

My jaw hung open when I saw what she was wearing. It felt like my eyes were going to bulge right out of their sockets at the sight. I scrubbed a hand along my eyebrow, praying that I could get through these next few hours.

I gripped the steering wheel, squinting my eyes through the windshield of the car. The sun wasn't the only thing warming my skin. Ava was carrying a box to the end of the driveway, wearing a pair of white shorts that were so small you could practically see her bottom sticking out. She couldn't possibly think that they were going to cover anything. The blue tank top that showed hints of skin underneath every time it blew in the breeze wasn't much better. There was no doubt that my self-restraint was going to be tested today. Groaning in frustration, I silently debated turning my truck around and peeling out of here before anyone could notice.

Brina's fingers were tapping against her iPad. She had her headphones in, listening to "Shake it Off" by Taylor Swift. She was distracted, and I was grateful for the silence. I needed a minute to clear my head.

"Dad." Brina's feet pressed against the back of my seat. "Can you unlock the door please?"

Unbuckling my seat belt, I turned sideways to face my daughter. "I'll let you out of the truck as soon as your iPad is turned off and put away?"

My eyes followed her movements as she shut her screen down and slid it into the storage bin on the floor. I scratched the side of my cheek, debating on whether or not I should scold her for eating a bag of goldfish when she knew I didn't want crumbs in the back seat of my truck. But when she looked up, giving me a gapped-tooth grin, I decided to let it go.

As soon as I hit the unlock button, she jumped out and ran straight over to Madison. I slid a baseball cap over my head and stepped out of my truck. Just because Ava and I kissed and spent a night under the stars last week didn't mean things had to be weird between us today.

"Hey." Ava smiled, blowing a strand of hair out of her eye that had fallen out of her ponytail. She seemed different today. Her face was free of makeup, showing off her natural beauty, but that wasn't all I noticed. Maybe it was the bright morning sun, or perhaps it was the dimples I was seeing for the first time poking out of her cheeks, but she seemed less guarded today. She reminded me of the woman I first met. She seemed more put together and a little less broken.

"Looks like your helper is taking a break." I pointed to where the girls were sitting on the grass, showing no signs of moving. Brina was showing Madison her new bead-making kit. I don't know what my mother was thinking when she bought that thing. It was so messy it should have come with a warning label.

"Yeah, apparently." She scrunched up her nose. "The

funny thing is, most of what we are moving is her stuff. I'm leaving a good amount of the furniture for the new owner. It still amazes me though how much junk accumulates in a house over a few years."

I swept my eyes across the yard. Marco and Quinn were loading the stuff into the small U-Haul. "Starting fresh, huh?"

She looked down at the ground. "I figured a clean slate would be best."

I adjusted the hat along my forehead. "Sounds like a good plan to me."

I had no idea what the hell to say. Clearly, she was sad about leaving her former life behind. This was a huge step for her, and I couldn't even imagine all the mixed feelings swimming through her head.

She glanced up and gave me a small smile. "I hope so."

I rubbed a hand over my face, noticing a bead of sweat rolling down her neck, moving straight toward her cleavage. I did my best not to follow its path, but I'm pretty sure she caught me staring.

I started backing away before I made things more uncomfortable. "All right, Captain, what do you need me to do?"

"There are a few odd and end pieces of furniture that I'm taking, but it's mostly boxes. Everything is labeled, so I just need you to load as much as you can into the U-Haul. There is coffee and bagels on the kitchen counter. Help yourself." I turned to walk away, but her hand reached out and touched my arm. "Logan, thank you for coming to my rescue today. I'm sure you have a million other things you would rather do on your weekend off. I can't tell you how much I appreciate it."

"I told you I don't mind."

"Well, then I'm glad Marco thought to ask for your help today." She removed her hand, and I followed her into the house.

I felt guilty for lying to her on the phone the other day. Marco never asked to borrow my truck. When he called, explaining why he had to cancel our plans to go fishing, I jumped at the chance to help. I was taking advantage of every opportunity I could get to be around her again.

I peeled my eyes off her backside and reminded myself to keep things friendly. That's what she needed right now, a friend.

I breathed a sigh of relief when I stepped inside the air-conditioned house. It was way too hot and sticky for this early in the morning, so the cooler air was welcome.

Amelia was fixing herself a cup of coffee when she saw me. "Good morning."

"Morning," I said, making my way over to kiss her on the cheek. "How does it feel to be kid-less for a few hours?"

"Marietta showed up an hour early." She set her cup down to secure the lid and sighed. "I barely got to hug my daughter before she was whisked away for the day."

I chuckled. "Sounds about right." Marco's mom dedicated her entire life to her family. She lost her husband a few years ago, so spending time with her two boys and grandkids is what she lived for.

I placed my hands on my hips, surveying the room. Everything was well-packed and organized, making for a quick move across town.

"All right." I rubbed my hands down along my gym shorts. "I better get started."

Two hours later, Brina and I were pulling into Ava's new neighborhood. We had to make a quick run back to my place to grab her inhaler. She hasn't had an asthma attack in a while, but I wanted to be prepared just in case.

I looked down the street to check out her new house. It was everything I pictured it to be. It was situated in an upper-middle-class neighborhood and only a mile away from the elementary school. The two-story colonial looked to be in great condition. The landscaping was another story. The overgrown hedges along the front needed a good trim, and some of the bushes needed to be replaced. The lawn was even worse. It had a number of spots that would require some reseeding. I was meticulous about my yard, something that drove my neighbors crazy. My head was already filling up with ideas of what I could do to give this outdoor space a new look.

I carried a couple of boxes up the driveway and set them on the front porch. As soon as I stepped inside, I could tell it had been recently renovated. It wasn't an older house, but it wasn't exactly new either. As a matter-of-fact, the more I looked around, the more I liked it. It was open and bright with a killer backyard. I could totally picture Ava and Madison restarting their lives here.

"Where do you want this?" I yelled over to Ava, who was carrying a bucket of cleaning supplies in one hand and a mop in the other.

She tilted her head to the side and studied the box. "That goes upstairs in my bedroom. It's the last door on the left."

Nodding my head, I gripped the end of the box and trudged up the stairs. When I opened the door, it squeaked a little bit, and I made a mental note to fix it before I left.

"You can just set that box next to the closet," Ava said from behind me.

"You got it." I followed her instructions and moved

backward to make room for her as she carried a set of curtain rods over to the window. "This is a nice place you have, Ava."

"Thank you." She gave me a smile, one that reached her eyes. "It may be more house than I need, but I'm excited about having the extra space. The townhouse that Drew and I lived in was fine, but it was small. Plus, this neighborhood is a lot more kid-friendly."

"Not to mention the kick-ass pool in the backyard."

"It definitely sealed the deal."

"So, when's the pool party?"

I tried not to look at her as she made her way up the stepladder in those tiny shorts. I knew thinking about her like that was wrong, but my eyes, no matter how hard I tried to pull them away, seemed to have a mind of their own.

"As soon as I get the house in order."

"Am I going to get an invite?"

"It depends on how fast you can assemble that nightstand."

I looked at the box and frowned. "If it's like every other piece of Ikea furniture, it should take me a few days."

She placed a hand on her hip. "I have faith in your abilities, so let's see what you got, Detective."

I arched an eyebrow. "You know, you really shouldn't say that to a man."

She shook her head. "And you really shouldn't turn everything into a sexual innuendo."

"I can't help it. I need to think of something to help pass the time. This project is going to take me forever."

She let out a carefree laugh. "Are you complaining about spending time with me?"

"Never." The word slipped out without thinking.

Before I had a chance to make light of my comment, there was a light tap on the door.

Charlotte poked her head inside, and I'd never been so thankful for an interruption. "Hey, Amelia and I just finished putting Madison's bed together. As soon as Quinn is done helping Marco with mounting the TV brackets, we are heading out."

"Oh, that's right, Emery has her big lacrosse game today."

"Yeah, she does, otherwise we would stay longer and help get you settled in."

"I'm just thankful for all your help. As soon as I get this house all squared away, I'm having everyone over for a pool party." She looked over, giving me a smug smile. "Well, Logan is a maybe. He hasn't quite made the list yet."

Charlotte regarded us with interest. "I look forward to it." Her gaze shifted to mine. "Bye, Logan. I'll keep my fingers crossed that you make the list."

"Thanks, Charlotte. Good luck with the game," I called out as she walked out of the room.

Ava and I spent the next hour getting her bedroom all set up. I tried not to look down her shirt every time she bent over or make a big deal and tease her when I caught her checking me out. She needed my help as a friend, and I felt like a selfish bastard for even feeling the things I was feeling. If she knew how deep my desire for her ran, she would have second thoughts about being in this bedroom with me.

"I'm going downstairs to get a few things out of my truck," I announced once I was finished with the night-stand. I was eager to get away from her before I did or said something stupid.

"Okay." She leaned forward to grab the screwdriver off

the mattress. "But don't forget about the other night-stand," she said, pointing to the box in the corner.

I cursed under my breath, causing her to laugh out loud.

"I don't understand why you need two stands for one person."

"Because it helps create symmetry."

"Whatever you say," I yelled as I walked out of the room. "I should arrest you for slave labor." The girls came running up the stairs, their little giggles filling up the hallway.

"Where are you two troublemakers going?" I asked, stepping in front of them. I held my arms out wide, keeping them from going forward.

"I'm showing Brina my room," Madison said, looking a little too guilty for her eight-year-old self.

I bent down to peek inside the bag that she was clutching in her hands. "Did I miss Halloween or something? There's enough candy in there for the entire neighborhood."

Madison put the paper bag behind her back as if she was afraid I would take it away. "We aren't going to eat it all."

"Where did that bag come from?"

Madison's eyes widened as they shifted to my daughter. "My friend Julia gave it to me. Her parents own a store that sells candy."

"Does your mom know about that candy?"

She nodded her head. "Yes, she lets me eat a little bit at a time."

"Okay." I patted her head and looked at my daughter. "You know the rules, Brina. Only a couple pieces."

She huffed out a breath and rolled her eyes. "I know,

Dad, I don't want to eat too much or I'll get a stomachache. I'm not a baby, remember?"

I didn't like her tone, but she was in front of her friend and at the age where she got embarrassed easily. I was going to let it slide for now. I learned a long time ago to pick your battles.

"All right." I lowered my hands to the side. "You girls can pass. Just remember that you have to eat dinner later."

They both ran so fast I chuckled under my breath.

I picked up a few bags of garbage on my way down the stairs. I rounded the corner of the kitchen, spotting Marco fiddling with something on his phone. "It's hotter than the hubs of Hades in this house," I said, feeling my T-shirt stick to my skin. "Is her AC working?"

Ava came sprinting down the stairs. "The thermostat is on the wall in the front room. Feel free to turn it down." She snatched the measuring tape off the table and dashed back upstairs. My eyes followed her, and I must have looked a little too long because my friend shot me a suspicious look.

He threw me a water bottle. "Please don't."

"Don't what?"

"I'm not dumb. I see the way you look at her. The way you have always looked at her."

I glared, not liking where this conversation was headed. "What's your problem?"

He lifted the lid of the recycling container and shoved a piece of cardboard inside. "She's off-limits to you."

I narrowed my eyes. "Really? And why is that?"

"She's my wife's best friend, who just lost her husband last year."

"And?" Not that I was going to ask her out anytime soon, but still.

He ran a frustrated hand along the top of his hair. "No offense, Logan, I love you like a brother, but you come with a lot of baggage. She has her own shit to deal with. The last thing she needs is to get tangled up in that mess and have Vanessa sniffing around. And don't tell me she won't."

My ex was not a nice person. When I thought about all the hell she could bring to Ava's doorstep, it made my stomach drop. People who didn't know me well assumed I just didn't date. The truth was, Vanessa made it almost impossible for me. My last attempt at a relationship ended up turning into a disaster. When word got back to Vanessa that I was seeing someone, she went all *Fatal Attraction* on me. She sent threatening messages to my friends and family, harassed me at work, hacked my Facebook account, and keyed my brand-new truck.

My jaw ticked with frustration. I couldn't argue with facts. It was just another reminder of why things would never work between us.

"I understand."

His head shook slowly. "I still don't get why you put up with her shit."

"I don't have a choice, Marco. We share a kid."

Ava and Amelia took that minute to walk into the kitchen. Our eyes met briefly before she darted them to the floor. Ever since that kiss, things shifted between us, and the hours we spent getting to know each other under the stars have been all I've thought about.

Amelia came to a stop and looked between us. She grinned so wide it practically split her cheeks. "Well, I wish we could stay longer and help, but Marco and I have to get going."

Marco lifted his eyebrow. "We do?"

"Yep." She glanced at her watch and smiled. She looked like she knew something we didn't. "I have to run an errand before we pick Gia up from your moms."

The girls raced into the kitchen while Marco leaned against the counter.

"Mom," Madison said, "Brina and I put all my clothes away. Can we watch a movie now?"

Ava shook her head. "I'm sorry, but the cable isn't hooked up yet."

My daughter cut in. "We can watch one on my iPad."

Amelia clapped her hands. "I have a better idea. Your mom still has a lot of unpacking left to do, and Logan still has to help her hang a few pictures and put some things together."

"I do?" That was news to me.

"Yes." Amelia smiled, looking pleased with herself. "That's why it makes sense for the girls to come with us for a couple hours while you guys finish up."

Wow! Talk about being discreet. I looked over at Ava, wondering what she was thinking. I could see the uncertainty in her eyes about being left alone with me.

"Amelia…" Marco slanted his head, letting her know that he could read between the lines.

She waved him off with her hand. "It makes sense." She turned to me and smiled. "You don't mind sticking around for a couple of extra hours to help, right?"

I tried to think of an excuse for why I couldn't, but there really wasn't one. I could say I had plans later, but I didn't want to lie. It was just a few hours. Ava and I could make small talk while we worked. It didn't have to be a big deal.

Brina raced across the room and tented her fingers under her chin. "Please, Dad."

She was bouncing on her feet, giving me a pleading look that she knew I couldn't refuse.

"Of course, I don't mind." I leaned down, touching her cheek with my thumb. "You promise to behave?"

"Yes," she squealed, unable to hold in her excitement about getting more time with Madison. The girls have really hit off, and that was both good and concerning to me.

Ava grabbed Amelia's elbow and glared at her best friend. "I don't know what you think you're doing, but you're going to pay for this."

"Oh, stop it. I'm doing you a favor and you know it."

"The only thing I know is that I hate you right now."

Amelia laughed it off, but Ava still looked pissed.

I tried not to take offense that she was throwing a fit about being alone with me. However, if my intuition was right, it was because I made her nervous. This attraction was no longer one-sided. Even Amelia picked up on it. I was close to finally getting my chance with her, so I needed to tread carefully.

Marco leaned against the wall, not looking happy about this setup. I nodded my head for him to meet me outside. I quickly shut the door and tried to keep my voice down. "Will you relax."

"I hope you know what you're doing."

"What exactly is it that you think I am doing? Because it's your wife in there who is playing matchmaker."

"I'm not trying to be a dick here."

"I didn't plan this." I leaned against the porch railing. "Look, it's clear you don't want me here alone with her. I'm trying not to let that bother me, but your attitude is starting to piss me off."

He tilted his head and stared at me. "I told you it's not you."

"Right." I rolled my eyes. "It's my crazy ex-wife."

He sighed. "If you tell me that I have nothing to worry about, then I believe you. I'm sorry I came across as a jerk. I care about both of you. I don't want to see either one of you get hurt."

Marco still didn't know what happened that night I drove Ava home. I'm actually surprised he hasn't asked me about it. I've kept that kiss to myself, and I sure as hell wasn't going to say anything about our little trip to the state park. I felt sleazy lying to my best friend, and I knew the right thing to do would be to come clean about how I felt, but I was one hundred percent certain it would only make things worse.

The front door was yanked open; Amelia stepped forward. "The girls are getting their things. You can swing by and pick them up whenever you're done. No rush."

"Thanks." I swallowed hard and looked over her shoulder. Ava and I stared at each other for a few seconds, neither one of us knowing what to do. Brina and Madison came skipping around the side of the house.

I waved my daughter over. "Don't forget your inhaler," I reminded her, running my hands along the top of her hair.

She patted her shorts. "It's in my pocket."

"Good. Now give me a kiss."

She groaned, almost on the edge of whining. "Dad, I'm too old."

"You will never be too old, and if you want to go to the movies later like we planned, you'll give me a kiss right here." I pointed to my cheek.

She gave me a kiss that lasted all of a half-second

before running over to the car. Sometimes it felt like she was nine going on nineteen, and it made me want to scoop her up in my arms and lock her away.

Ava hugged Madison goodbye, and I listened as they made plans to paint nails and do something with face masks later.

We stood on the porch side by side, waiting for everyone to load into the car, buckle their seat belts, and drive away. Once we were alone, she gave me a nervous smile and disappeared into the house, leaving me no choice but to follow her.

TEN

AVA

"You invited him to dinner?" Kara gave Michele, our other stylist, a high-five. I already regretted telling them.

"As a thank you," I stressed, making quick work of cleaning up my station. "We are just friends." The words felt like a lie coming out of my mouth. There were so many lingering glances and innocent touches that I questioned my sanity at times.

Logan stayed for most of the afternoon to help me unpack and put everything away. I knew it was his weekend with Brina, and I felt guilty taking that time away from him. It was a long day, and by the time he left, he looked exhausted. I told myself the least I could do was cook him a meal. So, why was I feeling so nervous about it?

"I can watch Madison for you," Kara offered.

"It's not a date." I turned to my friends, who looked like they didn't believe me.

"If you invited him to dinner, I'm pretty sure he's thinking it's a date," Michele pointed out.

"Clearly, I have no idea what I'm doing." Saying the

words out loud was embarrassing. It made me realize how out of touch I was. "It's been over a decade since my last first date. What the hell do I even wear?"

When Drew picked me up for the very first time, all he had to do was walk across campus and pick me up outside my dorm room. We went out for pizza and a cheap movie. Every college student back then lived in jeans, so the only thought I put into my night was how much makeup I wanted to wear or if my hair looked better up or down.

Michelle squinted her eyes at me, considering my words. "Honey, things haven't changed that much. You'll be fine."

I shifted my attention to the hairstyling products at my station. "I was with the same man for ten years." A flush took over my cheeks as I looked over my shoulder, making sure no one could hear me. "Drew and Logan are complete opposites."

Drew and I were both young when we started dating. We grew up and matured together. We were familiar and predictable. There was nothing about Logan Blake that was predictable. He was unexpected and had a way of surprising me. Just when I thought I had him all figured out, I would unpeel another layer and find something else I liked about him. He was new and exciting, and I worried at times if I would end up in over my head.

Kara placed her hands on her hips. "You need to stop comparing him to Drew. It's not fair and won't do you any good. I understand this is new, but every relationship is different. Take things slow, see if it blossoms into anything. Have a little fun, enjoy the adventure and hopefully the mind-blowing sex."

I held my hand up. "This isn't a relationship." No matter how many times I tried to explain, she still didn't seem to get it. I wasn't even going to address the sex. Not to mention, her advice wasn't helping my stress level at the moment. "It's a thank you dinner."

"It's a fresh start."

"I understand that." I gave Kara a pointed look as Michele walked away. "That's why I'm asking for your help. Now, can you please just give me a little advice on what to wear?"

She took her time looking me over. While I wasn't embarrassed about my looks, I wasn't confident either.

I pulled my hair back and adjusted my skirt while she walked around me in a circle like she was getting ready to carve a statue from a block of marble. "I'd say something tight and low-cut." I rolled my eyes and grumbled under my breath as she continued. "Show some skin, maybe some high heels and accessories that will draw attention to your assets."

"Maybe I should just answer the door naked."

She smirked. "I don't think he would mind."

I waved her away with my hand. "I don't even know why I bother with you."

Thankfully, Kara's customer was done with the dryer, so she had no other choice but to check on her. As she was walking away, she stopped and placed her hand on my arm. "I don't think he cares what you wear, Ava, that's what I'm trying to tell you. Just let me know if you want me to watch Madison. I think this dinner will be good for you. It's a step in the right direction."

I looked at myself in the mirror and played with the ends of my hair. There was a smile on my face that wasn't there a few weeks ago. All thanks to a handsome, green-eyed detective who made me blush like a teenager. There was a small knot of guilt in my stomach, but it quickly passed. I needed to stop feeling guilty, like I was doing something wrong. Drew wouldn't want me to dwell on the past. He would want me to live my life.

I made my way over to the reception desk to go through some paperwork. I needed a distraction because the more I thought about this dinner, the more nervous I became.

I was tapping some numbers into the computer when a leggy brunette stepped through the front door. I stopped typing and looked up.

"Hi, can I help you?"

"I'm here for a trim." She smiled, but it seemed a little forced to me. There was something about her face that looked familiar, but I couldn't place it.

"Do you have an appointment?" I closed out the spreadsheet I was working on and pulled up the calendar.

"I was hoping you took walk-ins."

"I'm sorry, we don't." A flicker of annoyance crossed her face. "But let me check the schedule and see if there is a way to squeeze you in. What exactly is it you're looking to have done today?"

She twisted a strand of hair around her finger. "I just want a quarter inch off the ends."

I stared up at her; she was really pretty. Her long, dark hair looked like it was recently done, which had me confused on why she was here. She also wore expensive clothes and heavy makeup. She didn't look like the type that just strolled into a random salon off the street.

"What's your name?" she inquired, edging closer to the desk. I scooted my chair back slightly, not liking how she was invading my personal space.

"I'm Ava and you are?"

She stared at me for a minute, and I did the same. I

kept my face neutral even though she unnerved me. She was tall for a woman, probably five nine; while I wasn't short, her presence seemed to tower over me. My eyes squinted in confusion, trying to figure out if I knew her from somewhere. I was pretty sure I would have remembered her if we had met before.

"My name is Vi." Her eyes darted down to my left hand. "I like your rings."

My fingers paused on the keyboard. "Thank you."

I shifted uncomfortably and went back to look over the schedule. Maybe if I avoided eye contact, she would stop talking. I brought my hand up to itch the end of my nose; her expensive perfume was overpowering.

She leaned her elbows on the desk and folded her hands. "How long have you been married?"

"My husband passed away last year."

"You're a widow. That's interesting." I gave her a blank stare, not sure if I heard her correctly. "Sorry," she said when she noticed my expression. "I wasn't expecting that. You look so young."

"Right," I said, averting my attention back to my computer screen. I was relieved when I noticed there were no openings. The lady caused the tiny hairs on the back of my neck to tingle. My instincts were usually right about people, and I had a hard time believing she was sincere.

She extended her hand and lifted it so I could see the glistening diamonds on her finger. "I still wear my rings too. My husband and I are separated, I'm just waiting for him to come to his senses." She sighed heavily, and I got the impression she was telling me this for a reason. "We're taking a little break right now, but I'm not worried. I'm the love of his life and you just don't get over that. He's goes through his little playthings, and then moves on. He tires of them easily. That's why I don't mind waiting for him to get his shit together."

"I hope it all works out for you." I looked over her shoulder, praying my next customer would walk through the door. I just wanted to get back to work. This woman was either lonely or had mental issues. I tried not to judge, but there was something off about her.

"Have you had any work done?"

"Excuse me?"

"You know, Botox, lip injections, boob job?" This had to be one of the strangest encounters I've had in my life.

"Um…no."

"It can't be easy trying to find someone at this point in your life, especially with the way men lie and cheat. They only seem to want one thing and once they get it, they are on to the next willing participant. If you're going to put yourself out there, you're going to have to get a little work done. There is too much competition out there. You're going to want to stand out."

I didn't even know where to begin or why she was even telling me this. I wanted to feel sorry for her, but my gut told me there was a reason behind this visit. She made me feel highly uncomfortable, and there wasn't a chance in hell I was cutting her hair.

"I'm sorry to hear about your relationship troubles. I understand how that could be upsetting. Let me take a look at my schedule." I peered down at the computer and pretended to look it over. "I'm afraid we don't have any available appointments today."

Her mouth pressed into a firm line. "When's your next opening?"

"One of our stylists has an opening next Thursday at three p.m. I can pencil you in if you're still interested."

She tapped her red-painted fingernail to her lips. "I'd like to request you. When's your next available?"

This entire encounter was bizarre. "I'm sorry, but I'm not accepting any new clients at this time."

Her head jerked back. "Really?"

"Yes, I'm afraid that I'm all booked up. I didn't realize how full my schedule was until I just looked at it."

She was about to respond when Kara walked over and placed her hands on the back of my chair. "Everything okay over here?" she asked with concern, obviously picking up on the tension.

"I'm trying to convince Ava here to fit me in."

Kara's eyes slid to mine, glancing between me and the Megan Fox lookalike. I could tell she wasn't sure how to take this woman any more than I did. She smiled tightly while rounding the desk. "Your name is?"

"Vi."

"Hi, Vi, I'm Kara," she said quickly while leaning forward to look at the computer monitor. I pushed back from the desk and stood up so she could sit. "Let me take a look and see what we can do."

Kara opened up her calendar and looked over the screen. "I can fit you in next Saturday at one p.m."

I pulled my phone out of my bag, trying to act like I wasn't paying attention.

"Ava said there was an appointment for next Thursday."

"That was a mistake. I forgot to add a client in that day."

I bit back my smile. There was no mistake. She purposely scheduled her on my day off.

"Fine." She huffed in frustration. You could tell she

wasn't happy, which made no sense. My psycho meter was going off because the woman was clearly nuts.

Kara handed her an appointment card, and I breathed out a sigh of relief when she spun on her heels and strode away.

She raised her hand and waved goodbye like we were long-lost friends. "Bye, girls, I'll see you next week." She threw an overstretched smile over her shoulder. It seemed insincere, and I didn't trust it.

I waited until she was out the door before turning to Kara. "Is it just me or did she seem a little crazy?"

"She was definitely two cans short of a six-pack."

I massaged my temples, trying to get myself to relax. I couldn't quite kick the feeling aside that I had a target on my back, and I had no idea why.

ELEVEN

AVA

THE PUNCTUAL KNOCK ON MY DOOR HAD ME DRAWING IN A deep breath. Glancing in the mirror one last time, I convinced myself that this was just dinner. There was no reason to be nervous. After all, it was just Logan.

I smoothed a hand down along my stomach. The diamond princess cut stone on my left finger glinted in the dim lighting.

"I'm so sorry, Drew," I whispered, looking up at the ceiling as if he could hear me.

I placed a hand over my racing heart and swung the door open. A wave of heat sprung to my cheeks, and my mouth watered at the sight of him. He looked devastatingly handsome in his dark, fitted jeans and white button-down with the sleeves rolled up to his elbows.

It was a simple look, but it worked for him.

His eyes traveled along the length of the cute and flirty romper Kara convinced me to wear. "You look gorgeous."

For a moment, I couldn't even form words. I just stared and prayed I didn't have drool hanging from the corner of my mouth.

"You clean up pretty good yourself."

My heart fluttered at the way he stared at me. It's been a long time since a man has looked at me like that.

Logan handed me a big bouquet of pink roses and a bottle of wine. Kara was right, this seemed more like a date than just a simple dinner between friends.

"Thanks." I closed the door and took the flowers from his hand. "These are beautiful." I carried them into the kitchen and set them down on the counter, searching for something to set them in. I opened the cabinet, my eyes landing on a crystal vase I received as a wedding gift. I swallowed and grabbed a tall glass out of the top cupboard to place them in that instead.

"I have a bottle of wine already opened. I wasn't sure what you liked, so there is beer in the fridge too."

"I'll have a glass of whatever you have opened."

I slid the extra wineglass across the counter and poured him a glass of cabernet. He settled into the seat across from me on the kitchen island. He was close enough to where I caught the scent of his cologne. It had hints of sandalwood and cedar. It was woodsy and totally him.

Tearing my eyes away, I picked up my wine and took a huge sip. I silently willed my senses to shut down. My nerves were all over the place, probably because I hadn't been this attracted to a man since I met my husband.

"This place looks great." He reached for his wine, swirling it around before bringing it to his mouth. My eyes instantly followed his movements. I took another drink from my glass and reminded myself to slow down. Otherwise, I would be drunk before we even sat down to dinner. I wasn't kidding when I told Kara I was out of my element.

"Thanks." I walked over and grabbed the salad off the

counter to set it on the table. "I've been adding little touches here and there."

He glanced around. "I may have you come decorate my place."

I placed my hands on my hips. "I'm not sure you could afford me."

"What's your hourly rate?" He grinned. "Are you a pay by the hour type girl?"

"You are being awfully brave for someone who is about to eat the food I just cooked," I said, moving across the kitchen to grab some utensils out of the drawer.

His eyes filled with amusement. "Seeing that you still need me to hang a few pictures in the family room, I think I'll take my chances."

I stepped over to the stove so I could put the meal together. "Why don't you put those muscles to good use and toss that salad before I decide not to feed you."

I poured the pan of chicken, artichokes, and sundried tomatoes over the pasta. I set it on the table next to the salad and a fresh loaf of bread.

Logan let out a low whistle. "Wow. This looks and smells amazing."

All those years I spent helping my mom in the kitchen have paid off. This Mediterranean chicken recipe was one of my favorite dishes and one I cooked well. I gave myself a mental pat on the back.

"Thanks. It was nice to cook an adult meal for a change. If Madison had her way, she would live off of hot dogs and macaroni and cheese."

He sliced off a piece of chicken and brought it to his mouth. "I'm a bachelor, so I don't cook much. This is a nice treat."

"Don't tell me you live off of takeout and fast food."

"My cooking skills are limited. I can grill and boil water. That's about it."

"Poor Brina."

"I wouldn't feel too sorry for my little picky eater, all she does is complain about the way I cut her sandwiches." He shook his head. "I've never understood why kids refused to eat the crust. I think it's the best part."

The thought of him taking care of his young daughter had my body filled with warmth.

"What about the nights that you don't have Brina?"

He rested his elbows on the table and grinned. "You're cute."

I leaned back in my chair. "What makes you say that?"

"You don't think I can't tell that's your subtle way of asking me what I do in my free time?"

I tipped back the rest of my wine, feeling a blush hit my cheeks. I was so busted.

"I'm sorry to disappoint you but I really was just curious about your eating habits."

He threw his head back in laughter. "Let me put you out of your misery. I haven't been celibate since my divorce, but I'm not out every night collecting notches for my bedpost either."

It felt like all the air had left the room and my kitchen suddenly felt tiny.

"That's good to know, but I'm sure you still embrace the bachelor life and all the perks that come along with it," I said, going along with this silly conversation because, damn it, I was a little curious.

"That doesn't happen as often as you think. And just to be clear, it's been a while." His head cocked to the side. "How about you? I shared with you, I think it's only fair and square you do the same."

"I'm flattered that you would think I even have a social life, let alone a love life."

"Why's that?"

"The only thing I've been focused on these past eighteen months, is raising my daughter and putting my life back together." I shook my head and looked away. "Besides, trying to date would have been pointless. I can't imagine there are a ton of men out there looking for a widowed, single mom. And truthfully, I'm not just looking for casual sex."

I regretted the words the second they left my mouth. It was the last thing he probably wanted to hear, but it was the truth.

"Ava, you're gorgeous. You don't give yourself enough credit." A thrill ran through me as he continued. "I also have to be honest with you. I'm glad you didn't put yourself out there, otherwise there would probably be some other asshole sitting here right now instead of me."

He took a casual sip of his drink as if he didn't just lay it all on the line for me.

My eyes dropped to my plate, needing a few seconds to get my thoughts in order. I wanted to believe that I could do this flirting and dating thing, but part of me was scared. Logan seemed almost too good to be true, and I was afraid to get pulled under his spell.

"You really know how to flatter a girl," I said, trying to go with the flow, and sound casual. But he could see right through me.

"Relax." He reached for my hand across the table. "There are no expectations right now." His thumb brushed over my wrist. "This dinner can be whatever you want it to be. It can be a dinner between friends, or a get to know you. I just want you to enjoy it."

His warm eyes met mine, and I held his gaze. I might have been out of practice, but the connection was too strong to ignore what was happening between us.

"I want to get to know you better, Logan."

"Good," he smiled, "because I'm not going to lie and pretend that I want to be just your friend."

I was headed into dangerous territory with this man. I needed to be careful because hearing him say that he wanted to be more than just my friend made me feel things I wasn't sure I was ready for. But I liked Logan a lot, probably more than I should have.

"Let's start with the get to know you."

He released my hand and spread his arms out. "I'm an open book, ask away."

"Tell me a few random facts."

He scratched his cheek like he was thinking it over. "I like beer over hard liquor. I'd rather fish off the back of a boat than surf on a beach. My idea of relaxing is doing a project around the house and spending time with Brina."

"Fishing." I groaned. "Why am I not surprised? That last one though, is pretty sweet."

"Your turn." He picked up a sun-dried tomato and popped it in his mouth.

"You're going to be disappointed, because I am the exact opposite of everything you just described." I laughed. "I'm a city girl whose ideal vacation is to do absolutely nothing. Give me a beach chair, toes in the sand, and a margarita in my hand and I'm happy."

"Opposites attract, right?" He flashed me a grin that made me want to reach across the table and kiss him. Instead, I took a sip of my wine and averted his gaze. I didn't need to focus on his lips. Or remember how they were just the right amount of soft and firm. Or think about how much I wanted to feel them against my mouth again.

"They do sometimes," I said, finally finding my voice.

He swirled his wine around in his glass. "Tell me about your business. Did you always want to be your own boss?"

"I guess you could say that." I grabbed a piece of bread and applied a little butter. "You might find this hard to believe, but I don't like being told what to do."

He laughed. "I don't think anyone likes being told what to do."

"What about you? Did you always want to work in law enforcement?"

He sat back in his seat and rubbed his thumb along his bottom lip. "I had no idea what I wanted to do. I just knew that I didn't want to get stuck behind a desk every day."

"Don't you do a fair amount of desk work as a detective?"

"Not if you're a good one." He winked before picking up his fork and twirling it around his pasta.

"For someone with a small head, it sure does seem pretty big. I'm surprised it doesn't get swollen." His fork paused on the way to his mouth at the exact moment where I realized how that sounded. "Oh, my God." I threw my hand over my eyes in embarrassment. "Forget I said that."

"Not a chance," he teased as we both erupted into a fit of hysterics. "And you say my jokes are bad."

Once our laughter died down, I sat back in my seat and shoved a fork full of pasta in my mouth. Maybe that would stop me from saying anything stupid. Logan didn't seem to mind having a little fun at my expense, though. I loved how he didn't take things seriously and how we both participated equally in the conversation. I might have been nervous earlier, but there was nothing awkward about this dinner. Feeling comfortable was a good sign. I felt like I could be myself around him.

"You realize, you're the first official guest I've had in my new home."

He leaned forward with a devilish glint in his eyes. "I'm honored to be your first."

I moved some of the tomatoes and artichokes around on my plate. "I told Amelia you were coming over. I hope that was okay?"

He wiped his mouth off with his napkin. "Yeah, I figured when Marco called me and handed me a stern lecture on how to behave."

I cringed. "I'm sorry. He means well. He's just doesn't want to get caught in the middle of any drama between us."

"I can handle Marco." He rested his hands on the table. "Do you think Amelia is okay with me being here?"

I rolled my eyes. "You're not a very good detective if you didn't pick up on the clues she dropped on moving day."

He grinned, and he really needed to stop doing that because it wasn't helping my situation. "At least we have someone rooting for us."

Us? What exactly were we? I didn't give it much thought when I extended the invitation. All I knew was that it was an excuse to see him again. He was slowly chipping at the walls I had built up. But what would happen when he finally got what he wanted? Was he just interested in me because I was new? How long would it take him to get bored and move on to the next challenge?

"Hey." His eyes filled with concern. "Did I say something wrong?"

"Of course not." I shook my head. "I just don't want Marco to be mad at you," I lied.

He blew out a relieved breath. I guess I was more convincing than I thought.

"I don't want to waste any more time talking about Marco. Tell me more about you. Tell me more about what a rebel you were growing up. Tell me all your embarrassing stories."

"Okay." I held my fork out and gave him my "mom" voice. "If you hold anything against me or tease me in any way, I will…." I paused, trying to think of something. "I don't know what I'll do but I'll think of something good and you'll regret it."

His lips twitched. "Understood. I won't tease you in any way. Scout's honor."

My eyes narrowed on the little liar. Like I would ever believe he was a boy scout. Whatever, I was thankful for the switch in topics.

I started telling stories from my teenage years. I loved how he listened intently and seemed to hang on to my every word. We laughed throughout the entire meal. He ate every last bite on his plate and even ate a handful of chocolate chip cookies I baked for dessert. I pushed my plate to the side and refilled our wineglasses. Never in a million years did I think things would be this easy between us.

He leaned back in his chair and patted his stomach. "That meal was outstanding."

"Thank you. I'm glad you enjoyed it." I looked out through the sliding glass doors, noticing the glass streak with raindrops. "I was going to suggest that we sit outside by a fire, but seeing that it's raining, would you be interested in a movie instead?"

"Sounds great. Let me help you clean up."

It didn't take us long to get everything wiped down and put everything away. The time passed quickly, and I found myself not wanting this night to end.

———

"This is such a horrible movie."

I smirked over the rim of my wineglass. "Are you not a fan of Kevin James?"

"Kevin James is all right, but this movie is stupid."

"I wanted to learn more about what you do for a living," I said, trying and failing to keep a straight face.

He set the bowl of popcorn down on the table. "I think there has been some miscommunication here. I'm a few levels above a mall cop, sweetheart."

"So, what movie would you have suggested?"

"Oh, I don't know. Maybe *Training Day*, *The French Connection*, or *Dirty Harry*. Any of those would have been better than this crap."

"Oh...I would definitely pick Denzel Washington."

He narrowed his eyes. "You mean *Training Day*?"

I nudged his leg with my foot. "Sure."

"You do realize that he's as old as my grandfather, right?"

"Shut your mouth." I laughed. "He's still hot and so is Clint Eastwood."

"Do you have a thing for older men, Ava?"

I stuck my tongue out and threw a kernel of popcorn at him.

"Real mature." He rolled his eyes, scooped a handful out of the bowl, and tossed it at me.

"Hey." I laughed while plucking a few kernels out of my hair. "That was uncalled for." I started to inch toward the bowl to get my revenge when he snatched it off the table and held it out of my reach. The hem of his shirt lifted, showing off his tanned stomach. Holy shit, was he hot. My breathing picked up; there was no way he didn't notice it. His eyes dropped to my lips, and instead of leaning back like I should have, my body slanted forward. It felt like there was no space left between us. I didn't want to rush things, but the urge to kiss him grew stronger by the second.

Very slowly, I moved closer, searching for any signs of hesitation. He took a deep swallow, and I could tell he was just as nervous as I was. I took the bowl out of his hands and set it back on the table. He looked like he was holding his breath as if he wasn't sure this was really happening.

I rested my hands on his shoulders. "If I kiss you right now, will you pull away like before?"

"Ava," he said with a tortured look on his face. "Don't think for one second that I didn't want that kiss. Hell, if I had my way, we would have done a whole lot more than kissing that night."

"What if I want you to have your way tonight?" I pressed my lips softly against his.

His hands framed my face. "I'll give you whatever you want, if you're sure this is it. What I don't want is for you to regret it."

I wasn't sure about anything other than I would hate myself later for not exploring these feelings. With a sense of bravery I had never felt before, I dropped my mouth to his and blocked out whatever doubts I had lingering in my head.

He hesitated at first, but slowly moved his lips in sync with mine. I closed my eyes and tried not to think about how different his lips felt. I tried not to compare how he threaded his hands through my hair, instead of how Drew would glide them along my back. I tilted my head as he brushed his tongue tentatively against mine. He let me take the lead as I skimmed my hands along his chest. It surprised me how easy it was to kiss him. How much I wanted to be kissed by him. His muscles were tense, and I could feel his apprehension. Whatever thoughts and worries I had faded into desire. His tongue delved deeper into my mouth. Everything felt like it was too much and not enough. There was a mixture of desperation and self-control in his touch. A million thoughts raced through my mind, but there was no regret, no remorse. This kiss was everything I needed. Everything I wanted and certainly wasn't what I expected.

I pulled back and gazed into his eyes. "Thank you."

"For what?" He swallowed, holding my stare.

I held his face in my hands, hoping he would be able to understand how much this meant to me. "For making tonight one of the best nights I've had in a really long time."

A smile tilted his lips. "You don't have to thank me. Do you know how long I've been wanting to do that? I've wanted to kiss you since the second I laid eyes on you."

I played with a lock of his hair. "I don't know what I'm ready for, but I know I want to keep seeing you. I like having you around and spending time with you."

He pressed his forehead against mine. "Why don't we take it one day at a time? The last thing I want to do is push you into something you're not ready for. But I would like to keep kissing you."

I rested my head against his chest and tried to fight the smile that was taking over. "What a coincidence, I'd like to do the same thing."

And kiss we did.

TWELVE

LOGAN

I forced myself out of my car, walked up the steps like a man condemned, and hesitantly pushed the doorbell. Pete, one of my old neighbors, was out walking his dog. I gave him a wave and a nod and turned my back before he could strike up a conversation.

Vanessa swung the door open and leaned against the frame. "Well, look who's here. It's my long-lost husband." Her tone was anything but pleasant. "Have you already gotten bored with your little hookup of the month?"

"I'm not your husband anymore." I looked over my shoulder. There were too many curtain twitchers peeking through their windows on this street. The last thing I wanted was to have an audience for this exchange. "And Ava isn't a hookup."

She folded her arms across her chest. "What exactly is Ava to you then?"

I stared at her, unsure how to respond. I should have anticipated Brina would say something. Not coming prepared was no one's fault but my own.

"I don't really think that's any of your business."

"Oh, that's where you are wrong. Everything you do is my business."

I swore to myself that I wouldn't lose my cool no matter what she said, but if anyone knew how to get a reaction out of me, it was my ex-wife. Honestly, it seemed like she went out of her way to irritate me.

"Ava is no one you need to concern yourself with. So, don't bring her up again."

She studied me carefully. "She obviously means something to you if you're so defensive about her?"

I wasn't sure what she wanted me to say. If I told her about Ava, then she would call me insensitive. If I didn't tell her, then I was hiding things from her. There was no winning with my ex-wife. Vanessa would only twist my words around and hold them against me. I was going to get shit either way.

"Leave her name out of this conversation." My voice was low, but the warning was clear.

"I don't want you bringing random women around my daughter."

"Our daughter," I reminded her. "You seem to forget that Brina is my child too, along with the fact that we are no longer married."

Her eyes turned glacier. "Oh, I remember all right. I remember how you walked out on me and your daughter because you needed to focus on your own happiness. How you went and started a new life and never looked back. You knew that I still loved you and wanted to stay married, but you left me anyway." You would have thought we divorced yesterday instead of almost three years ago with how worked up she was. "Meanwhile, you're bringing random women around a daughter that you claim to love, but if you really did, then you wouldn't have left us."

"Are you done?"

If I had a dollar for every time she spewed this crap, I could buy my own island in the Caribbean. Her recollection of events is a hell of a lot different from reality, with one exception. I was the one who left. I spent six years of my life trying to make things work. I didn't realize until the end that we were doomed from the start. I ignored so many red flags because I assumed everything could be changed or fixed. That was very naïve on my part. Being married to Vanessa was like a bad cold that never went away.

I tried. God, did I try, but I could only take so much.

"Why are you such an asshole, Logan?"

I sighed. "I'm not trying to be. I just don't see the point in arguing. I came here to talk to you."

She did her best to smooth out her frown. She was expecting a fight. I wasn't going to give her one. "What do you want to talk to me about?"

"I want to take Brina on a trip this summer."

"What kind of trip?"

"Are you going to let me in so we can talk, or are we doing this out here?"

"Fine." She huffed. "You can come in."

She held the door open but didn't leave much room. I had to brush past her, and of course, she pushed her breasts out as soon as our bodies touched. I internally rolled my eyes.

"Are you still taking her to the carnival tonight?" she asked, walking over to the counter to pour herself a cup of coffee.

"I am." I pulled out a barstool and took a seat.

"Don't forget she has dance tomorrow at ten, so don't keep her out too late."

I wasn't worried about her being tired the next day. I was concerned about Vanessa finding out that Ava and Madison were going with us.

"My parents rented a house up in the Adirondacks for two weeks in August," I said, getting straight to the point. The sooner we finished this conversation, the sooner I could leave.

She walked over to the fridge to get her almond milk to add to her coffee. "Send me the dates and I'll let you know."

I gritted my teeth. She acted like an HR director who had to approve my time off. Tension crept up in my spine.

"Also, while I'm here." I pulled the envelope out of my back pocket and smacked it down on the counter. "I believe this is yours."

"What's that?" she asked, sliding onto one of the barstools.

"It's a bill with my name on it for lawn service."

"You're right it is. What's your point?"

"Why the fuck am I getting charged for this?"

She huffed and threw her long dark hair over her shoulder. Vanessa was a beautiful woman, and I was the stupid son of a bitch who allowed her beauty to cloud my judgment when we first met.

"You seriously expect me to mow the lawn and trim the bushes that you planted?" She played with the diamond pendant necklace I gave her and trailed her fingers to her cleavage. "I told you from the beginning that I wanted minimal landscaping, but you got what you wanted and now I have a damn forest growing around my house."

This was an ongoing battle during our marriage. She fought me tooth and nail on everything. The fence. The deck. The landscaping. I let her make every other decision without any protest. She picked everything from the paint, the furniture, to the SUV she drove. Whoever came up with the phrase "happy wife, happy life" never met Vanessa.

"Yes, I expect you to pay because it's part of being a responsible homeowner. If you don't like the bushes, then tear them out and pour cement across the entire property, I don't care. I don't live here anymore and I'm not paying that bill."

"We had an agreement. You said you would help me out."

"Yeah, I meant if the hot water tank went or the furnace shit the bed. I'm not paying for this."

Vanessa came from money. She was a pampered princess who was used to getting her way. My ex-wife also suffered from major mommy and daddy issues. When she dropped out of college to pursue a career in modeling, her parents cut her off. Once she realized that her looks weren't going to pay the bills, she started bussing tables to make ends meet. That's where we met.

When I saw her wearing that little plaid skirt with a low-cut green top, I was stunned, speechless at how stunning she was. I thought I hit the mother lode when she agreed to go on a date with me. I was young and dumb and full of cum. No matter how beautiful or how great the sex was, no woman is worth what I went through.

She parked her hands on her hips. "You know I don't make a ton of money working at the doctor's office. The one thing I splurge on is these nails." She held them out.

"I'm not breaking them by pulling out those damn shrubs I didn't even want in the first place."

"But you wanted this house, right?"

"Damn right I did."

I pushed the letter toward her and tapped my finger over the amount due. "The bushes came with the house, so pay the bill."

"I'll tell you what. You pay that for me and I'll let you take Brina on your family vacation."

My back went straight. "You're serious?"

"As a heart attack."

"This is low, even for you. Using Brina to blackmail me."

She rolled her eyes so far back in her head I was afraid her fake eyelashes would fall out. "I'm not blackmailing anybody. You can either pay the bill and take your daughter camping or not pay the bill and go alone. Completely your choice." She smiled smugly, seeming so damn pleased with herself. I had officially reached my limit.

I smacked my hands down on the counter and leaned in. "I'm taking you back to court."

"What?" she shrieked. "What the hell would you do that for?"

"Because I'm sick and tired of your games and trying to drain my life savings."

There was nothing I wouldn't do for my daughter. That was the only reason why I tolerated her bullshit. I gave her the house, and the car in the divorce. I paid off all the credit card debt. I covered all Brina's doctor and dentist appointments. I even paid for her dance classes, her clothes, and added lunch money to her account at school every month. All this on top of the monthly support checks she got from me. Not once have I ever complained. I would give every last cent to my name if it meant my daughter had what she needed.

"Drain your savings? Really? How about the fact that I had to go get a job because my husband left me without an income?" She blinked at me like working was completely beneath her. The biggest mistake I ever made was allowing her to become financially dependent on me. All the overtime I worked was never appreciated. All she did was whine that I was never home. On the days where I was home, she would complain we didn't have any money. I couldn't catch a break to save my life.

"Maybe you should save that speech for the judge." I tapped my knuckles on the granite countertop and stormed out the door.

THIRTEEN

AVA

My body vibrated with anticipation while Madison and I waited for Logan to pick us up. I've spent the last week trying to wrap my head around that kiss. I've worried about what to say and how to act tonight. I tried to play it cool when he invited us to go to the carnival a couple of towns over, but truthfully, I was freaking out.

I spotted his black truck coming down the street. I locked my front door, grabbed Madison's hand, and led her down the walkway. He pulled into my driveway and jumped out to greet us.

Jesus! Why did he always have to look so damn good? It was utterly unfair. He slid his aviators on top of his head and smiled at us. "Hello, ladies. Are you ready to have some fun tonight?"

Madison let go of my hand and skipped over to him. "We are going to have so much fun," she stuck her foot out, "even though my mom made me wear sneakers. I really wanted to wear my sandals, but she said my feet would get dirty."

"I have to agree with your mom on this one, kiddo.

Besides, some of the attendants won't let you ride if you don't have the proper shoes."

She tilted her head up in confusion. "What's an attendant?"

He laughed. "A worker. The person who lets you on the ride."

"Oh, well, I like rides, especially the ones that go upside down. Does Brina like those?"

"She's not a fan of going upside down, but she likes the rides that spin and go really fast. Don't worry though, I'll go on whatever you want."

I smiled, watching him give Madison his full attention. I tried not to stare too much at how good he looked in a simple pair of jeans and a black T-shirt. My tongue darted out to wet my dry lips. He looked up at that moment and quirked an eyebrow, letting me know that I'd been caught.

"I'm going to grab her a sweater in case it gets cold later." My daughter gave me the stink eye. She could be so stubborn at times.

"No need. Brina has an extra sweatshirt in the back of my truck if she needs one." He winked at Madison like they were in on a secret.

Brina rolled her window down and waved us over. "Come on, guys, we have a lot of rides to go on."

I chuckled at her enthusiasm.

Logan slid into the driver's seat and buckled his seat belt. He shot a glance my way and almost reached for my hand but stopped himself. I shifted in place, looking out my window. I really wanted him to hold my hand, but it wouldn't be appropriate in front of the girls.

He cleared his throat and started to back out. "You can push your seat back if you want. They have plenty of leg room."

"I'm fine." I stretched my legs out, showing him I had more than enough space. The girls' laughter coming from the back seat had me turning around. "What are you two troublemakers up to back there?"

"Brina just told me what her dad is going to try to win you at the carnival."

I slanted my head to the side. "Really, and what's that?"

Brina reached over and flashed a finger over Madison's mouth and whispered to keep quiet.

"It's a secret," Brina offered up, meeting her dad's eyes in the rearview mirror. He gave her a warning look which I thought was funny until I realized what it could be.

My head snapped to his. "It better not be what I think it is."

The smirk on his face gave it away. I smacked his leg. "If you even think about winning me a goldfish, that thing will be sent right back out to the ocean where it came from by morning."

"You would really kill an innocent little goldfish?" He sounded offended and was laying it on thick for his audience in the back.

Both girls gasped on cue. "No! You can't kill the fish."

I groaned and leaned against the door. I was tempted to bang my head against the window. He set me up on purpose. He knew bringing them in on his plan would leave me stuck with the damn thing.

The girls were talkative during the entire ride, and by the time we pulled up to the carnival, they were both pretty wired. I thought giving them my phone to watch YouTube videos would calm them down, but they were too excited to sit still. They couldn't stop talking about which rides they wanted to go on first.

Brina jumped out of her seat and looked out the window. "Woah…look at that Ferris wheel."

The parking lot attendant came over to take our money and placed a ticket on the windshield. Logan's hand brushed up against mine as we weaved our way through the gravel lot. Once we reached the entrance, the girls ran straight to the ticket booth. After looking at the prices, we decided to buy the unlimited wristband instead of individual tickets. Well, I should say Logan bought the girls wristbands. He insisted on paying, which made me feel guilty. These carnival rides weren't cheap.

The girls were beside themselves as we walked by the blinking neon lights from the rides. Teenagers screamed as they were being flipped around and thrown in the air. The girls paused as we passed the swings; one of their favorite rap songs blared through the speakers. It was amusing watching the ride attendant try to egg them on the ride. Oh, to be young and fearless again.

There were so many attractions; they weren't sure where to start. After riding the swings and The Round-Up, they made a beeline for the Scrambler, which had a short line.

Logan and I stood back and watched them while I pulled my phone out and snapped a few pictures. Once the Scrambler came to a stop, they jumped out of the car; their smiles were infectious.

"What's your favorite ride, Ava?" Brina asked while Madison looked through the photos I had just taken.

"She likes the Tilt-A-Whirl," my daughter stated without looking up.

Logan nudged my arm. "You're quite the daredevil, huh?"

"I prefer rides that don't toss me into the air defying gravity."

"She doesn't like upside-down roller coasters either," Madison offered up and handed me back my phone. I glared at her while tucking it away.

Logan shook his head like he was disappointed in me. Whatever, at least I didn't have to worry about throwing up and having a killer headache from screaming so much. Plus, these rides were taken down and put together once a week. No, thank you.

We reached the end of the midway and stood in the long line, waiting for our turn for the Tilt-A-Whirl; the girls demanded that they ride alone. Logan and I walked along the unsteady platform, climbed into the car, and pulled the safety bar down on our laps. He put his arm around me and grinned. "Don't go squishing me." He winked, and I stuck my tongue out because I was mature like that.

He looked around briefly and surprised me when he leaned in and closed his mouth over mine. I no longer cared about where we were because there was no way I could resist him even if I wanted to, which I didn't. The kiss was needy and quick and way too short. He pulled back with a smirk, and I wanted to cry because that kiss was nowhere near enough.

"I've been wanting to do that since I picked you up tonight," he confessed while running the pad of his thumb along my bottom lip. "Just needed a minute alone with you away from prying eyes."

I was pretty sure my cheeks were the same color as the matching apple cars we were sitting in. The man made me feel like a damn teenager.

The ride started out slow at first before we started spinning in different directions. I gripped the bar, trying and failing to stay on my side. We laughed as the car turned us around and around. Logan's body kept crashing into mine; there was no way it wasn't deliberate. I leaned my body as far away as I could, but he refused to give me space.

Once we stopped, I shifted to face him. "You did that on purpose."

"What are you talking about?" The corners of his eyes were crinkling in humor.

"You banged your body up against mine. I'm going to be sore for days."

"Banged your body, huh?" He laughed as we made our way off the ride.

I groaned, trying to act put off, but really, I was having the time of my life. The two minutes spent in that hot rusty car wasn't nearly long enough. My thighs stuck to the ripped leather seats, and I would bet my life savings that these rides hadn't been cleaned in the last decade, yet I was already dreading when this night would come to an end.

"Did you guys get dizzy?" Madison asked as we exited the ride.

I quickly pulled her hair into a ponytail, brushing the strands back with my fingers. "We did, but it was fun. What's next?"

"The fun house," they both said at the same time.

"I'm going to grab a cold beer, want one?" Logan asked, pulling out his wallet.

"No, thanks. I'm good for now."

Logan got his drink and brought back a couple of waters. I smiled, watching all the little kids crawl along the moving tubes and squeal through the maze of mirrors. "I love carnivals. They remind me of how much fun it was to be a kid."

"The girls are having a good time," he said, stepping aside as a little boy came running toward us.

"I am too. Thank you for inviting us." He squeezed my hand while I met his gaze. His touch was comforting, and it was impossible not to feel the insane connection between us.

We stood there in the middle of the crowd, just staring at each other. So much was spoken without a single word. Logan's phone rang in his pocket, breaking our connection. He pulled it out and rolled his eyes when he looked at the caller ID.

"Excuse me for a minute," he grumbled and walked a few steps away.

Whoever it was on the phone, he didn't look all that happy. He shook his head and moved his hands animatedly. From my view, it looked like he was yelling into the phone, but I was too far away to hear, especially with all the noise. A few minutes later, he was back.

"Is everything okay?" I asked, noticing his shift in mood.

"Yeah. That was Brina's mom. She was calling to remind me that Brina has dance in the morning and not to keep her out too late."

His phone chirped with a message. He looked at the screen; his jaw ticked, and his shoulders tensed. He pocketed the phone and brought his hand to the back of his neck.

"What kind of dance does she do?" I asked, trying to distract him.

"Ballet and sometimes hip-hop."

"That sounds like fun. I wish Madison had an interest in dance."

"What does she like to do?" he implored, ignoring the vibration from his cell phone in his pants pocket.

I cleared my throat and folded my arms in front of my stomach. Logan's ex-wife was starting to put a damper on our evening, and she wasn't even here. "She plays softball and basketball."

He laughed. "Yeah, Vanessa would never allow that."

"Why not?" I questioned, even though his ex-wife was the last person I wanted to talk about. We were having the perfect night up until she called. He tried to hide his annoyance, but I could still sense it.

"Well," he reached up and scratched his scruff, "softball would require her to play in the dirt, and basketball is too much of a contact sport."

"It can be, but at this age, it's all about teamwork and making friends."

"Hey, you don't have to tell me. I grew up playing hockey and lacrosse."

"Really, what else did you play?" I pictured him as captain of the football team with a fan club of teenage girls following him around everywhere he went.

He laughed. "I pretty much dabbled in every sport out there except soccer. And even though I played little league when I was younger, it was never my thing."

"Really, why is that?" I was curious about the baseball part but didn't want to bring attention to it because it was Drew's sport.

"Soccer I just found boring to watch, so I never had an interest to play. And baseball is the opposite. I love to watch an MLB game, but I hated playing as a kid because it wasn't fast-paced enough for me. I had a ton of energy and needed to move around. For me, the best part about playing baseball was goofing around with my buddies in the dugout. And," he looked at me and laughed, "the snacks the moms would pass out after the practices and games." I shook my head and laughed along with him.

Logan spent the next few minutes telling me how he played hockey and lacrosse but had to quit hockey once he reached varsity because lacrosse was too much of a commitment, and that's where his heart was.

We stopped talking as the girls came closer. Brina came up and tugged on his hand. "Dad, can we play games now?"

"I told you earlier, we can play games when you're done with the rides." He bent down and kissed the side of her head.

Madison placed her arm on mine. "I want to go on the Fireball."

"You know I won't go on that one." There was a good chance I would puke my brains out if I did.

She hung her head in disappointment. "Brina won't ride that one with me either."

Logan glanced over as she crossed her arms and did nothing to hide how upset she was.

"I'd be happy to ride with you." He looked from me to her. "As long as it's okay with your mom."

I raised an eyebrow. "Are you sure you don't mind?"

"Not at all. I'd be happy to take her." He paused and looked at Brina as she chugged the water bottle he gave her. "She's getting hungry. Maybe the two of you can go order some food and we'll meet you when we're done."

I put my hand on Madison's shoulder. "Are you okay riding with Logan?"

She nodded her head enthusiastically, causing me to

laugh at her eagerness. "Great." I turned to Brina. "Why don't you and I go take a break while these two daredevils go hang their heads upside down on the ride."

I watched Logan and Madison as they weaved their way through the crowd. He angled his head to the side, listening to her intently as she talked a mile a minute. It was so endearing to watch; I had a hard time taking my eyes off them.

I placed my hand on Brina's shoulder. "Come on, let's go find some food."

We strolled over to one of the food trailers. I stopped and let her get a bag of cotton candy, something I could tell by the way her face lit up that her mother would never allow her to do. Whatever, you're only young once. We found a picnic table under a big white tent. I sent a text to Logan telling him where we were. We ordered burgers and fries and sat down with plates and drinks.

"Does Madison's dad like to go on upside rides too?" she asked while dipping her French fry in ketchup.

Answering these questions never got easier, and I couldn't only imagine how my daughter felt when people would ask her about Drew.

"Her dad is in heaven, honey," I tried to explain gently. I wasn't sure how much she understood about death. It could be very confusing and overwhelming for a young child. I was about ready to explain that his body was no longer here but resting someplace else when she surprised me.

"You mean he's dead?" Her little forehead wrinkled, and I blinked, trying to scramble for an answer.

"Yes, he is." I gave her a sad smile, and twisted my hands in my lap.

"She must be sad not to have a dad anymore," she lamented, and went back to eating her food.

"She misses him, but thankfully, she has family and friends like you that make her not feel so sad."

She seemed to think that over for a minute. "My dad is a really good dad, and a lot of fun. She can come hang out with us when she gets sad."

Oh, my heart just filled with joy and sorrow at the same time. "That is awfully nice of you. She loves spending time with you and your dad."

I shifted on the wooden bench seat, twisting my ring on my finger. Sometimes it felt like just yesterday when Drew and I would do fun things like this as a family. It worried me how much Madison would remember as she got older. The last thing I wanted was for her ever to forget her father or how much he loved her.

Madison spotted me from across the crowd, running full speed ahead. She jumped into my lap, too excited to sit still. "Mom, that was so much fun. We tipped around like twenty times and I didn't even get dizzy."

I looked over at Logan, who looked a little green, and bit back a laugh.

"Can we go on the bumper cars now?" she asked me but looked to Logan for permission.

"Why don't you take a break and eat something and then you can go on another ride."

She hopped off my lap while Brina made room for her dad to sit next to her. He pressed a kiss on her forehead. "Having fun, sweetheart?"

She pulled her bag of cotton candy out from her side and grinned. He took the bag out of her hand, broke off a piece, and stuffed it in his mouth. I handed Madison hers and let her eat a small amount before she dug into her dinner.

Logan and I carried the plates to the trash can while the girls discussed which rides they were going on next. The four of us made our way up and down the midway, stopping at the long line for the bumper cars. An hour later, we were standing in front of Arcade Alley.

"Time to win my lady a prize," Logan whispered in my ear playfully.

I backed up and put my hands in the air. "I'm not participating in this."

"You know, that's not very nice. You sound a little ungrateful."

"Couldn't you just win me one of those over-sized stuffed bears?"

He ignored me and ushered the girls over to the tent. I spotted a wine slushy stand a few feet away and headed in that direction. I leaned up against a pole, sipping on my frozen drink, and watched Logan and his playful antics. He was trying to show off for the small crowd that gathered around as he went through the bucket of ping-pong balls that he spent a fortune on. His eyebrows folded together in concentration before each throw. I wasn't even paying attention to see if those little white balls reached their target. I was too busy laughing along with everyone else.

The girls came racing up to me, holding a clear plastic baggie in each of their hands. "Look," they held the goldfish up, "you got two, so we each get to name them."

Logan tucked his hands in his pockets with a sly grin on his face. He looked pretty damn pleased with himself.

"Well," I sipped my slushy, wishing I could kiss that

stupid grin off his face, "it looks like I'm the proud owner of two new pets."

"That you are," he confirmed. "You better take care of them. They are very expensive goldfish." He backed away. "Now I think it's time I go win these girls a prize. I can't let them go home empty-handed."

"Of course, they get stuffed animals and I get these," I gritted out in annoyance.

After throwing darts at balloons, shooting BB guns at targets, tossing rings on posts, and firing water guns, Brina walked away with a huge brown bear and a baby dolphin. Madison was carrying a gigantic SpongeBob and a little stuffed dog.

"You do realize you could have saved yourself a lot of money and just stopped at the Dollar Store on our way home?"

"Yeah, but this right here," he pointed to the girls as they walked in front of us, "is priceless."

My daughter's smile lit up her entire face that was sticky from the cotton candy. Brina's hair was falling out of her ponytail; she had a face painting on one side of her cheek and grass stains all over her white shorts.

I couldn't agree more.

FOURTEEN
LOGAN

"WHAT WAS SO IMPORTANT THAT YOU NEEDED TO MEET WITH me outside the office, Renee?"

Renee Alvez was an assistant district attorney. She was a no-nonsense, no-bullshit type of person. I wasn't all that surprised when she got straight to the point.

"How are you making out with the Wilson case?"

I eyed her skeptically, trying to figure out what her angle was. "I'm hoping to wrap it up soon?"

"I need a favor."

"You know better than to ask me that."

"Please." She batted her eyelashes in a way I was all too familiar with. Renee wasn't just a coworker. She was someone I hooked up with a few times in the past. It was nothing serious, but I got the impression she was more into me than I was with her.

I set my turkey sandwich down and pushed it aside. "Renee, this is a sensitive case. If you want a conviction then let me do my job." I leveled my gaze on hers. "The right way."

The case she was referring to would most likely be one

of the biggest trials of her career. Doug Wilson was a prominent dentist, and our number one suspect in the murder of a topless dancer found in an alley outside the Landing Strip, a gentleman's club just south of the airport. Right now, all we had was circumstantial evidence tying him to the murder. Surveillance was getting heavy, and while our IT department was making progress combing through his digital footprint, time was running out. I wanted a warrant for his arrest before another woman was found sexually assaulted and murdered.

"I just want to help move this case along."

What she was really saying was, she wanted her moment in the spotlight. She was one step away from a promotion, and this would be the case that would seal the deal.

"Patience," I reminded her.

"Fine." She pushed back in her chair. "I knew it was a long shot. It was also the only way I could get you to meet with me."

I knew this lunch was an excuse, but against my better judgment, I agreed. The last time she called and asked if I'd meet her out for a drink, I told her I wasn't interested. With things picking up with Ava, there wasn't a chance in hell I was going to give Renee any false hope. Our fling was over and done. She knew this but used this case to get me here. I was busy and didn't have time for her games.

"Renee, there are two things I won't do." I placed my arm along the back of the chair next to me. "Jeopardize this case or go back to being fuck buddies."

She folded her arms along her chest and glared. "You could have phrased that a little more gently, don't you think?"

Renee knew the shit I went through with my ex-wife.

She understood why we ended. She wasn't stupid. I never misled her, and I certainly never made her any promises. When I said something, I meant it. My blood heated with frustration as I stared at her. Renee was used to getting what she wanted, and she hated that I wasn't willing to give it to her.

I wadded my napkin up and placed it in the middle of the tray next to my half-eaten sandwich. "I'm just being honest. I thought you of all people would appreciate that."

She tossed her long auburn hair over her shoulder. Renee was gorgeous. You would never know by looking at her that she was in her mid-forties. She had a fan club of admirers following her around the office everywhere she went—some of them straight out of the academy. Age didn't matter when it came to an attractive woman, especially one who was into fitness like Renee. She had a body of a twenty-one-year-old.

"There has to be something I can do to change your mind." She brought the heel of her shoe up to my pant leg and started trailing it up to my calf. "None of the men I've been with lately know how to handle me. You're a tough act to follow."

I laughed, not knowing what to say to that. Renee had a very active sex drive. She'd been around the block a few times and was comfortable in her own skin. Our relationship was satisfying for both of us while it lasted, but things just fizzled out on my end. "C'mon, you know damn well that's not true. There is plenty of young blood in that precinct with enough stamina to keep you entertained."

Hell, at forty-five, she could probably teach them a trick or two.

She twirled her hair along her finger. "You know what I like. You're fun and…" Her eyes darted over my shoulder.

A little hand tapped me on the arm. I turned in my seat, shocked to see Madison grinning from ear to ear. "Hi, Logan."

"Hey, kiddo, what are you doing here?"

My eyes moved over to the older lady that was standing behind her. "I'm sorry to interrupt your lunch date, but my granddaughter said you were her friend, and she wanted to come say hello."

Granddaughter? Great! This was Ava's mom, and she thought I was on a date. This wasn't awkward at all. I ran a hand through my hair, praying she didn't overhear my conversation with Renee.

I held my hand out. "I'm glad you stopped by. I'm Logan Blake, it's nice to meet you."

If her daughter mentioned my name, she didn't show it. It was stupid to let that bother me, but it did anyway.

"Judith." She shook my hand.

I took her in; she was a picture of class and elegance, yet her demeanor was friendly and warm. I shifted my attention back to my little friend. "Isn't today a school day?"

"It's summer break, duh."

I snapped my fingers and played dumb. "Oh, that's right. Aren't you supposed to be at summer camp?"

She shook her head back and forth. "Not today, Wednesday is my day with Grandma."

"Well, lucky Grandma." I looked up at the woman with short, brown hair the same color as Ava's, except it had a little gray peppered in. "What do you ladies have planned for the day?"

"We're going to Independence Hall and then going on a carriage ride," Madison said with her eyes lighting up. I could tell she was getting impatient and wanted to get moving. "Do you want to come with us?"

"Wow. That's sounds like fun. I wish I could, but I'm working today. I'm just finishing up my work lunch with ADA Alverez, and then I have to head back to the station."

I could feel Renee's gaze on me. No doubt the wheels were spinning in her head.

Madison's smile turned into a pout. I hated disappointing her. I reached out and adjusted the small backpack around her shoulders. "If I didn't have to worry about getting in trouble with my boss, I would be happy to tag along. Maybe we can pick another time when Brina and your mom can go too."

That seemed to appease her, but damn, for someone who probably weighed no more than fifty-five pounds, she knew how to throw one hell of a guilt trip.

"Why don't we let Mr. Blake get back to his lunch," Judith said, reaching for Madison's hand.

"Okay." She didn't look too happy about that, but she knew throwing a fit wasn't going to do her any good. "Are you coming over this week? My mom bought an aquarium for the fish you won her at the carnival."

My lips quirked up at that. "Did she? I'll have to come by later and check it out."

"Yay." She clapped her hands and surprised me when she threw herself into my arms. I held her tight, inhaling her strawberry-scented shampoo. This little girl was slowly working her way into my heart, just like her mother.

I kissed the top of her head. "Have a good day, sweetheart."

Judith looked mildly intrigued. She seemed to have a

million questions to ask me but instead gave me a tight nod and walked away.

I watched them stroll out of the restaurant and turned back to Renee. "Sorry, about that."

Renee placed her hands under her chin and arched an eyebrow. "It makes sense now. You're seeing someone."

She didn't sound pissed off or annoyed, so I took that as a good sign. "It's new."

Her eyes narrowed slightly. "You better hope your ex-wife doesn't find out."

Renee knew about Vanessa's craziness. It was another reason why I liked her enough to keep seeing her on the regular. She went through a messy divorce herself and wanted to keep what we had private and casual. With Ava, though, there was nothing casual about her.

———

The sun was warm on my back as I peered through the windows of Ava's salon. I watched her, completely mesmerized as she moved around with ease, laughing lightly with an older lady sitting in the chair at the end. Her long dark hair was loose, tickling her back as she retrieved something out of the cabinet. Memories flooded my mind as I recalled the soft and silky texture beneath my fingertips. That kiss on the couch wasn't enough. I didn't know what it was about her, but I wanted more, and not just physically.

I ran a hand through my hair, wondering what had happened to me. Typically, I was the guy waiting for the girl to walk my way. Truthfully, I didn't have to try or chase a girl. It just happened. I could call Renee and have simple and easy. But simple and easy got boring after a while. It seemed lately I wanted messy and complicated.

Before I could talk myself out of this any further, I squared my shoulders and took confident strides toward the front door.

"Hi there," a blond woman called when I stepped inside. "Can I help you?"

I leaned my elbows along the counter and flashed her a friendly smile. "I'm looking for Ava."

On the walk over, I debated on calling her first but didn't want to risk the chance of her telling me she was too busy. Showing up unannounced and getting a glimpse of her was better than calling and hearing the sound of her voice.

Ava's feet paused halfway on the wood floor; a smile appeared immediately on her face.

I took that as a good sign.

"Logan, what are you doing here?"

"Isn't it obvious?" I touched the top of my hair, trying to sound casual. "I'm here for a trim. Plus," I held out the iced coffee that Amelia said she loved, "I heard this is your favorite."

The blond behind the desk grinned, like she was in on a secret. "I'm Kara." She held out her hand for me to take. "We met briefly on Ava's birthday."

"Ahh…yes." I shook her hand, pretending to remember her. Honestly, I only had eyes for Ava that night. The Pope could have been standing right in front of me, yet I still wouldn't have noticed. "Good to see you again."

She gave me a look like she knew I was full of shit.

"So, Logan." Ava stepped closer, a smile tugging at her lips. "What are you looking to have done today exactly?"

She reached for the extended coffee. "Thank you for this, by the way. That was very sweet of you to think of me."

I stroked my chin, pretending to consider it. "Just looking for a little cleanup around the ears and back of my neck."

She leaned forward and grabbed the ends of my hair, rubbing it between her fingertips. "I don't usually take walk-ins, but for you, I'll make an exception. Follow me." She started moving toward the back, where there was a row of black sinks.

My eyes were glued to her hips as she swayed them across the salon. Damn, her ass looked pretty good in those black pants, but then again, it always looked good to me. She wiped off the leather seat with a rag before I sat down.

I stretched my legs out and rested my hands on my knees. "You're never going to believe who I just ran into?"

She let out a laugh while securing the black cape along my body. "I heard, my mom just texted me and asked who you were."

My eyebrows popped up. "What did you tell her?"

"I haven't responded yet."

A small part of me wanted to press her on how she would explain our relationship, but the bigger part was afraid of her answer.

"So, how are Splish and Splash doing?" I asked, deciding to be a smart-ass instead.

"Oh, you know, shitting all over their aquarium and stinking up my house."

I rolled my eyes as she stood over at the sink. "You're not feeding them too much, are you?"

"Of course not, they could die." She tucked a towel behind the back of my neck and wrapped it around my shoulders. "And that would be a tragedy." She patted my chest and turned the faucet on.

She was such a ballbuster.

Once the water reached the right temperature, she started washing my hair. I had to suppress a moan when she bent forward to get the shampoo bottle. There was nothing sexier than having a beautiful woman with her boobs right in your face, especially one with a skin-hugging top that left little to the imagination. It was damned near impossible to look away. I was tempted to bury my cheeks in between her cleavage and sniff the scented body lotion she had coating her skin. I patted the front of my pants, acting like I was searching for something but secretly checking to see if I had a bulge.

"Did you find what you were looking for?" she asked, screwing up the corners of her lips.

"I don't know, I can't really see with my head back like this. Maybe I should have you check."

She lifted her eyebrows. "You would like that, wouldn't you?"

A laugh flew from my chest. "You have no idea."

Visions of how good the swell of her breasts felt up against my chest popped into my mind. Those memories weren't helping.

"And here I thought you were a gentleman."

"Give me a chance and I'll prove exactly how nice I can be." I winked and gave her a sly grin.

"Is that right?" Her fingers massaged my scalp. My eyes closed at the feel of her hands kneading and pressing against my skin. "And here I thought you were a bad boy."

My eyes popped open. "Which one do you prefer?"

"It depends. During the day, I like a nice guy who

opens doors, pulls out chairs, and buys flowers and jewelry for no reason. But at night, I like the unexpected, the rebel who takes what he wants and keeps me on my toes."

I hissed out as her hands dug deeper into my scalp. "That sounds like a lot of pressure on a guy."

"You asked." She dragged her hands down my neck. My mouth fell open when the little tease leaned in closer and dropped her voice. "Do you happen to know anyone who fits the bill?"

"I might. Is there a sign-up form I can fill out?"

Her throaty laugh caused her hair to drift forward. Unable to resist, I pushed it back away from her face. A touch of pink, the same color as her top, crept up to her cheeks. Our gazes lingered for a moment, her lips parted, and I wanted to reach up and taste them. Our eyes stayed locked; I could feel that spark between us intensifying, the one that made me forget about everything else going on in the world but right here.

She cleared her throat and turned the water off. "All right, funny guy, follow me."

She guided me to her station, filled with styling tools, hair products, combs, and brushes. There was a lot jammed into the small space, but surprisingly it didn't look cluttered. I slumped in the chair and glanced around, noticing the framed cosmetology license on the brick wall, as well as a few pictures of Madison and Drew.

She squeezed my shoulder and spun me around. "No looking into the mirror until I'm finished."

"That requires a certain level of trust. I'm not sure we're quite there yet," I teased as she ignored me and started running a comb through my hair.

She pushed my hair off to the side, grazing her fingers

along my stubble. My bulge was getting bigger and bigger. There was no way she couldn't see it. It practically tested the restraint of my zipper.

"You've got great hair. I don't want to take too much off."

"I want you to cut it however you like it. Your opinion is the only one I care about."

She shook her head and started trimming away. "You're too smooth for your own good. You know that?"

She thought I was joking. I was dead serious. I didn't give a shit about what anyone else thought but her.

I glanced around the salon. It was small and trendy, with dark brown flooring and a sitting area with dark chairs and white table lamps. It had a good vibe, and it was a hell of a lot cleaner than the barbershop I usually went to.

"So, Kara is the other owner, right?" I asked, rearranging the black cape along my chest.

"Yes, we worked together when we were both starting out." She held my hair up by her fingertips and started snipping away.

"How did you end up in business together?" I was eager to learn every little detail about her life.

"When Madison came along, I wanted to have the flexibility to make my own hours. And I figured it would be the perfect way to put my business degree to good use. When the previous owner was looking to sell, I approached Kara with a marketing plan and asked if she wanted to go into business together. She's a couple years younger than me, but she's very driven and we just clicked."

"Not to mention, I'm one of the few people who can

put up with her," Kara added as she walked by with a customer.

Ava shook her head and laughed. "There is no privacy in here."

I kept my hands folded in my lap to keep myself from doing something stupid. Seeing that Ava seemed to appreciate my sense of humor, I kept my well-timed jokes coming as she worked on my hair. The ladies around me laughed their asses off at my antics. I tried to explain to Ava that it was all part of my charm.

"Whoops." She cringed and stood back. Concern filled her eyes.

My gaze jumped to hers. That didn't sound good. "What's the matter?"

"Shit, I accidentally shaved a bald patch up the back of your head."

"What the hell?" I sat up straighter in my chair and tried to turn around, but she stopped me by pressing her hands to my chest. "How the hell did you do that?"

"I wasn't paying attention and used the wrong attachment," she said with a straight face while holding up the razor.

"Ava, I swear to God, you better not be fucking with me." That earned me a dirty look from the elderly lady in tight curlers next to me.

She burst into a fit of giggles. I spun around in the chair, no longer waiting for her permission. When I looked in the mirror and felt the back of my head, I was relieved to feel nothing but hair on my scalp.

"You're going to pay for that," I said, standing up and pulling her into me by the hips. It was probably more PDA than she wanted, but I was taking advantage of the fact that she wasn't pushing me away.

She patted my shoulder. "Just giving you a taste of your own medicine."

She had no idea how badly I wanted to kiss her. If we weren't in a shop full of people, my tongue would already be down her throat.

"How much do I owe you for the haircut?"

She waved me off. "Free of charge."

"How about dinner?" I offered up, hoping I wasn't moving too fast for her. I didn't want to get ahead of myself, though I was feeling very uncertain with the way she blinked at me.

"Dinner?" she asked as if she had never heard that word before.

"I'd like to cook you a meal as a thank you, like you did for me when I helped you move."

I also wouldn't mind another make-out session on the couch, but I kept that thought to myself.

"But you can't cook," she blurted out and immediately blanched. "Sorry."

"Why don't you let me worry about that. Amelia already offered to babysit, so if that was your next excuse you're out of luck."

She crossed her arms and tried to act put off. "Why am I not surprised?"

"So, it's a date?" I asked as the hairdryers and chatter stopped at once. The noisy salon went quiet. All eyes were on us as she took her time mulling over my invitation. My palms started to sweat while I waited for her answer. If she shot me down in front of these people, it would make things really awkward.

"If you don't say yes, I will," the older lady in the station next to us shouted. She looked to be as old as my grandmother.

"You better hurry up," I chuckled, "you've got competition."

Honestly, I never had to work so hard to get a woman to go out with me. Then again, this was Ava, so I expected nothing less.

"Okay." She smiled, and it felt like I had just won The Nobel Peace Prize and found a cure for cancer all in one.

FIFTEEN

AVA

I shifted my car into park, and turned off the engine. Logan's house was nothing like I pictured. It was tiny, in a rundown neighborhood. The outside, however, was immaculate, which didn't surprise me, considering how much he loved the outdoors. He probably spent every ounce of his free time, doing yardwork.

Butterflies erupted in my stomach, thinking about the text messages we exchanged today. We tried to fit in a lunch date earlier in the week, but we couldn't make it happen between our work and parenting schedules. So, we settled on FaceTiming and late-night phone calls every chance we got. Sometimes he was out in the field working on a case; other times, I was at the salon or just settling down for the night. No matter what, we just couldn't seem to get our schedules to align until tonight.

I pulled down the visor and glimpsed at my reflection in the mirror, fixing a few flyaway strands of hair. I wasn't sure what was going to happen tonight, but I prepared myself regardless. I shaved in all the important places, especially the spots I've neglected over the past year and a half. I gave my outfit extra thought as I mulled over my options earlier, deciding on a pair of curve-hugging jeans that gave my backside a little extra lift. Logan was always staring at it, so I made that a priority. Now, I just need to find the courage and walk up the front steps.

My phone buzzed in the cupholder. I picked it up and laughed when I read the message.

Logan: Are you planning on coming in tonight, or should I bring your dinner out to the car?

I slipped my phone into my purse and stepped out onto the driveway. My heart seemed to pound harder with each step I took toward his house.

The front door opened, and I was greeted with a soft smile that immediately put me at ease. "Welcome to my home."

"Thanks for having me." I adjusted the strap of my purse along my shoulder.

He angled his head, brushing his lips across the corner of my mouth. "Come on in, I'll give you the grand tour, which should take about five seconds."

He stepped back to let me enter. His familiar scent lingered in the air as I passed by.

I followed him through the house, which consisted of a small galley kitchen and an open family room that extended into a dining room. He had the table decorated with candles and a bottle of wine. I thought it was sweet that he put that much thought and effort into tonight.

"Would you like a glass of wine?"

"I would love one."

He poured my wine in a glass, handed it to me, and fetched a beer out of the fridge for himself. "This is a cute little house," I said, taking a seat on the couch and looking around. I picked up a piece of cheese that he had set on the table along with a few crackers.

"Thanks! It was a real fixer-upper when I bought it." He set his beer down on the glass table and plopped a cracker in his mouth. "I left the house to Vanessa in the divorce. I wanted Brina to grow up in a nice home. That left me with little money to work with. I guess it's a good thing I'm good with my hands and don't mind doing a few small projects."

I shifted my attention to the spot in the corner with a desk and a bookshelf with a blend of books, board games, and crafts. Logan's house was simple, but it was clean and lived in. It was a home, one that he put thought into, knowing his daughter would be spending time here.

"I love it. It's cozy."

"Right." He stood up, looking uncomfortable. "I should probably get the steaks on the grill."

"What can I do to help?" I asked, following him into the kitchen.

"You can grab the salad out of the fridge." He looked at his watch. "The baked potatoes are in the oven but still have a few minutes to go."

"Got it." I walked over to the fridge and smiled at all the artwork and school pictures of Brina covering the door. Once I got everything assembled, I placed it on the table and waited for Logan to finish up with the grill outside. Only he didn't come back in. It felt like he was avoiding me, so I poured myself another drink to take the edge off.

When he finally did make it back inside, our dinner conversation was forced and awkward. Something was seriously bothering him, and I couldn't quite figure out what it was. He was polite but cautious with his words. He didn't crack one joke, and I hated how cordial this felt.

He was wound tight, like one little tug and he would come undone.

Finally, I set my silverware down and decided I had enough. "Logan, what's going on?"

I wracked my brain, trying to figure out what I could have said to cause this much tension.

He ran a shaky hand through his hair. "I'm trying not to screw this up. I know we're walking a thin line here, I just wish I knew where that line was. I know you haven't been with anyone since Drew." He swallowed hard and studied my reaction. My heart tangled up at the emotion in his eyes. "I'm not sure where your head is at or what you want. I just want you to know there are no expectations. You set whatever pace you're comfortable with and I'll follow."

I angled my body closer to his. "You've been more than patient with me, but I'm not made of glass, Logan. I'm not going to break." I brought my fingers up to his cheek. "Am I a little nervous, yes, but not for the reason you think. I don't need more time. I want to be with you. I'm just scared of the unknown. I'm scared of putting my heart out there again."

He brought my hand up to his lips and froze when they touched my wedding ring. I dropped my hand so fast you would have thought it was on fire. I forced a steady breath, trying to even out my breathing. Guilt swirled in my gut, and it couldn't have come at a more inconvenient time.

"I'm sorry." There was worry in his eyes as I curled my hand under my thigh.

"It's fine," I lied, and he knew it. The last thing I wanted was for him to feel worse than he already did. But the reality was these feelings were a constant ebb and flow, and for every upward turn, there was a downward spiral.

"Don't lie to me, Ava." He pulled my hand out from underneath my legs and stroked his thumb along my wrist. "We need to be honest with each other if this is going to work."

He was right. I couldn't keep these feelings bandaged up forever. If we were going to move forward, I needed to be candid about my fears. He deserved the truth.

"Before I say this, I want you to know that this isn't a competition." I let out a slow exhale. "I was with the same man for ten years, but when I'm with you," I wiped a tear that escaped my eye, "I feel things I've never felt before, and that scares me for many different reasons. The way you kiss me with such passion, the way your arms make me feel safe, everything about you is just different. I don't want to disrespect my husband because we had a good marriage. If Drew were still alive, we would probably still be together, but he's not. You're here, and I'm happy. And I refuse to feel guilty about that."

Those damn tears started to fall, no matter how hard I tried to stop them. He gathered me up and placed me on his lap. His arm snaked around me and held me tight. I felt vulnerable, like I was leaving my heart unguarded, but if I trusted anyone to keep it safe, it was Logan.

"Tell me about him." He pressed a gentle kiss to my temple.

"What?" I asked, unsure if I heard him correctly.

"You never talk about him. I don't want you to feel like you need to hide that part of your life from me."

Resting my head against his chest, I wasn't sure where to begin. Would he draw the wrong conclusions? Would I say the wrong thing? Why did this conversation feel like a betrayal to both men?

I pulled my head back so I could look into his eyes. "What do you want to know?"

"How did you meet?" His thumb stroked along my cheek.

"We met during our sophomore year of college. Drew and his baseball buddies strolled into the café acting like they were too cool for school." I laughed at the memory. "I was studying for a math exam and he approached me with these cheesy pickup lines. Like most jocks, he was a known player around campus who didn't like being told no. He eventually wore me down, and used to tell everyone that I made him work for every date we went on. We eventually spent more and more time together. I started showing up at all his games and he ended up spending every night in my dorm room because the base-ball house he lived in was disgusting," I added, trying to bring a little light to the conversation.

Logan laughed. "Our lacrosse house probably wasn't much cleaner."

I smiled gently. "Our families took us out to dinner after our graduation ceremony to celebrate. He proposed that night, and we got married a year later." I played with the hem of his shirt.

"You mentioned Madison was a little earlier than planned."

"Yes, she was." I shook my head, curling deeper into him. Talking about this felt strangely therapeutic. "Drew was a planner. He had a journal with dates and events and when they would happen. I was nervous when I found out we were expecting. We were supposed to enjoy being married for five years." I laughed. "But as you know when it comes to kids, you have no choice but to adapt, and he turned into a wonderful father, and a good provider." I swiped at another tear. "He was my best friend, always had my back and I'm not going to lie, we had a good life and there isn't a day that goes by where I don't think about him."

His thumb reached and wiped the moisture under my eye. "I'm sorry you lost him."

"I am too, but I'm also thankful that I found you."

His eyes grew warm with affection. My heart was heavy from talking about this. I had a sudden need to lighten things up."

"Tell me about your days playing lacrosse. I don't know much about the sport. Do you have any pictures from college?"

He pulled out his phone, pressed a few buttons, and handed it to me. "That's me and a few of my fraternity brothers after we won our first championship against Cornell."

I looked at the picture and smiled. Of course, he was hot, even all sweaty and muddy. "Wait a minute," I said, looking more closely. "You have a Facebook account? How did I not know that? Why are we not friends?"

He went to the home page, typed in my name; his finger hovered over the friend request. "Are you going to accept?"

"As long as you promise not to spam me with stupid memes and comment on every single picture."

He rolled his eyes, clicked add friend, and set his phone down. "I hardly use the app. I mostly use it to keep in touch with old friends."

"What other apps are on your phone?"

He picked it up and handed it to me. "It's all yours. The password is 0420."

I leaned back with my mouth hanging open. "You trust me with your phone. What if I snoop through your text messages?"

He nuzzled his nose into my neck. "I've got nothing to hide."

"Logan, what are we doing?" My throat burned with how transparent he was being. Trust wasn't something to take lightly. It was something earned, not given. I don't know how we ended up here, but it was too big to ignore.

"We're taking this one step at a time."

"What if I'm done taking things slow?"

His hand touched my lower back, sending a path of goose bumps up my spine. "What exactly are you saying, Ava?"

"I'm done talking. Let me show you."

I moved in, brushing my mouth against his. He held his breath as I positioned myself on his lap so I could straddle him. I cupped his face, pulling him closer. He was allowing me to take the lead, and despite being in control, I was the one at his mercy.

He slanted his head and kissed me softly. The pads of his fingers tickled my scalp as he weaved his fingers through my hair. A million thoughts raced through my mind, but the best one of all was how amazing this felt. My teeth grazed along his bottom lip, begging for entry. He took my mouth in his, kissing me with more intensity. The way he responded to me was enough to send me over the edge. I rocked my hips into him, feeling consumed with need. This kiss was real. It was raw. It was everything.

Very slowly, he pulled away, letting his lips linger

against mine. "Are you sure you're ready for this?" he asked with a challenge or a question, I wasn't sure.

I leaned back so I could stare into his eyes. "Have you changed your mind?"

"Not a chance." His mouth came back down with a force that left no question on who was in charge now. His tongue stroked relentlessly against mine. I don't remember ever being kissed like this before in my life. I circled my hands along his neck, needing something to hold on to. The pleasure that was building was too much. He yanked me tighter, repeating the same torturous strokes of his tongue. I was strung so tight I was about ready to break. I gripped his hair and tried to move my hips, but he held me still.

"Logan," I begged, knowing I was one second away from losing complete control.

"What do you want, Ava?" he asked, kissing along my neck and tracing his mouth over my exposed shoulder.

"I want you. Only you."

"As long as you promise to stay with me," he whispered into my neck. "Please, just me."

How could this man break my heart and mend it back together at the same time?

I smoothed a piece of hair from his forehead. "This moment isn't about anyone else but us." I stood up and eased my top over my head. "Now take me to your bedroom." His eyes heated as they trailed over my lace bra. The need to connect with him was growing stronger with each passing second.

He rose to his feet. I knew lust in a man's eyes when I saw it, but there was something else too. There was an undeniable amount of emotion, strong enough that I could feel it in my bones.

"You are so beautiful." My heart skipped a beat as he dragged his hands along the straps, pulling them down and freeing me from the material. Logan's mouth closed over one of my nipples. He swirled the tip of his tongue over the peaks, taking his time with each one. My body arched into his, begging for more. I fisted my hands in his hair, bringing him closer. He cupped my breast. His thumb circled and teased over my sensitive skin. My head fell back in a gasp. It felt like I was about to have sex for the first time.

He brought his hand to the back of my head, tipping it back. My lips parted, his tongue slipped inside. He kissed me like a man who was dying of thirst and was on a hunt to quench it. How is it that he's been in front of me the entire time, and I never realized it? How did I overlook him for all those years?

I reached my hand out, needing to feel him. His eyes followed my every movement as I slowly pulled the shirt over his head. He sucked in a breath as I trailed my hands up his chest. The pads of my fingertips ghosted along his stomach. He shuddered when they landed over his beating heart.

"I'm going to ask you one last time." His breaths were uneven as he spoke. "Are you sure?"

"Yes," I said without hesitation.

I held my breath, waiting to see what he would do. His patience was wearing thin, and whatever resistance he held on to disappeared when he scooped me up and carried me into his bedroom.

SIXTEEN

LOGAN

There was nothing uncertain about what was going to happen next. I laid her down on the bed and crawled over the top of her. From the first day I laid eyes on her, I knew I wanted her, but she belonged to someone else. Now she was mine, and I had to force myself to relax, to slow down so I could savor the moment.

My hand curled around her neck; her eyes fluttered closed from my touch. "This is your last chance."

The last thing I wanted was to talk her out of this, but I wouldn't be able to handle any regrets.

She swallowed, locking her eyes with mine. "The truth?"

I weaved my fingers through her hair, taking her face in my hands. "Always."

"I thought I would have doubts, I don't know how to explain it." She paused. "There is something about you, about us that just makes sense."

Inhaling deeply, I allowed her words to soak in. "I feel the same way. It feels like you get me. This thing between us may feel unexpected, but you're important to me, and having you here means everything."

I brought my head down to hers and brushed my lips to the corner of her mouth. Desperation like I'd never felt before had me eager to touch and claim her in places I only dreamed about.

My lips traveled across her skin, sucking and tasting, drawing out a shiver of need. We've only kissed a few times, and I already knew what she liked. She didn't just like to be kissed on the mouth. She wanted to be kissed everywhere, her jaw, her neck, and especially behind her ear.

She traced her fingers down my chest. My breath hitched when they reached the waistband of my shorts. She undid the button on my fly, and I watched her hand disappear inside. The lightest feather of her touch had my pulse kicking up another notch. I've never had performance anxiety before, but I've never wanted to impress a woman so much in my life. I don't remember wanting anyone like this, ever.

Her hands were on the move, traveling up along my shoulders before landing in my hair. She leaned forward, pressing her lips to mine. The kiss started off soft, but as I reached her ass to pull her into me, it became frantic. I pulled my lips away so I could feel her skin under my tongue. I wanted this moment to go on forever. There were so many things I wanted to say to her, but I knew it was too soon. She wasn't quite there yet.

Tilting her face up so I could get a better angle, our eyes met, and my heart started to flutter. I knew that after tonight I would never feel the same again. Every fear I had about her being ready had me questioning if I should let things continue. I've had sex. Lots of sex. Great sex. But this was not just sex. This was intimate, even that wasn't the right word for what I was feeling. But my brain cells weren't working at the moment, so that was the best I could come up with.

I stood up and slid my shorts down my thighs. Her eyes widened when she saw how hard and ready I was for her. I quickly stripped off the rest of my clothing, not wanting to waste a single second. Ava did the same while keeping her gaze fixed on mine. There was a smart-ass comment on the tip of my tongue, but then I remembered that it's been a while for her.

I peered down at the woman who has come to mean so much to me, struggling to make sense of this deep connection I felt toward her.

"I'm not strong enough to stop once we get started." The emotion was thick in my voice as I laid it all on the line for her. "I want you, Ava. Not just for tonight, but you've got to promise me that it's only me you see. I can't be with you if your mind is on someone else. Do you understand what I'm saying?"

"Yes." She cupped my face as I planted a leg on the mattress. "Now stop trying to talk me out of this. I know what I want, and it's you."

I fused my mouth with hers in desperation. Her hand went to the back of my neck, urging me on. My pulse raced, and my heart thundered in my ears.

I pushed her legs apart with my knee and slid my fingers into her warmth. I wanted her to feel every inch of pleasure I could provide. She tightened around my hand as I stretched and curled my fingers, searching for that spot that would make her see stars. I pulled away from our kiss, to study the reaction on her face. Watching her come alive under my touch was like witnessing every fantasy I ever had come to life.

I kissed along her jaw and ran my mouth down her neck. My hand moved to her breast, and the other roamed along her thigh. I darted my tongue out to lick her nipple and grazed my teeth along the peak. She bowed her back off the bed, and her cries filled the room. She seemed to like it, and I wanted to find every spot on her body that would give me that same reaction. I don't think my dick could get any harder.

"God, Ava." I trailed my hands down to her glistening arousal. Her lips were parted, her cheeks were flushed, she was hands-down the hottest thing I'd ever seen. "Do you have any idea how long I've waited for this? How bad I want you?"

"You have me, Logan. Take me. I'm all yours."

I dipped my fingers inside her wetness. Her eyes flickered up at me, holding me captive. Everything I'd hoped to find, and all I'd ever wanted, was right here. It's never been like this with anyone. Where I've been this needy, where I would beg for any piece of her I could get.

I leaned over and grabbed the condom out of my night-stand. "Promise to tell me if this is too much."

She gave me a slow smile. "Feeling confident, are you?"

A small laugh escaped. "I just want to make you feel good."

I only wanted to bring her pleasure. The last thing I wanted was for her to feel pain.

"I trust you, Logan, but the only thing I'm questioning right now is what's taking you so long."

I bent down and kissed her. She was perfect, but as

much as I loved kissing her, I was ready to get acquainted with other parts of her body.

Once I was fully covered, I shifted forward and entered her. My eyes slid shut the second I felt her heat wrap around me. She felt like heaven, and I wanted to stay still, inside her, forever. Gripping her hips, I slowly began gliding in and out, I wanted to go deeper, but I kept my strokes measured and controlled.

We kissed and touched as our bodies moved together in a rhythm that had me craving to explore every part of her. I watched her facial expressions, not wanting to miss a thing. My hips rocked into her, taking everything she was willing to give me.

Ava's hands went to my hair, pulling and tugging at the ends. She stretched around me as I braced my arms alongside her head. The headboard banged against the wall in sync with our movements. There was something about having her here, in my bed. In my space, that made me frantic. I dropped my forehead to hers, trying to draw out this feeling as long as I could. We moved, each of us chasing and searching for that same release. My hips pounded into her, hitting that spot that would send her over the edge.

Every nerve ending inside me tightened. I threw my head back, knowing that I was headed to the point of no return. Each thrust grew deeper and more impatient. My hands went to her hips, needing something to hold on to. I slowed my rhythm to a torturous pace, sliding in and out. There was no way I was coming without her. I'd fuck her all night long if I had to.

"God, that feels so good. I can feel you everywhere," she whispered, hooking her leg around my back.

I pinned her hands to the bed, holding her in place.

"You're going to feel even better in a second." I drove in deep, increasing my rhythm. I was never going to be able to sleep in this bed again without thinking of this moment. My breathing grew uneven with each thrust. She was so damn tight that I had to change my angle so I could slide in deeper. Her nails dug into my back as I pushed her further into oblivion.

Ava squeezed herself around my shaft and fell apart with my name on her lips. That little move broke whatever restraint I had left. My thighs shook, and my shoulders tensed as I finished off inside her. She clung to me, allowing the aftershocks to settle down.

It took a few minutes to get my breathing under control, and I rolled to the side so I wouldn't crush her. My gaze dragged over her features, taking her in before planting a kiss to her lips.

"Wow." She sighed, snuggling into my arms. Never in my life had I been so content. So sated and blissfully happy. I pulled her close and stroked her shoulder with my thumb.

"Are you okay?" I didn't want her to overthink or regret what just happened. But the longer we laid there, and the longer I held her, the more I questioned how much of her heart still remained with him and how much she would be able to give to me.

She ran her fingers down my chest in lazy patterns. "I think you exceeded my expectations and that never happens."

"Is that so?" I grinned.

"Logan." Her expression sobered. "I care about you, a lot, but I'm still a work in progress." She swallowed and shifted her eyes away from me. "This relationship isn't always going to be easy, as a matter-of-fact, I can guarantee that things will get bumpy. I need you to promise me that you'll hang on, even when I give you every reason to push me away."

I moved up on my elbows to support my weight and dropped my mouth down to hers. "I promise to always hang on because letting go isn't an option."

SEVENTEEN

AVA

MY EYES OPENED, AND IT TOOK ME A MINUTE TO REMEMBER where I was. I adjusted my head on the pillow and ran my hands along the blue comforter. Logan's leg was covering mine, one arm was draped along my waist, and the other was trapped underneath his pillow.

A lock of hair rested over his forehead as he snored softly next to me. His scruff seemed darker and thicker than it was last night. I brought my fingertips up to his eyebrow to push the hair aside. He stirred at my touch as I watched him sleep like a stalker. I couldn't take my eyes off of him. I should feel sated and worn out, but when he ran his hand along my back and curved it around my behind, a need sparked back to life.

"Morning." His smile was lazy and automatic.

"Good morning." I found myself smiling back. I was afraid things would be awkward, but the guilt and the mixed feelings I expected, never came.

"Any regrets?" he asked, his gaze raking over my face.

I leaned forward and pressed my lips to his. "None."

His hand snaked around the back of my head, pulling

me in for a slow, lazy kiss. One of the things I loved about Logan was his attentiveness. Every touch, every kiss, every caress restored something inside me. He was bringing me back to life, one kiss, one touch at a time.

"Good, because I like waking up to you in my bed." He cupped my ass and pulled me tight against him. His teeth scraped against mine, and that's when it hit me. I tore my mouth from his.

"I need to brush my teeth. I have morning breath."

"I don't care." He scraped another kiss along my jaw. I wanted to protest, but instead, I found myself fighting another smile. "Your mouth is addicting," he murmured, trailing his tongue up over the seam of my lips. "And so sweet, just like the rest of you. Although there is nothing sweet about how I feel right now." He pressed his erection into me, proving his point.

"I think I'm going to have a hard time keeping up with you," I admitted, rolling my body into his. "I'm a little sore, but I ache in all the right places."

Logan flipped me over on my back and hovered over me. "Then you better stop looking at me like that, unless you want me to do something about it."

"What exactly are you thinking?" My eyebrows arched in a challenge.

His gaze dropped to my lips. "Lots of things." He peppered kisses along my jaw. "Multiple things." He ran his tongue along my neck. "Just you wait and see."

He lifted his head and stared at me with so much tenderness, I just wanted to drown in it. My need for him was only growing. I was afraid I would never get enough of him. He had no idea how much he was putting me back together, piece by piece.

The sound of my phone buzzing on the floor had me

twisting in his arms. "That could be Madison." He groaned when I pushed him off of me and bent over the side of the bed. The sheet was pulled up along my waist as I frantically searched for my phone. My clothes were scattered across the room, far enough away to where I couldn't reach them. But there was no way in hell I was dropping this sheet to get them. I wasn't comfortable with him seeing me naked in broad daylight. My skin wasn't as tight as it used to be, and the faint white stretch marks along my stomach weren't very flattering.

He arched his eyebrow when I allowed the ringing to stop. "I thought you needed to get that."

I threw my head back on a fake yawn. "It already went to voicemail. I'll check it in a minute."

He climbed out of bed and walked toward his dresser. Apparently, he didn't have the same insecurity issues I did. Then again, why would he when he resembled a Greek statue? He pulled out a T-shirt and boxer shorts. "Here." He handed me the clothes. "You can put these on while I make breakfast."

"Wow, I'm really getting the five-star treatment."

He slipped a pair of gym shorts over his legs, forgoing a shirt. Must be nice. "Why don't you just lie there while I go prepare us some food. You probably don't get a chance to relax very often, so take advantage of it."

Who was this man? He probably sensed my hesitation, and instead of calling me out on it, he discreetly put me at ease. I reached underneath the sheet and lightly pinched myself to make sure this was real. Scratching my head, I searched my brain for a flaw. He had to have one, right? No one was that perfect.

I gathered the clothes he left for me and dragged myself out of bed. While I was used to getting very little sleep, I was tired for an entirely different reason. My mind drifted back to last night. Sex with Logan was different. There was no doubt that he was more experienced than me. I don't remember Drew's touch ever being so needy and hungry. It was always controlled, sweet, and comfortable.

I shook my head, trying to rid the memories that I needed to move on from. They had no place here in another man's bedroom, especially after what happened last night. I padded across the room and smiled when I walked into the bathroom. There was an unopened toothbrush sitting on the counter, a pack of face wipes, and a bottle of moisturizer.

I picked up each item, relieved that they were all brand new. He must have bought them with me in mind the last time he was at the store. That little gesture had me swaying on my feet.

I quickly got dressed, cleaned up, and followed the smell into the kitchen.

I bit my bottom lip at the sight of Logan's bare back. The gray athletic shorts hung low on his hips, and his hair was sticking up in every direction. His muscles flexed as he stirred and flipped the eggs around in the pan. I determined right then and there this was my favorite look.

"Are you just going to stare at me all day?"

I laughed and strolled over to where he was watching me in the glass of the microwave door. "I don't know, it's a pretty good view."

I slid my hands along his waist, pressing a kiss to his shoulder.

He set the spatula down on the counter and turned around. "Hungry?"

"Mm-hmm," I said, peppering kisses along his jawline.

Without a doubt, his facial hair was a turn-on for me. It reminded me of his laid-back, carefree spirit.

"How do you feel?" His expression softened as he reached out, tucking a strand of hair behind my ear.

"Confused."

"About what?" His arms fell to the side as he studied me.

"You told me you didn't cook." I tilted my head to the stove to the perfectly cooked eggs.

His face split into a smile while his fingers lifted the hem of my shirt. "I might have exaggerated a little bit."

"Why?" I swallowed and moved my gaze to his chest. It was such a distraction. "There's nothing sexier than a man who can cook."

"Maybe I was looking for sympathy. I was hoping you would feel sorry for me and invite me over for another meal."

I blinked at him and stopped his hands from traveling up any farther. "So, you played me?"

"I was desperate." He moved his hand up and pulled on the back of my neck, bringing his mouth against mine. "I would have done anything to get another date with you."

"Is that so?" I asked as he tried to give me a chaste kiss, but I arched my face away from him.

"Ava, don't be a tease."

I tapped his nose playfully. Sometimes our teasing turned into a competition to see who could get the other one worked up the fastest. He wasn't going to win this round. "I think you need to be taught a lesson."

"Why? It worked, didn't it?" He wrapped his hands along my back, linking his fingers. "Besides, I didn't hear any complaints from you last night."

"So, you used me to get in my pants."

"No, I played dirty to get what I want," he whispered against my mouth. "I think I made it crystal clear last night how bad I have it for you."

"While I don't agree with your methods, they were pretty successful."

"Does that mean I'm forgiven?" He trailed his hands along my sides. "I can feed you to make it up to you."

I looked up into his intense eyes and realized I wasn't going to win this round as easily as I thought I would. One touch and my willpower seemed to disappear.

"I'd rather you make it up to me in other ways."

He hissed in a breath and stepped away from me. "I can certainly make that happen, but first we need to eat." Logan walked me over to the small kitchen table and pulled my chair out.

"Now who's the tease?" I settled into my seat with a pout.

He leaned in and kissed my forehead. "Trust me, you will need to fuel up for what I have planned for you later."

"Is this your idea of foreplay?" I asked, my spirit perking up at the thought.

He aimed a devilish glint my way. "I think you became quite acquainted with my methods of foreplay last night and the fact that you're confused has me questioning my abilities."

I laughed, although there was nothing funny about the way he ravaged me last night. He took his time as if he cared about how I was feeling, and not just physically. He treated me like I mattered to him. Although Logan always had a way of making me feel special. I knew this wasn't love, but it didn't feel temporary either. I wanted to believe we were going somewhere; it was just too early yet in our journey to determine where we were headed.

Logan walked over and set down a white plate covered with scrambled eggs, diced peppers, cheese and crumbled sausage. My mouth watered. He went back to the counter and carried over two mugs of freshly poured coffee with a platter of wheat toast.

He took the seat next to me while I poked my fork into my eggs and brought it to my mouth. "This is really good. What else can you cook?"

He snagged a piece of toast off the platter and applied a little butter. "I was only half-joking earlier. My cooking skills are limited. I can cook a few things but not much. Eggs just happen to be one of them."

"Do you cook for all the women you bring home?"

His food paused on the way to his mouth, and I wanted to kick myself.

"Why would you ask me that?" He set his toast down and narrowed his eyes on me.

"I'm sorry, I shouldn't have. I don't know what possessed me to ask that. It's none of my business."

His expression became serious. "I think you do know why you asked me that. Just be honest with me and tell me why?"

I pulled my hair to the side, weaving the strands into a braid. It was something I did when I was nervous. This was a conversation I'd been trying to avoid, so I'm not sure why I had to go and open my big mouth. "I don't understand why you like me so much. You can have any woman you want. In fact, I'm sure you've had your fair share of women, so why me?"

"There is so much to unpack from that I don't even know where to begin, but first, let's get something straight.

Any woman who has sat here before you does not matter. Okay?" He looked me dead in the eyes. "I say that with all sincerity. Now let's get down to what this is really about. Why you?" He rubbed his hands along his legs and looked up to the ceiling. "Do you remember the first night we met?"

I nodded, visibly recalling that night. Marco and Amelia were going through a rough patch, and I ran into Marco and Logan when I was out with Kara and her sister.

His fingers skimmed along my knee. "I saw this gorgeous woman stalk across the bar and lay into my best friend." I laughed at the memory. Marco had just broken Amelia's heart, and I took the opportunity to let him know how I felt about it. "I was so damned turned on." I smacked his shoulder, and he grinned. "You're gorgeous, I'm not gonna lie. The physical attraction has always been there, but as I got to know you it turned into more than that." He ran a hand down my leg; I was unprepared for the vulnerability I saw. "You weren't mine then, and I know we wouldn't be together if he were still alive." Oh, my heart. I had no idea he ever felt this way. "I know I'm second best…"

"Stop." I shook my head and wiped my eyes. "I'm with you because I want to be with you. Let's leave it at that, okay?"

He cupped my face. "Ava, I was pulled in the second I saw you. These feelings I have, they've always been there. I know I don't deserve you and I sure as hell shouldn't have you, but I do. I promise, if you give us a chance, and let me in, I will give you *whatever you want*. I know I'm not your original plan, but sometimes what you thought would be isn't always what life has in store for us."

"Don't make me cry." I twisted in his lap. There was so

much I wanted to say to that, but I was too choked up to speak.

"You have no idea what you do to me." He swallowed hard. "How badly I want to promise you things."

"Shh." I pressed my mouth to his and moved my lips down his neck. "I like being with you, Logan. I can't imagine feeling this way with anyone else."

His arms folded around me. "Good, let's keep it that way."

EIGHTEEN

LOGAN

I LIFTED THE FRAME OFF THE DRESSER AND STARED AT THE happy family in the picture. Drew was holding Madison on his hip while Ava leaned against his other side. Even though I knew it was irrational, I was envious of a dead man, simply because he had everything I ever wanted.

My marriage to Vanessa was a mess. Hell, keeping her happy was a full-time job. There were no tender moments or soft smiles. It was a relationship filled with bickering and resentment—nothing like what Ava and Drew had.

"That's my dad," Madison whispered softly. I set the frame down to face her.

"I know. You look just like him." I moved across the room and sat next to her on the bed. It was clear that this little girl was still mourning the death of her father. I wanted to wrap her up in my arms and take her pain away.

"I miss him." My heart cracked open at the sadness in her eyes. I smoothed a piece of hair off her forehead as she snuggled into my side. It hurt knowing she was suffering, and there wasn't anything I could do about it. My throat got uncomfortably tight as I felt my dad instincts kick in. I thought about what I would want for Brina if the situation were reversed.

I would want someone to love her and look out for her. I wouldn't want anyone to step into my shoes and replace me; instead, I would want them to have their own relationship. I would want her to have a safe place to go, where she could express her emotions. More importantly, I would never want her to feel alone.

I brought the blanket up to her chin. "If you ever want to talk about him, I'm here. Although I didn't know him very well, I know he loved you and your mom very much and he wouldn't want you to be sad."

She pressed her head deeper into her pillow. "Okay."

She seemed satisfied with that answer, but I could sense the tiny gears in her head working on another question.

Her little nose twitched. "Are you my mom's boyfriend?"

I sucked in a breath and looked over my shoulder. Where the hell was Ava? We had just gotten back from the movies when she asked me to tuck Madison in. She had to be done folding the laundry by now, right?

"Why do you ask that?" I plowed a hand through my hair, stalling for time. I didn't know how to answer that question and was afraid if I said the wrong thing, Ava would kill me.

It's been two weeks since she'd spent the night at my house, and we've both been cautious around the girls. Sure, we've spent time together, just the four of us, doing simple things like going to the mall or out to dinner. If the weather was nice, Brina and Madison would spend their afternoons swimming in the backyard pool. Not once have we held hands or kissed in front of our kids. On the nights when Brina was with her mom, I came over after Madison was asleep and gone before she woke up. This was the first night where it was just the three of us.

She looked down at her light blue comforter. Her cheeks grew red. "I saw you guys kissing the other day."

Apparently, we haven't been as discreet as we thought.

"Oh, does that bother you?"

She shrugged her shoulders, and I reached for her hand, curling her tiny fingers underneath mine. "You can tell me if it does."

I held my breath waiting for her answer. What the hell was I going to do if she said yes? Be patient, I reminded myself. This wasn't about me.

She looked up at me. The innocence and concern in her eyes slayed me. "My mom is smiling again, so it doesn't bother me. I didn't like seeing her sad and crying all the time."

"I'm glad to hear that, but just because I'm here, it doesn't mean she still doesn't get sad sometimes. She's always going to love your dad, just like you do."

Her eyes floated over to the family picture on her dresser. "My mom said he is my guardian angel in heaven, and he can see me, that's why I talk to him sometimes."

"I bet that makes him very happy."

She sighed heavily, and I saw that faraway look creep back into her features. "He was the best daddy. He taught me how to ride my bike without training wheels, and how to play baseball." Her eyes got watery. "My mom isn't very good at throwing a ball, I don't want to hurt her feelings though. But I'm afraid I won't be good enough to make the team when I get to high school because I don't have anyone to practice with."

I wasn't sure if I wanted to laugh or cry. Instead, I smiled. "You've got plenty of time before you get to high school. While I wasn't a good baseball player like your dad, I played when I was younger. I bet Marco and Quinn would be happy to practice with you too."

She chewed on her bottom lip. "Will you help me with my pitching? My dad used to practice with me and coach all my games."

"I would be happy to throw a few balls with you. I might need a new glove though. Maybe you and I could go pick one out together."

I had a glove that would have worked just fine, but I thought she would enjoy helping me choose a new one. It would be a great way for us to spend time together.

"Can we go tomorrow?" she asked hopefully. I smiled at how fast her mind worked, how it could go from sad to happy within a few seconds. I wish it were that simple for me.

"Let's check with your mom first, okay?" I squeezed her arm gently. "Sweet dreams." I switched the light off next to her door and closed it softly behind me. Resting my back against the wall, I took a few minutes to let that conversation sink in.

Ava was in her bedroom putting clothes away when she spotted me in the doorway. "Hey, I was just going to go give her a kiss good night."

"She's already asleep." I walked over and wrapped my arms around her from behind. "You know that I adore her, right?"

She touched my hands that were resting on her stomach. "She thinks pretty highly of you too."

"She was asking questions."

"What kind of questions?"

I took her hand and entwined our fingers. "She saw us kissing. She asked if I was your boyfriend."

She turned around in my arms. "What did you say?"

"I evaded the question, but I also put a few feelers out." I cleared my throat and braced myself for her reaction. "I want to tell Madison and Brina about us?"

While I desperately wanted to bond with Madison, I had my own daughter's feelings to consider. I wasn't anticipating any problems, but I still needed to reassure her that she would always come first, that her feelings mattered. I would never do anything that would jeopardize her trust in me. Telling Madison before Brina felt wrong. Talking to both of them together seemed like the right thing to do.

"What exactly do you want to tell them?"

I could sense the panic in her voice. If I knew Ava, she would put this off for as long as possible. It might have only been a couple of weeks, but I was already sick of sneaking around. I wanted us to be official. Our girls would always be our priority, but if we were going to move forward, we needed to have this conversation with the people closest to us.

"We tell them that we are together and not just as friends."

Ava worried her bottom lip between her teeth. "Logan, it's too soon. They're not ready for that."

I tugged her arm, pulling her against my chest. "I don't want to keep sneaking around. We don't have to tell them tomorrow but I want to tell them soon." My fingers slid into her hair. "I'm crazy about you, Ava Donavon, and I'm sick of worrying about what people will think. I want the world to know that you are mine," I whispered over her lips as she folded her hands along the back of my neck. "Because make no mistake, I'm yours."

"Is that your way of saying we're official?" Her smile was so damn beautiful. Sometimes it felt like I didn't deserve her.

"You can use whatever label you're comfortable with, as long as I get what I want."

"And what exactly is it that you want?"

I moved my hands down her back and brought my lips to hers. "I want everything, Ava. I want your kisses." I touched my lips to hers and stroked her tongue softly. "I want your smile." I ran the pads of my thumb along her mouth. "I want this body." I gripped her curves, letting her know how much I wanted it all. "I want your heart." Our eyes met, and I knew, at that moment, that I was so far gone for this woman that I was done. "I'm not looking to replace him, I'm just asking for you to make room for me too."

She shook her head and looked away. I grabbed her chin, forcing her gaze to mine. "Do not hide from me."

"I don't want to hurt you."

"There is nothing about the way you make me feel that hurts."

"But I can't emotionally give you what you want."

And there it was. The truth that I tried to deny. Drew might have been buried six feet in the ground, but he still stood between us. Would she ever give me a chance? Would I always be second best? As a man, that was a hard pill to swallow.

I knew going into this that it wouldn't be easy. I was a

competitive person by nature, but I was realistic too. Drew would always be the gold medal winner in this race, and the most I would ever get was the silver, the second place.

This entire situation was unfair. Sure, she would give me her body, but I wanted her heart, which belonged to another man, and maybe it always would. So, where did that leave me?

A poor sap, that's where, because I would take whatever this woman gave me. As long as I got one more day, one more minute with her, it would all be worth it.

I ran a hand through my hair, hoping I could convince her to take a chance on us. "I know you have a past, and I don't want you to think you need to be someone you're not. This thing between us has evolved into something that I want to invest in. I can handle you being sad. I can understand why you're afraid." I swept my thumb under her eyes. "But I can't handle you doubting us."

"It's not *you* that I doubt. It's me. I don't have a whole heart to give you. Would you be okay with that?"

"Yes." My reply was automatic. "You don't have to stop loving him to fall in love with me. It doesn't have to be one or the other. You can still hold him in your heart. I'm just asking for you to make room for me too."

She shook her head as if she didn't believe me. "You say that now, but grief isn't something that can be controlled. There are still days where I cry, where a song will come on the radio and I'll think of him. Where a Philly's game will be on the television and I'll sit in his recliner and wrap myself up in his blanket just to feel close to him. There are birthdays and holidays that aren't always joyous. Why would you want to put yourself through that?"

"Listen to me." I grabbed on to her shoulders. "I can

handle all that as long as you're honest with me about how you're feeling. But right now, I want you to shut off your head and open up your heart to the possibility of more with me. You don't even have to let me in yet, just don't close the door on us without even knowing what's on the other side."

I wasn't naïve enough to know that everything would be smooth sailing. Life was messy and complicated, filled with mistakes and disappointments, but it could also be wonderful and amazing. That was the reality of life. You have to love through the bad, just like you love easily through the good. If I could convince her to give me the broken pieces of her heart, I would do everything in my power to mend it back together.

Her eyes watered and I worried that I might have pushed her too far. "You have no idea how much I've let you in."

"Ava..." She placed her hand over my lips, silencing my words.

"Please let me say this." She swallowed. "When I'm with you, I feel like I can breathe again. You make me happy and I know that's a step in the right direction, but I'm not quite ready to leap. And that's so unfair to you. You deserve so much more than this and I'm afraid I'll never be enough for you."

I kissed her nose. "You talk about not being enough for me, but you have no idea how much you mean to me." I brushed a piece of hair off her shoulder. "Like I said before, you're not the only one with a past. I have my own issues to work through. We might not be on the same page now, but our story isn't over yet, and there isn't a chance in hell I'll let it end before it even has a chance to get started."

She buried her face in my neck. "I don't deserve you."

I rubbed my hand up and down her back. "You're right. You deserve so much better than me."

She laid her head on my shoulder. "You're making me cry. Do you always have to say all the right things? It's kinda hard to resist you when you're so perfect."

"Ava, there is no such thing as perfect."

"Fine. But you still deserve someone who can give you so much more than I'm capable of giving you."

"I just want you to want to be with me."

Her thumb grazed along the top of my cheek. "I do want to be with you, but you scare me."

Our eyes met, and my heart began to race. "Why do I scare you?"

Truthfully, she terrified me. She was a widow with a young daughter who was trying to put her life back together. I shouldn't have wanted her as bad as I did, but she made me feel things I couldn't ignore. Now that I knew what it felt like to have her in my arms, I couldn't pretend not to want to be with her. I wanted to take her pain away, make her smile, and one day, hopefully, she would fall for me like I was starting to fall for her. I've been fooling myself by thinking this was something I could control. Because now that I have her, I don't ever want to let her go.

"The last thing I want to do is go through what I went through last year, but here's the thing, I can't pretend that these feelings between us aren't there. If I learned anything over the last eighteen months, it's that life is short." Her thumb grazed along my bottom lip, and I felt something shift between us.

My heart hammered against my ribs. "What are you saying, Ava?"

"I'm saying men like you only come around once in a lifetime. There is risk in every relationship. And you, Logan Blake, are worth the risk. I'm done worrying about what everyone else will think. The only opinions that matter, are Madison and Brina's. Let's tell them first and go from there."

NINETEEN

AVA

The girls' feet smacked against the hardwood floor above my head as I placed the last plate in the dishwasher. Logan and I were planning on having a talk with Madison and Brina today. I thought about the conversation we had in my bedroom last week, and he raised a lot of good points. We couldn't hide our feelings from the world forever. There was still a possibility that one or both of the girls might not be happy, but Logan was confident we would find a way to make things work somehow.

Madison still carried a good amount of anxiety, and I didn't want her to worry about how Logan and Brina would fit into our lives. And Brina, I really wanted her acceptance. I would be very disappointed if things didn't go as I hoped they would.

"Relax." Logan's lips pressed against my temple. My stomach buzzed with nerves at the sound of the girls running down the stairs. "Everything will be fine, especially since you let them eat chocolate muffins and donuts for breakfast."

"A little bribery never hurt anyone." I did my best to school my features as soon as I spotted them.

"Can we go outside now and ride our bikes?" Madison asked, pulling her hair back into a ponytail.

I wiped my hands along my shorts. Here went nothing. "Before you go outside to play, Logan and I want to talk to you both about something."

Brina's forehead wrinkled while Madison groaned in annoyance. "Come here." I walked over and patted the cushion next to me on the couch. "Have a seat."

I've never been so nervous to talk to my own daughter before. I was a freakin' mess.

"Logan and I want you both to know that you girls are the most important people in our lives." Two sets of confused eyes searched my face, wondering where I was going with this speech. God, I sucked at this, and I was making this situation more awkward than it needed to be. You would think I could do a better job of easing into this conversation. "The four of us have been spending a lot of time together, right?"

They both nodded as I forced the rest of my words out. "Well, during that time, Logan and I have developed feelings for each other. I know this is probably very confusing and I'm not sure how much you understand, but we make each other happy." I exchanged a look with Logan, who was casually sipping his coffee in the chair across from me. I wanted to throttle him for acting so composed while my heart hammered away in my chest. I gave him the evil eye and turned back to the girls. "Now, I'm sure you both have tons of questions and we will do our best to answer them."

"You mean you like each other like boyfriend and girlfriend?" Brina asked, and it was hard to tell, but she didn't seem too excited about that.

Logan scooted forward so they were at eye level. "Would you be okay if I asked Ava to my girlfriend?" he asked, all steady and calm.

"Will you be Madison's new daddy?" She looked down at the floor; the worry in her voice was unmistakable.

I held my breath, waiting to see how he would answer that question.

Emotion swam in Logan's eyes as they shifted to my daughter briefly. "Drew will always be Madison's dad, but he's in heaven now. I was thinking that maybe we could include her in some of the things we do together, wouldn't that be nice?"

Brina pursed her lips; she seemed to ponder that for a minute. "Will we still get to do things together, just the two of us?"

"Absolutely." He bent forward and squeezed Brina's knee.

Madison grinned up at Logan. "I knew you liked my mom."

I let out a relieved breath while Logan laughed. I thought if anyone would have asked questions, it would have been my daughter.

I pulled her into a tight hug. "I love you."

She looked up at me. "Love you too. Can we go outside and ride our bikes now?"

That was a lot easier than I expected. Things couldn't have gone any smoother.

"Sure, let me grab the helmets out of the garage." I stood up and made it halfway across the room when my phone started ringing. "Madison, can you get that, please?" I pointed to my cell phone that was sitting on the table.

I was just about ready to open the side door when I heard Madison's high-pitched voice.

"Uncle Jeremey." My hand froze on the doorknob. "Yes, we are home. Okay, I'll tell my mom. See you soon."

I rested my palm against the wall for support. "What did your uncle Jeremey want?"

"He's on his way over. He'll be here in thirty minutes." She set my phone down. "Come on, Brina, we can get the helmets. I know where they are."

I looked across the room in a panic, searching for a way out of this.

"Who is Jeremy?" Logan asked, watching me cautiously.

"He's Drew's best friend."

His eyes continued to study me. I hated feeling like I was being scrutinized. "Okay, I'm assuming he doesn't know about me?"

Leave it to Logan not to miss a beat. "You are correct."

"Why haven't I heard of him before?"

"He lives in Colorado."

He placed his hands on my shoulders. I was hyperventilating. "Ava, breathe."

"I know you probably think I'm overacting." I paused, waiting for him to tell me I was being ridiculous, except he didn't say anything. Great.

"How can I make this easier for you? Do you want me to leave?"

"No...yes." I blew out a breath, wishing I could bang my head up against a wall. "I don't know."

Hurt flashed in his eyes, but he recovered quickly. "I'll do whatever you want me to do."

"Maybe you could run an errand, just to give me enough time to tell him about us."

"And where do you suggest I go?" he asked in disbelief. He wasn't very happy, and that made me feel ten times worse.

I chewed on my bottom lip, trying to think of something that would keep him busy. "How about the carwash?"

"The carwash?" He raised a brow. "My truck is already cleaned. I washed it yesterday in my own damn driveway."

"Well, my Nissan is filthy. Come on." I wrapped my arms around his neck. I hated this, and if I didn't think he would be okay with this, I wouldn't have suggested it.

He sighed and leaned his forehead against mine. "I understand why you want to handle things this way, but that doesn't mean I have to like it."

"I'm not hiding us, I promise." His face filled with understanding, but I still felt so damn guilty. I wanted to kick something.

"I know." He looked away, unable to meet my eyes. "This just feels like a setback."

"It's not. And if you're not comfortable with leaving, then stay. Jeremey's feelings are not more important than yours. I'm sorry if I made you feel that they were."

He kissed me briefly before gathering his keys and wallet off the table. "Brina and I will go for a drive. We will come back later."

"No, let her stay, and you don't have to go far. Just give me a few minutes alone with him."

He walked out the door without another word. He was right, this did feel like a setback, and I was already regretting asking him to leave. I didn't even have to question my decision because I already knew I made the wrong one.

Jeremy's thirty-minute drive seemed to take forever. I tried calling Logan multiple times, but he refused to pick up. I sent him a dozen text messages pleading with him to come back, but they've all gone unanswered. I had a feeling I'd be doing a good amount of groveling when he returned.

I was pacing around my house when the doorbell rang. I took one last look around, making sure everything was put away. This would be the first time I've seen Jeremey since the funeral, and I didn't want things to be awkward.

I swung the door open, and a familiar face smiled down at me. "Well, hello there, stranger." He pulled me into a hug, wrapping his strong arms around me. I hadn't realized how much I missed him until now. He reminded me of happier times. When life was easier and a hell of a lot less complicated.

"It's good to see you." I smiled, noticing he was still in his captain's uniform. I patted his chest playfully. "I see you're still giving those flight attendants something good to look at." His hair was a little shorter than usual, and it looked like he had filled out a bit. He looked good, but he already knew that.

He grinned. "Don't forget the female passengers on the flights too."

I stood off to the side. "Get in here, Romeo."

He held me out at arm's-length. "You look great, Ava. I'm sorry for the short notice. I wasn't sure I was going to have time, and I didn't want to make any promises."

I held the door open for him. "How long is your layover?"

He looked at his watch. "I have about an hour or two to spare."

"Jeremy, now I feel terrible. Did you have to rent a car too?" I glanced outside to the small black sedan in front of my house.

He flashed me that pearly white smile that pretty much got him whatever he wanted. "Yes, but it was worth it because I get to see two of my favorite girls." He glanced over his shoulder to where Madison and Brina were playing hopscotch. "Although one has already ditched me for a friend. Story of my life." He dramatically rolled his eyes.

I touched his elbow gently, guiding him inside. "Come on in, I haven't seen you in forever."

"Wow, this place is a lot bigger than the pictures you sent." His eyes scanned my living room, and I was glad I tidied up before he came.

"Let me give you a quick tour." We took our time walking through the house, and I caught him up to speed on everything concerning Madison. If he noticed most of Drew's things missing, he didn't say a word. After showing him the inside, we headed out to the backyard and sat at the outdoor table. I kicked my feet up on the deck railing while he sipped his ice water.

"I'm sure Madison loves having an in-ground pool."

"This house was the best investment I ever made," I said, twirling my hair into a messy bun on top of my head.

He squinted at me through the bright sun. "You sure you're doing okay financially?"

"Yes, Jeremy. Drew left us a good sized life insurance policy. Plus, I got a great deal when I sold our townhouse."

He took his time looking around. "Drew would have loved this place."

I hummed in agreement, unable to speak over the knot in my throat. He was right; Drew would've loved it. He was definitely on my mind when I signed the paperwork. Although, I'm not sure he would have been thrilled with the in-ground pool. He always thought they were too expensive and not worth the trouble for only using them four to five months out of the year.

"So, other than the house, what's new?"

Now would be the time to tell him about Logan, so why couldn't I get my mouth to cooperate?

"Not much." I shifted in my seat. "How's Beth doing? Have you guys set a date yet?"

Jeremy and Beth have been together for as long as I've known him. Whenever I would ask Drew why they never got married, he told me Jeremy had commitment issues. Well, no shit. It's been twelve years. I'm not sure I could wait that long.

"If I didn't know any better," he leaned forward, resting his elbows on his knees, "I would think you're trying to throw me off topic."

I sighed; the man was too smart for his own good. Lord help his future children. I sat back in my chair and crossed my arms. I couldn't believe we were going to have this conversation. Might as well just rip off the Band-Aid.

"I'm dating someone."

He was quiet. Too quiet. Jeremy never had trouble making conversation. I could practically feel his brain shifting through our phone conversations and text messages, trying to remember if I had hinted at anything.

"Wow, I wasn't expecting that." He grabbed the back of his neck. "Who's the lucky guy?"

"Logan Blake, nice to meet you." I sucked in a breath as Logan walked through the sliding glass door. I didn't even hear his truck pull up in the driveway. My nerves spiked with how uncomfortable this could get.

They shook hands, and Logan took the empty seat next to me. Jeremy's eyes narrowed when Logan placed his arm around my shoulder.

"Uncle Jeremy." Madison came barreling through the backyard, breaking through the tension. "I finished the bag of candy you gave me."

He shifted forward in his chair and ran his finger along her cheek. "I can see that. Did you happen to get any in your tummy?"

She giggled. "Yes, silly, and I shared with Brina." She plopped down in his lap, making herself comfortable. "We're going to swim in the pool. I can swim with my head under water now and no more floaties in the deep end."

"Nice. Where did you learn that?" He gave Brina a little wave as she snacked on a bag of pretzels.

"Logan showed me. He's a really fast swimmer too."

I couldn't tell what he was thinking, but my own thoughts were running wild. This couldn't have been easy for him, but hopefully, he would come around when he realized how good Logan was for us.

Jeremy scratched his chin. "I'll have to bring my swim trunks next time I visit. Or," he tickled her side, "maybe you and your mom could fly to see me in Colorado, and I can take you guys white water rafting."

She twisted in his lap. "Yes, we can see grandma and grandpa too."

Jeremy glanced at me briefly. He still had dinner with David and Karen once a month. He knew exactly what happened the last time they were in town. I wanted to ask how they were doing and if Karen still hated me, but I didn't want to spend this visit talking about them.

"I'd bet they would love to see you." He shifted her on his lap. "I'll even make sure you and your mom get bumped up to first class again."

"Is that the one with the big seats and good snacks?"

He smiled down at her. "Nothing but the best for my goddaughter."

"Madison," I cleared my throat, "why don't you and Brina go upstairs and get your swimsuits on."

She rested her head against his shoulder. "Are you going to be here when I come back down?"

He rubbed her back softly and kissed her cheek. "And miss watching you do cannonballs and dive into the deep end?" He shook his head. "No way am I leaving until I see that."

The girls rushed off, leaving us alone. I don't know why I suddenly felt nervous; maybe I should have thought this through, instead of just winging it.

Logan stood up and squeezed my shoulder. "I'm going inside to get changed and give you guys time to catch up."

Jeremy's eyes followed him with curiosity as he disappeared into the house. He leaned back in his chair and took a sip of his drink. "I guess you forgot to mention a few things."

Jeremy and I have always gotten along. He was Drew's best friend, and suddenly it felt like we were at odds with each other.

"Whatever you want to say, just say it."

"This is a lot to take in, Ava. I want you and Madison to be happy, but I also want to look out for you."

"I appreciate that, Jeremy, but I'm capable of taking care

of myself." I laced my fingers together and took a calming breath. "There isn't a day that goes by where I don't miss Drew. I will always love him, but I'm ready to move on. I'm sick of being lonely. It sucks. I want to be happy again."

"You're human, of course, you'll want to move on, but I have questions." He ran his hand through his hair and looked off to the side. "I don't know this guy. You and Madison have been through so much. Drew and I talked about this. I promised him that if anything ever happened that I would make sure you and Madison were okay." I wiped my eyes, not being the least bit surprised by that. Drew didn't trust many people; Jeremy might have been the only one. "Look, Ava. I'm not trying to upset you, but seeing you with someone else is weird."

I took his hand in mine and squeezed it gently. "He's a great guy. Give him a chance."

He swallowed thickly. "I've known you long enough to know that this wasn't an easy decision to make. As long as he treats you and Madison right."

"He does," I rushed out.

"I will always be here for you both, no matter what."

I burst into tears, overwhelmed with so many different emotions. His approval meant more to me than he ever could imagine. We sat for the next hour, while the girls splashed around in the pool, and the guys talked about sports. It didn't take them long to ease into friendly conversation. By the end of the visit, I was beginning to feel like a third wheel. Logan went out of his way to be respectful of Jeremey, and it was noticed and appreciated. When it was time to leave, it felt like we had turned a corner.

TWENTY

LOGAN

"Dad." Brina's soft voice woke me up from a sound sleep. "Can I sleep with you?"

I lifted the covers and sat on the edge of the bed. "What's wrong, sweetheart?" This is the second weekend in a row where she's come into my room in the middle of the night.

"I miss sleeping in your bed like I did when I was little." I brushed a piece of her hair back and studied her. Brina used to have a hard time falling asleep when she was younger. Either Vanessa or I would have to lie down with her until she passed out. I was convinced it was because of all the arguing that took place between her mother and me. After our divorce, I suggested she see a therapist to help with the change and transition. Vanessa was against it. She thought it was just a phase that she would grow out of. Things did get better for a while; it wasn't until Ava and I talked to the girls about us being together that I noticed a slight change in her behavior.

I ran a soothing hand up and down her arm. "Honey, you're getting too old to sleep in my bed."

Cuddling with my daughter when she was three and four wasn't a big deal, but I wasn't sure if it was appropriate at age nine.

Her bottom lip trembled. "Can you lie down with me then? Just until I fall asleep."

I rubbed at my eyes. "Sure."

I stopped in the kitchen and poured her a glass of water. She climbed into her bed, and I set the glass on her nightstand.

"Do you want to talk about what's bothering you?" I asked, knowing this wasn't just a bad dream where she woke up scared.

She played with the hem of her nightgown. "I don't want to get in trouble."

"Brina," I said, my body filling with concern. "You will not get in trouble for telling me whatever it is that has you upset. Let's talk about it and see if there is anything I can do to help."

She worried her bottom lip between her teeth. "Are you going to move in with Ava and Madison?"

I drew back, unprepared for that question. "I don't have plans to do that at the moment. Why are you worried about that?"

Ava and I have been taking things slow. We were slowly easing our girls into this new dynamic. Both girls have already been through so much change, so the last thing we wanted to do was push them into something they weren't ready for. It was surprising that Madison was handling things better than Brina. While the four of us still did things together, we kept those visits to one or two days a week. Brina seemed clingier than usual, and it baffled me because she loved Ava and Madison.

"I overheard Mom talking on the phone." Her big blue

eyes stared back at me. They were the same color as Vanessa's, yet so full of innocence. "She said if you moved in with her that I wouldn't be allowed to see you anymore. She called Ava some bad names."

I fought the anger that immediately swelled inside me. No matter how hard I tried to be the better person, the truth was, my ex-wife was a hateful and malicious human being. The world was full of bad people that I desperately wanted to protect my daughter from. It sucked that one of those people had to be her own mother.

"I'm sorry that you had to hear that." If there were a way to make that woman disappear from this planet, I would do it in a heartbeat. "Sometimes when people are hurt or angry, they say things they don't mean. Your mom doesn't know Ava well enough to say those things about her. She has the right to be concerned because things are changing, but she doesn't have the right to speak like that. That's not okay and I don't want you to think badly of Ava because of it."

Never ever would I want to put my daughter in the middle or make her feel like she had to choose between her parents. She had a relationship with both of us. If only I could get my ex-wife to understand that.

"I like Ava, she's really nice."

"She is very nice, and she loves spending time with you." I kissed her head. "I'm glad you were open with me about this. I also want you to know that as long as I'm alive, no one will ever keep you from me. You are my entire world, Brina Marie, it doesn't matter who I date or who I marry, you will always be my little girl. Nothing and no one will ever change that. So, please don't worry about what your mom said. I'm sure those words slipped out and she didn't mean them." That was a lie, but I wanted to ease her discomfort. "I'll talk to your mom about this, okay?"

"She's going to be mad."

000My heart pinched at the concern in her eyes. "You let me worry about that. But you know what you should be worried about?" I tickled her side gently, not wanting to get her too wound up. "If you don't get back to sleep, I'm going to be very grumpy in the morning."

She giggled and squirmed underneath the covers. "I love you, Dad."

"I love you too, princess. More than anything."

I laid on my side and waited for her to fall asleep. I knew Vanessa was going to be a problem. Sometimes I wondered how I even lasted so long in that marriage. Maybe it was because she wasn't always this bad. It wasn't until she had Brina that I started to see how spiteful and unrelenting she was. Over the years, her obsession with me has only gotten worse. It made no sense to me. She could have any man she wanted with a snap of her fingers. It was keeping the man that was the issue. I knew for a fact that she's dated since me. She loved to throw her hookups in my face, hoping I would get jealous. What she couldn't seem to get through her head was that we were never getting back together.

I stood up and tucked the covers up to Brina's chin. There was no way I was getting back to sleep now, so I went downstairs to my workout room and took my frustration out on my punching bag.

———

I set my coffee down on the counter when the chime of my

doorbell rang. I walked over and unlocked the storm door. "I want to talk to you."

Vanessa stood against the door and looked around. "Where's Brina?"

"My mom took her out to breakfast so we could have some privacy."

I held the door open for her to step inside. I looked across the street; my elderly neighbor was sitting on her front porch in her rocking chair pretending to knit or crochet or whatever the hell they called it. The last thing I wanted was an audience to what was about to go down, especially with her two grandkids running through the sprinkler in the front yard.

"I don't have time for your games today, Logan. I have things to do and places to be."

"Make time, your Botox injection can wait."

She rolled her eyes as she passed me by. "Real mature."

"Have a seat." I pointed to one of the empty high-top chairs in the kitchen. I've had all night to rein in my fury. I didn't sleep a wink, so I stayed downstairs and worked out until three a.m. After an intense workout of pull-ups, sit-ups, and a few extra rounds with the punching bag, I felt slightly better. Now, as I looked down at my ex-wife, I wondered what the hell I was thinking when I married her. My brother asked me before if I ever loved her. I think I convinced myself to try to love her, but the feelings never came. I married her because it was the right thing to do. It was times like this where I wished I had never met her. But as they say, you can't put the toothpaste back in the tube, so here we were.

"Logan, what is this about?"

"Brina had a hard time sleeping last night."

Genuine concern jumped in her eyes. "What was wrong with her?"

I leaned against the fridge and crossed my arms. "I think the better question is, what the hell is wrong with you?"

Her body locked up at my harsh tone. "Excuse me, could you repeat that please, because I'm not sure I heard you correctly."

I pushed myself off the fridge and stalked toward her. "Your hearing is just fine but let me fill you in." I leaned forward, getting up in her face. So much for trying to be calm and collected. "Brina was upset because she heard you on the phone talking shit about Ava and threatening to keep her from me."

Her head tilted to the side, and her eyebrows drew together. "Oh, when I was talking to Debbie?"

I wanted to laugh, but it wasn't funny. Her friend Debbie was a psycho bitch who made Vanessa look like a saint. I should have known it was Debbie who stoked the fire.

"Unless you make a habit of spilling your hateful words to someone other than your only friend then yes, and I see you're not all that surprised either. Did you intend for our daughter to hear that conversation?"

"Of course not." I studied her, searching for any signs that she was lying. I wanted to believe that even she wouldn't stoop that low, but there wasn't much I wouldn't put past her.

"You can't think that shit is okay?"

"I was being honest. The only woman who will be raising my daughter, will be me."

My forehead wrinkled. "Is that what you're worried about?"

"I want to believe that this chick is only temporary, but I don't know you anymore, so I can't be sure. I wouldn't put it past you to shack up with her and try to take my daughter from me."

"Vanessa, that's absurd."

She folded her arms and glared at me. "Which part?"

"Okay. Let's get something straight." I held my hands out. "Things between Ava and I are new. There are no plans for us to live together yet…" I stopped and ran a hand through my hair. "But I'm not going to lie, I see a future with her. When the time comes, not if, you will have to accept that."

"No, I don't."

"Vanessa." I sighed. "This needs to stop. You and I are never getting back together. Stop with the games. Stop with the drama and stop putting Brina in the middle."

She leaned across the breakfast bar, putting the tits that cost me six months of overtime on full display. I knew exactly what she was doing. My hands folded along the countertop in frustration. She smirked when she caught me looking, thinking I was checking her out when really, I wanted to take a hot shower and scrub my eyes out. I wouldn't touch her if she were the last woman on earth.

"I don't understand why you're doing this? You know you're never going to get what we had with anyone else."

"You're right." I gritted my teeth. "I already have better."

"You bastard," she shouted, and I glanced across the room to make sure the doors and windows were shut. "I'm not going to let some bitch and her sad story take you away from me. You don't get a happily ever after with the pitiful widow. That happily ever after belongs to me."

All I saw was red. "News flash! I don't belong to you!

You stopped getting a say in how I live my life the day the ink dried on those divorce papers. We ended for a reason. I've moved on and I won't let you fuck this up for me. You may have gotten away with it in the past, but I'm warning you." I pointed my finger at her. "Mark my words, you mess with her and you'll regret it."

She reached out and slapped her hand across my cheek, sending it sideways. "I've got a news flash of my own. If I can't have you, then neither can she. Consider yourself warned. I'm about to make your life a living hell!"

I wanted to reach out and throttle her, but I couldn't. Putting my hands on a woman went against everything I believed in. Instead, I stood there and watched her storm for the door.

She whipped around; her body was vibrating with rage. I gripped the back of the chair to keep myself still. "You can bring Brina to me when she gets back. And when you're done, you can go fuck yourself!"

I picked up my coffee cup and threw it across the room.

That went well.

TWENTY-ONE

AVA

I COULDN'T EVEN SLEEP LAST NIGHT KNOWING WHAT TODAY was. Every day this month, I would look at the calendar, stare at the date, and hope it would disappear. No matter how much I tried to fight the sadness, everything inside me ached. Drew and I should be getting ready for our anniversary dinner. He would be on the bed, telling me to hurry up because I was always late. He'd tease me while scrolling through his phone and kiss me when I was done and tell me how beautiful I looked. God, I missed him so much.

I stroked his face through the glass frame as the memory of our wedding day played out in my mind, making it hurt even more. I hugged the picture to my chest and sobbed. I knew I wasn't the first woman to lose her husband, and I wouldn't be the last, but it didn't make it hurt any less.

My eyes drifted over to my ringing cell phone. I've already gotten calls from Amelia, my mom, and a few of our mutual friends. All have gone unanswered, but ignoring Logan was the last thing I wanted to do.

The ringing stopped and started again. I grabbed a tissue out of the box and tried to pull myself together. Just when my life was finally getting more manageable, today had to show up and punch me in the face.

"Hey," I answered, trying to sound strong and not like I'd been crying nonstop. He didn't need to worry about me or how I wanted to hide away from the world today.

"Ava." There was stress in his voice. "Is everything okay?"

I guess I wasn't good at faking it. I wanted to downplay things and pretend everything was fine, but he would only figure out I was lying, so what was the point.

"Today is my wedding anniversary." I wiped my hand across my cheek, trying to get the tears to stop falling.

The line went silent.

"I …" he started and stopped. "I didn't know. I'm sorry."

I rubbed at my stinging eyes, feeling physically and mentally exhausted. "You don't have to apologize, but I bet you're sorry you asked."

This time, he didn't even hesitate. "I'm glad you told me. I just don't like hearing you so sad. It makes me feel helpless." He was quiet for a moment, and that only allowed the awkwardness to linger between us. "Do you want me to leave you alone?" he asked, giving me a minute to think that over. I liked that he was giving me a choice. That he wasn't pushing me to talk about it. He seemed to always know what I needed.

"No." My voice cracked as I tried to pull myself together. "It's okay."

"Where's Madison?"

I looked over my shoulder, the blinds were closed, and my room was void of any light. A lump grew in my throat.

"She's downstairs watching TV by herself. She has no idea what today is. Just that I've been sad all day."

I wasn't going to win any mother of the year award, that was for sure.

"I'm at Brina's dance class. We're going out to mini golf and ice cream when she's done. Madison is more than welcome to come with us. It might be good for her to get out of the house, and you sound like you could use some time alone."

"Oh, that's nice of you to offer. She would like that. Are you sure you don't mind?"

Was it wrong that my boyfriend was picking up my kid so I could stay home and cry over my dead husband? I looked away, feeling guilty. Sometimes, I wasn't sure what he saw in me or how much longer he would tolerate these ups and downs before deciding he's had enough.

"Of course, I don't mind."

This man was too good for me. I didn't deserve him, but there wasn't a chance in hell that I was going to let him slip through my fingers. My feelings were unfair to him, yet his main concern was making things easier for me.

"Okay, text me when you're on your way."

After hanging up the phone, I looked at the photo one last time and put it back in the box where I kept it for safe-keeping.

I quickly made my way to the bathroom and glanced in the mirror. My cheeks were blotchy, and my eyes were red and swollen. I was such a mess. Maybe a glass of wine would help. It couldn't possibly make things worse.

I walked downstairs and made grilled cheese sand-wiches for dinner. I threw a tray of French fries in the oven and a bag of frozen vegetables in the microwave. I was feeling slightly better by the time Logan and Brina showed up.

"Hi," I said, opening the door so they could step inside.

"Hey." He smiled while pushing his sunglasses on top of his head.

A piece of hair had fallen out of place, and without thinking, I reached up and pushed it back. His eyes softened with unspoken emotion. I wanted him to pull me into his arms and take all my pain away. I wanted this day over with, so we could get back to where it wasn't about anyone else but us.

"Are you guys hungry?" I took a step back and slid my hands in my back pockets. "I can whip something up really quick."

"We are all set. We stopped at a drive-thru on the way over."

"Okay, let me make sure she's got everything."

I started for the stairs just as Madison was coming out of the bathroom.

"Mom, are you coming with us?" Her eyes looked hopeful as she stared up at me.

I worried my bottom lip between my teeth and weighed my options. I could bury myself under the covers and cry my eyes out, or I could spend a few hours actually living my life. Spending time with people I cared about. Drew would want that for me. He wouldn't want me alone in this house, crying over him.

"It might take your mind off of things." Logan's eyes met mine. "But there is no pressure."

Taking my mind off of things sounded like the best idea yet. I wanted this misery to stop. Hadn't I shed enough tears? My eyes drifted to the clock on the wall. I decided right then and there that I had spent enough time in my own head for one day.

"You know what? I think I will. Just give me a minute to freshen up." Maybe being distracted for a few hours would help. If anything, it would make the time go by faster.

I ran upstairs to my bedroom before I had a chance to change my mind. I picked up my hairbrush and ran it through my hair. My eyes paused on my wedding band. I stroked my thumb over the diamonds, letting a few seconds pass. A lone tear slid down my cheek; my heart wanted to hang on to him for as long as I could, but my head knew it was time to let him go.

I slid my rings off my finger and held them up. It was completely unfair that Drew's life was cut short, but that didn't mean I had to stop living mine. I kissed my rings and slid them into a box.

Moving forward didn't mean I would have to forget him. Maybe I could start remembering him instead.

———

The girls walked in front of us. I could tell Logan wanted to reach for my hand but wasn't sure if it was a good idea. There was a family with young children in front of us, waiting for their turn while a group of teenagers finished up. The girls were sitting on the bench playing Rock Paper Scissors to see who would go first.

Brina went first, and Madison went second. I set my ball down and took a swing. It didn't even come close to the hole. Logan went last, and of course, the showoff got the ball in the cup on the second try.

He placed his hand on my shoulder as the girls did a little victory dance. "I take it golf isn't your thing?"

"I hate golf. I think it's stupid."

He laughed. "It just takes a little patience."

"I thought you didn't play golf," I said, standing off to the side while the girls went to fetch my ball out of the creek.

"I play occasionally, it's just not my first choice."

I eyed him skeptically. "How did you get so good?"

He grabbed me by the hips, pulling me close. I shivered when his lips brushed against my ear. "Haven't you learned by now that I'm good at everything." He looked off to the side to make sure the girls weren't listening. "Especially with my strokes."

I laughed while bringing my hand up to his cheek. The soft whiskers along his jaw scratched against my palm. "You're full of yourself, you know that?"

"I'd rather be full of you." His eyes twinkled in amusement.

I smiled up at him. This man was insanely good for my soul. What started out as an unbearable day turned into an enjoyable evening.

By the time we made it to the eighteenth hole, I looked at my card, noticing I was in last place. I didn't even try; I walked across the green felt and dumped my pink ball into the cup. The girls called me a cheater while Logan lined his ball up. He studied the path in concentration and swung with just the right amount of force, sending the ball sliding into the hole.

The girls pouted off to the side with their hands on their hips.

He held his hand up for a high-five, which no one returned. He might have been proud of his hole in one, but we were a little bitter. "All right, showboat, let's get you an ice cream cone."

We left Logan's truck in the parking lot and decided to take advantage of the nice weather and walk to the ice cream stand a couple of blocks away.

"Does everyone know what they want?" he asked, leaning up against the window to look at the board with the list of flavors.

"I'll have a vanilla and chocolate twist with rainbow sprinkles," I said, not even bothering to look at the menu. I ordered the same thing every time.

"Rainbow sprinkles, huh?"

I smacked his stomach playfully. "The sprinkles are the best part."

"If you say so." He looked over at a couple who had just walked away, leaving an empty picnic table. "Why don't you guys go grab that while I finish up with the order."

I started to follow the girls, but he reached out and grabbed my wrist. "You took off your rings," he said, sliding his thumb over my bare ring finger.

I was wondering if he was even going to bring it up. "It was time."

He cupped my face between his palms and pressed his lips to my forehead. "I'm not going to push you today, because you've already taken a huge step. Tomorrow." He stared into my eyes. "We're doing this."

"What exactly are we doing?"

"Moving forward."

TWENTY-TWO

AVA

LOGAN PULLED MY HAND AWAY WHEN HE NOTICED ME TOYING with the hem of my sweater. "Don't be nervous." He laced our fingers together, trying to put me ease. "They will love you."

"That's easy for you to say." I sighed nervously as we pulled into his parents' driveway.

He brought my hand up to his mouth and pressed a kiss. "Relax, Ava. You have nothing to worry about."

"I just want them to like me."

"I assure you they feel the same way."

He let go of my hand and stepped out of the car while the girls jumped out of the back.

The front door flew open before we even reached the house. A tall, slender woman with shoulder-length dark hair greeted us.

"Hi Nana, hi Papa." Brina waved her hands in the air. She ran into them, wrapping her arms around their legs.

Logan's dad held his hand out. "Hi there, I'm Patrick. It's nice to meet you." I looked up at the man who strongly resembled his son. Both men had a similar build, except

Logan had a bit more muscle and a few more inches in height.

"It's nice to meet you as well. I'm Ava, and this," I said as Madison slid up to my side, "is my daughter, Madison."

I tipped her head back, forcing her to make eye contact. "Can you say hello?"

She leaned into my side and waved, giving them a bashful smile. Funny how she was curious on the drive over, asking a million questions, and now she seemed to forget how to use her voice. Brina was still talking a mile a minute, thankfully taking the attention off us.

Logan's mother pulled him in for a hug. "I'm so happy you are here. I don't get to see much anymore. You're always so busy."

She sounded annoyed, but you could see the wrinkles around her eyes deepen with her smile.

He kissed her cheek. "Sorry, Mom. I've been busier than usual."

She rolled her eyes before they turned to me. "Sometimes I wish he had a normal nine-to-five office job."

"Unfortunately, the criminals I have to hunt down for a living like to do their work after dark, so that will never happen."

He wasn't kidding. His phone was constantly going off in the middle of the night. He kept a spare suit and tie in my closet for when he got called in. When I asked him why he had to wear a dress shirt and tie to go out at three a.m., he reminded me that there were usually camera crews at the crime scene, and he had to look professional in front of the reporters.

His mom wiped her hands on her floral apron. "Ava,

I've been dying to meet you. My granddaughter has not stopped talking about you and Madison."

"I've heard a lot about you, too, Mrs. Blake. Thanks for inviting us."

"Please call me Kelly." She gave my arm a gentle squeeze as we shuffled inside.

As we entered the living room, two black labs trotted toward us. The sound of their big paws thumping along the hardwood floor had me taking a step back. Logan moved forward and held his hand out. "Harley… Bentley…sit!" he commanded. Both dogs stopped, sat, and wagged their tails.

Brina rushed around her father and got down on her knees to greet her excited friends. She hugged them both tightly, and each dog took turns licking her face. "His breath smells like poop." She giggled, causing all of us to laugh.

Logan's father grabbed a few dog toys out of the basket in the hall. "I'm going to take them out back and let them run around for a few minutes." He looked to girls. "Would you two young ladies like to come with me?"

Madison looked up at me with pleading eyes. I gestured for her to go ahead.

Kelly held out her hand. "Shall we?" My gaze glanced at all the family portraits lining the walls as we followed her through the house. "I hope you guys haven't eaten today because I might have made a little too much food."

Logan laughed. "So, what else is new. You have a tendency to cook like you're expecting the Tenth Mountain division to stop by."

She gave him a stern look over her shoulder. "It's always better to have more than enough than not enough."

Logan leaned in and whispered in my ear, "Don't be

surprised if she sends us home with enough Tupperware containers that will last us a week."

We angled through a small cozy family room to the back of a kitchen that opened up to a large open sunroom.

"Whoa…" Logan stumbled to a stop, his mouth opened and closed as a man with dark hair rose from one of the gray couches. "What the hell are you doing here?"

The mystery man set his beer down on the coffee table and stepped forward. He drew Logan in for a one-arm hug. "Don't act so happy to see me."

Logan tipped his head to his mom. "Why didn't you tell me Gage was in town?"

"He wanted to surprise you." She shrugged, grabbed the pie from my hands, and set it down on a buffet table to the right.

Logan playfully pushed his friend in the shoulder. "Well, color me fucking surprised. How long are you in town for, man?"

"Just for one night. Lily and I are passing through on our way down to the Outer Banks."

Logan glanced over Gage's shoulder. "Hey gorgeous." His lips kicked up into a smile as the petite brunette set her drink down on a coaster. She ran her hands along her lavender dress as she walked around Gage to get to Logan. He scooped her up in a hug, practically lifting her off her feet. I had no idea who these people were, so I stood off to the side while they had their little reunion.

She pulled away from Logan and introduced herself. "Hi, I'm Lily and this is my husband, Gage."

Gage winked in greeting. It was hard to miss the subtle gleam in his dark eyes. He was handsome and looked like the type that knew it too. "So, you're the reason why my friend has fallen off the face of the earth."

"Gage and I are old friends," Logan explained, rubbing a hand along my lower back. "He's also a jackass, so don't pay him any attention."

Lily walked over to lean into her husband's side. He didn't seem the least bit fazed by being called a *jackass*.

"And don't forget asshole," a third man said, strolling into the room with a beer in his hand.

"Do you talk to your students with that same mouth?" Logan teased, but there was obvious affection between the two.

"Not if I want to keep my job." He looked at me. "I'm Luke by the way."

Ah, Logan's older brother. "I'm Ava. It's nice to meet you."

"Likewise." He raised his beer and grinned.

The two brothers had the same eyes and identical smiles. Except where Logan had facial hair and strong features, Luke was more clean-cut with a boy-next-door look. He wore a short-sleeved flannel shirt, skinny jeans, and a pair of Chuck Taylors. I liked Luke immediately, but the jury was still out on his friend.

Logan kissed my temple, and I tried not to squirm when I felt multiple sets of eyes on us.

After everyone grabbed a drink, Lily and I fell into easy conversation while Kelly and the guys told endless stories that had everyone laughing out loud. Every now and then, Logan would lean in and tell me not to listen to a word that came out of Gage's mouth. I loved the camaraderie between this group and the feeling of being included.

I was enjoying myself and feeling completely relaxed when Logan wrapped an arm around my shoulder and pulled me against him. "You doing okay?"

"I'm having a great time." I took a sip of my wine and glanced at Gage. "It sounds like you two have been friends forever. Did you grow up together?"

"Gage lived across the street. We worked together until he moved to New York. He works for the NYPD now."

Gage reclined back, stretching his long legs out. "I couldn't wait to get out of Filth-adelphia, although we did have some fun times." He smirked at Logan. "Do you remember when we got propositioned during our first drug raid?"

Kelly covered her ears and shot up from her seat. "I don't want to hear this story. I'm going to check on dinner."

As soon as Kelly left the room, Gage continued. "The girl was high out of her mind. She told Logan he looked good in a uniform and then said they could go in the back, do it missionary and forget the whole night ever happened."

"What did you say?" Lily asked, but I wasn't sure I wanted to know the answer.

"I told her I was pretty sure that wasn't allowed on the job."

"And then she turned to me and said, 'how about you, handsome? We don't even need to do it missionary. I can get on my knees right now and suck your dick.'"

Logan smirked behind his beer bottle. "One of my best memories."

Gage leaned forward, resting his forearms on his thighs. "Sometimes, I miss those badge bunnies and all the cop parties that never should have taken place."

Lily smacked him on the arm. "I've been to some of those cop parties with my brother. Some of those 'women' barely looked old enough to work at Dunkin' Donuts."

His eyes narrowed. "Your brother had no business taking you to those parties."

"You and I never would have met if he didn't."

He pulled her onto his lap and kissed her cheek. "That may be the only good thing Brad's ever done for me."

Lily looked at me and explained. "Gage and my brother hated each other."

"We still do," Gage offered up. He tried to make light of the situation, but I got the impression he couldn't care less what Lily's brother thought of him.

"How often do you get hit on?" I asked, knocking my knee against Logan's. His beer paused on the way to his lips.

"Um…Not as much as I used to."

Well, that wasn't very reassuring. Did I really want to know what he meant by that? No, I didn't. I wasn't an insecure person, but Logan's looks and personality could check off any woman's boxes. And despite my best efforts to not think about what a catch he was, a knot of jealously formed in my stomach.

He leaned in, pressing his lips to my forehead. "You have nothing to worry about when it comes to me. You're the only 'bunny' I'm interested in."

Gage placed a hand over his heart. "Aren't you two sweet, but Logan, you kiss like an old man. Next time aim for the lips not the forehead." I tilted my head to the side. He was such a smart-ass. "So, Ava, tell us about yourself."

I sat up straighter. "What do you want to know?"

"I heard you cut hair for a living. Other than playing with scissors and hairbrushes, what else do you enjoy?"

What a dick.

"Gage," Logan warned at the same time his wife elbowed him in the side.

"Will you stop being a butt-hole." Lily looked at me with an apology in her eyes. "Please ignore him. That's what I do. He's just teasing you. He's really not that much of an asshole."

Logan coughed next to me. "I'm not so sure about that."

Luke rose from his seat and glanced at my empty glass. "I'm going to fetch a beer. Can I get you another Chardonnay?"

Luke had been relatively quiet where Gage had been dominating the conversations. I knew that Logan was close with his brother, and I was eager to know him better.

"I was going to check in on the girls, they've been out back for a while. I can come with you."

I followed Luke into the kitchen. He walked over to the counter and quickly refilled my wineglass while I peeked outside. Brina was throwing a frisbee while Madison kicked a soccer ball around the yard. The poor dogs didn't know which way to turn. Patrick sat on the deck, seeming content.

I quickly closed the door. "I think Harley and Bentley are enjoying the attention."

Luke moved a scented candle out of the way and slid a coaster across the counter. "Let me guess. My dad has his ass parked in a chair while the girls tear up the yard."

I laughed at his accurate assumption. "Pretty much."

Once he grabbed a cold beer out of the fridge, he slid onto one of the empty barstools.

"Have a seat." He patted the spot next to him.

"Thank you." I held up my wineglass.

"My pleasure. It looked like you needed that." He looked off into the other room and back to me. "Gage was just being Gage. He grows on you once you get to know him."

I fidgeted with the paper towel in front of me. "It was that obvious, huh?"

He snorted. "Stevie Wonder could have seen it."

I bit the inside of my cheek. "My husband was an athlete in college who attracted a lot of attention. Gage's comment about the 'badge bunnies' just brought back a lot of insecurities. I know how hard it is to date a man when the temptation is always there." I shook my head, feeling stupid for saying that. "I'm sorry. I shouldn't be comparing Logan to Drew. Plus, I'm sure there are other topics you'd like to talk about other than my dead husband."

He reached out, placing his hand on my shoulder. "It's okay. You can talk about him. No one expects you to act like he never existed."

His tone was gentle and comforting. He was trying to ease my worry, and he reminded me so much of Logan at that moment.

I took a hefty sip of my wine. "You sound just like your brother."

"My brother is crazy about you." He rubbed his chin, seeming to weigh his words. "Logan will probably kill me for telling you this, but he's had feelings for you for quite a while now. Long before you two started dating."

That brought a smile to my face. "We talked about that, so no worries," I reassured him, recalling that conversation. "When we first met, I assumed that he just was a serial dater and huge flirt. It wasn't until this past year when he started coming around that I realized how badly I misjudged him. He's been there for me and my daughter in a way that I never expected." My words got caught in the back of my throat, and I felt a lone tear slip from my eye. "I'm sorry, I don't know what the hell is wrong with me."

"You don't need to apologize. Ava. You obviously still miss your husband. Your feelings are perfectly normal."

"That's just it. These tears aren't for Drew, they are for Logan. I feel guilty because he deserves someone who has a whole heart, not half of one. I feel damaged."

Luke shifted uncomfortably. "If anyone knows anything about a damaged heart, it would be my brother."

I wiped at my cheeks again to make sure they were dry. "I know his ex-wife did a number on him."

"That's not exactly…"

"Mom." Madison came running into the kitchen at full speed. "I have to go to the bathroom."

I looked away, trying to get my emotions in check. I probably seemed like a basket case.

Luke hopped off the stool. "It's down the hall, Brina can show you where it is," he said as his niece was shutting the door behind her.

Logan and his mom entered the kitchen. Kelly went over to check the roast in the oven while he came over and nestled his chest against my back. He dropped a kiss to the top of my head. "What were you guys talking about in here?"

Luke leaned forward, resting his arms along the counter. "I was telling her about what an asshole Gage can be."

Logan's hands tightened along my shoulders. "Are you upset about what he said?"

"No, I'm just not sure what to make of him."

Both men barked out a laugh. "He's definitely an acquired taste." Logan spun me around on the stool and caressed my cheek. "He's not that bad once you get to know him."

His words made me regret judging his friend. He might have gotten under my skin, but there were a few moments where he was charming, although I'd never admit that to him. I could get along with him if I had to. Lily was nice and sweet. How bad could he be?

Another glass of wine and a full belly later, I was feeling lighter somehow. Maybe because I had the best pot roast I'd ever tasted in my life. Kelly could cook, and if this was what Logan was used to, I needed to start watching more cooking videos on YouTube. After begging Kelly for the recipe because it was Logan's favorite, we moved out to the backyard and sat around the outdoor fire pit. A few neighbors came over and introduced themselves while the girls went inside the house to play a board game. Things could not have gone any better, and I determined that Gage Garrison wasn't so bad after all. By the time we reached my driveway, Madison and Brina were both passed out in the back seat.

Logan turned off the engine and reached for my hand. "Thanks for coming tonight."

I gazed at him through the dim lighting of the car. The only thing I could focus on were his lips and the smell of his cologne that filled the small space. He ran his thumb across my knuckles, silently watching me. Maybe it was the wine or just simply being near him. Whatever it was, it caused my heart rate to pick up, and I felt that familiar yearning pass through me.

I unbuckled my seat belt and closed the distance between us. "I always want to come, Logan," I said, brushing my lips against his. He responded immediately, and I moved my palm up to his stubbled cheek, feeling the coarseness against my skin. He made a noise in the back of his throat, one that had goose bumps rising along my bare arms. He gently swept my hair off to the side of my neck and kissed me deep and slow. I could taste the beer on his tongue and the warmth from his lips. This was the kind of kiss that you wanted to go on forever. I moved my hand to the back of his head, pulling him closer. My breast swelled, and my nipples peaked. Logan's thumb gently skimmed along my side, and I hissed out a breath.

He pulled back from the kiss, his lids were low and heavy. He glanced in the back seat, his expression looked pained. "Do you think they'll be okay if we let them sleep in the car tonight?"

I laughed while resting my head against his shoulder. The sound caused the girls to stir. Logan groaned in frustration and tried to slide away, but I grabbed his shirt and whispered in his ear. "Don't worry, we'll pick up where we left off once we get them inside." I lightly stroked his bottom lip with my finger. "You are so getting laid tonight."

"On one condition." He pulled my hand away and held it in his firm grip.

"What's that?"

"You let me show you all the different ways I can make you come."

My lips quirked up. "I have a condition of my own."

He lifted an eyebrow. "What's that?"

My gaze drifted down to my wrist. "You bring your cuffs upstairs tonight."

"You got yourself a deal, sweetheart." He unlocked the door, and I laughed at the speed at which he woke up the girls and raced inside the house.

TWENTY-THREE

LOGAN

I GRABBED THE ROSES OUT OF THE BACK SEAT AND STARTED heading toward the front entrance of the school. Judging by all the cars filling up the parking lot, it looked like it was a packed house. I walked behind a young family that I recognized from Brina's dance class.

A smile touched my face when I spotted Ava and Madison standing off to the side with my family. There was something about seeing them all together that felt right.

Luke spotted me first and waved me over.

"Sorry, I got stuck in traffic." I pressed a quick kiss to Ava's mouth and stared down at Madison, who was beaming up at us. The kid was too cute for her own good.

"Look, Logan. My mom and I painted our nails the same color, so we match. See." She stuck out her hand and twirled around in her sundress that was the same color blue as Ava's. "Luke said we look like twins."

I laughed and handed her the single pink rose I had wrapped for her. "You both look beautiful."

"That's for me?" she asked, her eyes going big.

"Of course it is." I smiled. "You got all dressed up for Brina's dance recital. You deserve something special too."

"Thank you, Logan." She hugged my waist. "I love it, and I love you too."

My heart squeezed, and I had to take a deep swallow. "I love you too, pretty girl."

I reached for Ava's hand, noticing the tears in her eyes. My mother snuck a tissue from her purse and handed it to her. I wanted to ask her if they were happy or sad tears, but I didn't want to make her uncomfortable in front of everyone.

"Why don't we go inside before the auditorium fills up?" my mother suggested as we followed her up the steps.

I handed everyone their tickets once we got to the door. I grabbed a program off the table and bought Madison a drink and a small snack before we found our seats.

The place was a zoo. There were babies crying and young toddlers being chased around by their parents. I nodded to a few people I recognized holding flower arrangements similar to mine.

Ava grabbed my arm. "I'm going to the bathroom before we sit down. Madison, do you have to go?"

She shook her head. "No."

"She can go in with us. I'll text Logan and let him know where we are." My mom placed her hand on Madison's shoulder and guided her around all the young children and parents.

Once they were out of sight, I pulled her into me. "I'm sorry I made you cry." I wiped at the corner of her eyes where there was a smudge of mascara.

"They are happy tears."

"Those are my favorite kind." I brushed my lips against hers. "You taste like cherries."

She laughed and wiped at the corner of my mouth. "It's my lip gloss."

"What the hell do you think you're doing?" a familiar voice shrieked, causing people to turn their heads in our direction.

I threw my head back and groaned. I had hoped to avoid Vanessa, even though I knew it was very unlikely. Things were already strained between us as it was, and bringing Ava here was only going to set her off.

"Lower your voice." I could feel my neck prickle as she got closer.

"Don't you dare tell me to lower my voice," she gritted out, gearing herself up for a tantrum. "This is family only. If you were going to bring a guest, you should have checked with me first."

"Wait a minute." Ava stepped closer; her brows creased in confusion. "You're the woman that came into my shop."

"What?" I swung my head to my ex-wife because What. The. Fuck?

Vanessa scowled at Ava. "So, what? I was interested in who my husband was sleeping with. Sue me."

My eyes narrowed. "Tell me you didn't."

"You should have known that I would go digging into your latest flavor of the month. I told you before I did not want you bringing random women around my daughter."

"Ava is not a random woman."

I knew bringing my girlfriend here wasn't going to go over well, but I was not going to exclude her from things that were important to me.

"Logan." Ava's soft hand touched my arm. "Maybe we should go find our seats."

"Are you deaf?" Vanessa's cheeks were getting redder by the second. This was turning into a complete shitshow. "I said leave."

Vanessa took a step forward, but I moved in front of Ava. "Back up."

I did not trust my ex-wife and wouldn't allow her to take one step closer.

"You really have nerve bringing your whore here."

"Ava," I said, never taking my eyes off my ex. "Go find my family."

She placed a gentle hand on my back. "I'm not leaving you here alone with her."

"Excuse me," Vanessa bellowed. Eyes from all over the auditorium started to draw our way, not that she cared. "You don't get a say in this."

"People are watching," I reminded her in a low voice. "Do you really want to embarrass your daughter like this?"

"You bringing your skank here is what's embarrassing."

I took in her face and studied her, wondering how the hell we ended up here. She was out of control, and I didn't see this ending unless I put my foot down once and for all.

"Vanessa. I'm not going to tell you again." I started and stopped when one of the dance instructors walked by with one of her students.

She folded her arms across her chest, not even caring about her surroundings. "I won't repeat myself either." She leaned her head over my shoulder and tried to get around me. "You are not welcome here!"

My ex-wife was seriously crazy. This little showdown would only get worse if I didn't get her to calm down.

What I really wanted to do, was grip her by the arms and drag her ass out of here.

Ava stood tall and squared her shoulders. "I'm sorry that my being here is upsetting you, but Logan wanted me here. And the last time I checked, this was public property."

Vanessa looked Ava up and down. "You think that just because you're spreading your legs for him, that makes you someone important? News flash, that only makes you a tramp. So you can go spread your STD somewhere else."

I inhaled slowly through my nose. Rage, thick and hot, flowed through my veins. I was about to respond when Ava's hand squeezed on my shoulder. "It's fine, Logan, I can handle this."

I spun around and begged her with my eyes to let me deal with this. "You shouldn't have to."

She patted me on the chest, letting me know she was going to square off with my ex-wife whether I wanted her to or not.

Ava moved around me, appearing calm and confident. I knew she was capable of holding her own, but that didn't mean I had to like it. "I've been warned about you, Vanessa, and I'm not afraid of you. You can call me all the names you want, and do your best to drive me away, but I'm not going anywhere."

"You are hilarious. You act like you have a say in any of this. You are a nobody. You will be forgotten like yesterday's news. So don't think you're so special, sweetheart."

Ava sighed. "This is getting nowhere." She looked to me and then around as if she wasn't sure what to do. "I don't want to draw anymore unwanted attention. I'm going to find your parents."

My eyes closed in relief. There was no doubt that if Ava

wanted to, she could wipe the floor with my ex-wife. Instead of taking her down, she chose the high road. I squeezed her hand, letting her know how grateful I was.

Vanessa tried to lunge for her as she walked away, but I grabbed her by the arm. "Don't even think about it."

I watched Ava disappear through the double doors and get lost in the crowd. Thank God, she was now far enough away from this train wreck. God, it went off the rails quick.

I spun around, trying and failing to keep the anger from showing on my face. "Don't ever talk to her like that again."

"How could you blindside me like this?"

I dragged her by the arm down the hall, away from prying eyes. "You want to talk about blindsiding? How about you showing up at my girlfriend's place of business, huh?" My mind was still swirling with that bit of information. "How about the stunt you just pulled? Calling her names and throwing a temper tantrum like a spoiled little brat. You need to get over yourself."

"Stop manhandling me." She tore her arm out of my grasp. "All this over a piece of ass that you've known for two point five seconds?"

"Watch it." My jaw clenched tight. "And you want to talk about manhandling. If you ever lay a hand on her, I will have you arrested for assault."

Vanessa's face screwed up in anger. "I don't need to lay a hand on her. If I want her gone, I will find a way to make it happen."

"Is that a threat?" You would think my height and my size would intimidate her. Or, at the very least, the thought of being arrested would scare her, but no. My ex-wife was too crazy to see straight.

"It sure as fuck is." She seemed so proud of herself, and she just proved to me that nothing I said was getting through that thick head of hers. I never thought it was possible to hate someone as much as I hated this woman.

"You just earned yourself a restraining order."

She stomped her foot. "You can't do that!"

"Oh, but I can. Did you forget what I do for a living? I finally have something good going on in my life and I'll be damned if I let you ruin it."

"Logan, please," she begged, her eyes now filling with tears. She could cry all she wanted. I would not comfort her, no matter how badly she wanted me to. I learned that lesson a long time ago. "How could you do this to me?"

"Do this to you?" She had the nerve to look hurt. She was the one who was acting crazy and making a big fuss.

"You and I both know that this is just a phase. I'm the one you love, so go have your fun now. I know you'll be back."

She couldn't seriously believe that, could she? I wasn't even going to address that nonsense. I've already wasted enough time.

"Vanessa, I've told you a million times we are never getting back together. I don't know how much clearer I can make that for you."

She smirked. "I noticed how you didn't say you don't love me anymore."

I wanted to tell her the truth, that I never really loved her. What I felt for her was lust, but she would never be able to handle that.

"You are the mother of my child and that is all you will ever be to me. You don't have to like Ava, but you will be respectful to her. If you can't do that then you'll have to find a way to keep your mouth shut and get the fuck over yourself."

She drew back, shocked that I was being so harsh. Honestly, I felt like it was about damned time. Maybe because I finally had something worth fighting for.

"God, you can be such an asshole."

I looked down the hall and noticed the lights were dimming, and everyone was scurrying inside to find a seat. Continuing with this conversation would be pointless, and I wasn't going to miss seeing my daughter up on that stage.

"There will come a day, Vanessa, where Brina will be old enough to understand." I looked off into the distance. "I hope to God she never sees this side of you."

With those parting words, I stormed away. I slipped inside the men's room to get my temper in check. I gave myself a few minutes and glanced at my watch. From the schedule they sent home last week, I knew that Brina's act would be coming up soon. I splashed some cold water on my face as if that would help cool me down.

I smoothed my tie along my dress shirt and blew out a deep breath before I walked out. I spotted my family and ducked my head as I made my way down the aisle, trying to keep out of everyone's way. I slid into the end seat next to Ava.

"Everything okay?" she asked as Madison and my family focused on a group of little girls lined up on the stage.

I reached for her hand and laced our fingers together. "I hope so. I'm sorry she treated you like that."

"I'm a big girl. I can handle it."

"I know you can. It doesn't mean I'm happy about it."

She squeezed my fingers. "Let's not talk about her anymore, okay."

My jaw clenched. I was frustrated and pissed off. Yet my shoulders slumped with relief that she was letting this go.

As soon as my daughter stepped onto the stage, my mood shifted in a different direction. Brina looked so damn adorable in her black leotard and pink tutu, spinning around to the music. Pride swelled in my chest as I watched her bend her little body and float around the stage. It was impressive and worth every penny I spent on her classes.

I smiled proudly as she bent forward for a bow. She'd been so nervous and afraid she was going to mess up. I looked off to the side, seeing Vanessa sitting alone. Her parents were a no-show, which wasn't surprising. It shouldn't have bothered me that they didn't want anything to do with my daughter, but it did. Brina didn't need to deal with their bullshit. It was their loss.

I rested my hands along the armrest of my chair and focused my attention on Ava and my family. My dad had slid Madison onto his lap so she could see the stage better. Luke was snapping a million pictures, and my mom was still standing, clapping her hands, not even caring about how loud she was.

These people sitting in this row were all my daughter would ever need. She loved her mother, and I prayed like hell that Vanessa would get her shit together before she ruined everything.

TWENTY-FOUR

AVA

I sat on the bench, licking the frosting off my red velvet cupcake, while Madison rode her bike in circles in front of me.

"Do you think Brina can come over and play later?" she asked, handing me the wrapper once she was finished.

"I think she might be with her mom tonight," I said, brushing the crumbs off my legs. "But I'll check with Logan when we get home. Does that sound good?"

She scrunched up her nose. "I guess."

She didn't seem happy about that, but at least she wasn't whining or complaining.

I pinched the tip of her nose, causing a giggle to break free. "All right, now come here so I can take a quick picture of us."

She groaned, but I didn't care. She was getting so big and changing every day. I was afraid if I blinked, I would miss something. After snatching a couple of quick selfies, I smiled at her goofy grin. She was missing one of her top teeth, and a new one was coming in next to it.

I glanced at the time and pushed to my feet. "It's

getting late." I crumbled up the bag and walked it over to the trash can. "Ready to get going?" I bumped her shoulder as a little orange golden retriever dropped a tennis ball right at our feet.

"Rex," the owner hollered as he jogged over. He slowed his pace as he got closer, grabbing the dog by the collar. "Sorry about that." He picked the ball up and threw it across the grass, and the puppy took off after it.

"No worries. He didn't bother us, right, Madison?"

She pushed her bike to the side as the pup came running back. "Can I play with him for a few minutes?"

"I don't mind." The man smiled politely. "He'll probably enjoy it." He pulled the ball out of the dog's mouth, wiped it off on his shorts, and handed it to Madison. She wrapped her fingers around it and threw it as far as she could.

"Wow." The stranger's head tilted to the side, his eyes going wide. "She's got quite an arm for a girl her size."

"Thanks." I sat down and pressed my hands under the wooden bench. "She plays softball."

He nodded. "I can tell. Let me guess, pitcher?"

I laughed. "What gave it away?"

"Oh, I don't know." He whistled. "Maybe that fact she can throw better than most teenage boys I know."

Pride swelled in my chest. "She's a natural." I smiled while watching her closely.

"I'm Will, by the way."

The wind was picking up, so I tucked a strand of hair behind my ear. "Ava."

He looked at my bare finger and smiled. "So, is it just the two of you today?"

I knew interest in a man's eyes when I saw it. Now that Logan and I were officially together, I wasn't sure how to navigate this. Did I announce right off the bat that I had a boyfriend? Yeah, that wouldn't sound presumptuous at all. He hasn't even hit on me yet.

"Yes, it's just the two of us. She had a doctor's appointment today, so I took the rest of the afternoon off."

"Hopefully, your boss didn't give you too much trouble."

I grinned. "I am the boss."

He laughed. "Beautiful and successful. That's a great combination."

Will spent the next few minutes telling me about his job as a freelance writer for a local newspaper and about his recent divorce. I let Madison play fetch with the dog, all the while keeping a friendly distance. I didn't want to give him the wrong impression, so I looked at my phone and decided it was time to go.

I stood from the bench, gathered up our things, and called Madison over. "It was nice meeting you."

Will's dimple popped out. He had a warm personality and was easy on the eyes, but he was no Logan. "I'm headed out too. We'll walk with you to your car."

I retreated a step back, hoping I wasn't misreading things. "You don't have to do that."

He shoved his hands in his pockets and looked down at the ground. "I'm going that way anyway, so it's no trouble at all."

Not wanting to be rude, I adjusted the bag along my shoulder and started making my way toward the parking lot.

"Did you call Logan yet and ask if Brina can come over later?" Madison asked as she walked her bike beside me.

"Not yet."

"Please, Mom, Logan's your boyfriend. Don't you want to see him?"

That caught Will's attention. Maybe now things wouldn't be awkward once we parted ways.

I looked down at her little freckled face. "I told you I would ask him when we got home."

"So, are you and your boyfriend serious?" Will asked as we winded our way through the parking lot. It was packed when we got here, so I parked on a side street around the corner.

I searched for a way to let him down easy, but the sight in front of my eyes stopped me cold. All the color drained from my face.

I gripped Madison's hand, pulled her back, and sucked in a breath at the smashed windshield. Someone threw a brick through my fucking window. I turned around in a circle, searching for what, I had no clue. I inched closer to look at the damage, and my heart seized when I noticed my slashed tires and the spray paint along the side.

My hands shook as I pulled my phone out to call 911. Strangers were starting to gather around. I swallowed against the lump in my throat as the dispatcher asked question after question. I hated that I couldn't get my brain to cooperate. I took a cautious step back because I didn't trust anybody at that moment.

Once they told me an officer was on the way, my body sagged against an oak tree. Will's eyes filled with concern.

"Do you want me to stay here until the police arrive?"

My mind spun, trying to come up with a face or a name of anyone with an axe to grind. The only person I could think of was Logan's ex-wife, Vanessa. Was she that fucking crazy? How would she even know where I was? My heart banged against my chest at the thought of her following me. I thought her showing up at my work was bad; this was much worse.

"You don't have to do that." I pulled Madison tight against me. "I'm sure you've got to get on with your day."

"I don't mind. Rex and I will keep you company."

"Thank you." I swallowed, taking in my surroundings and noticing my car was the only one damaged.

Madison slipped her hands around my waist and rested her head against my stomach. "Mom, what's going on?"

I pressed my lips to the side of her head. "I'm not sure, but I need you to stay with me, okay?"

A few minutes later, a sheriff's deputy pulled up to the curb. The big, beefy man with a military crew cut stepped out of his car and surveyed the area. I put my hand up, letting him know I was the one who called.

He walked over to my car first, roaming up and down from front to back, inspecting the damage. Once he was finished, he made his way over to us.

"Good afternoon, I'm Deputy Michaels. Is that your vehicle over there?"

"Yes. I'm afraid so."

I pulled my phone out of my purse and handed it to Madison. "Can you call Logan and tell him where we are while I talk to the sheriff?"

I didn't want to bother him at work, but I knew he would want to know. Plus, my car wasn't going anywhere, and we were going to need a ride home.

Deputy Michaels glanced over his shoulder to where the other sheriff took pictures of my car and looked back at me. He took out a small black notebook and clicked a pen. "Can you tell me what time this happened?"

"I don't know. I called nine-one-one as soon as we got to the parking lot and saw my car."

"Do you remember what time that was?"

"I'm not sure. I'd have to look at my call log."

He jotted something down. "How long were you away from your vehicle for?"

"I don't know." My brain was so scrambled, and I couldn't think straight. "If I had to guess, maybe an hour or so."

"Did you notice anything suspicious? Anyone following you?" I shook my head as he continued. "Did you notice anything strange or out of the ordinary?"

I knew these were standard questions, but didn't he realize that I would have called sooner if I had suspected anything.

"No, but seeing that my car was the only one vandalized, I don't think this was random."

I had a sick feeling about who it was, but I didn't want to point them in her direction until I was sure. I was hoping that maybe it was just a couple of teenagers looking for a cheap thrill. But the more that thought spun in my brain, the less likely it seemed.

"I agree. We don't have any other reports of vandalism in the area. Normally, if it's random, it would happen at night and there would be more than one car targeted."

One of the other deputies walked over. He wore a pair of black gloves and was holding a clear plastic bag. "We are going to send this to the lab for prints."

I bent forward and squinted my eyes. "STAY AWAY IF YOU KNOW WHAT'S GOOD FOR YOU" was written in bold black letters on the brick.

Well, there went the theory that this could have been a couple of bored teenagers just trying to piss off their parents. This looked more and more like a bitter ex-wife trying to scare away the new girlfriend.

Once the sheriff was finished with my statement, he went to talk to a few bystanders to see if anyone saw anything.

It wasn't long before a familiar black truck pulled up to the curb and slammed on the brakes. Logan jumped out, not even bothering to turn the engine off.

"Ava," he called out, looking frantic.

"Over here."

His shoulders sagged with relief once he saw us. He jogged over and didn't even hesitate before lifting Madison and throwing her around his waist. "I got you. I'm here. Don't be scared," he whispered into her hair.

The tightness in my chest loosened at the sight of him.

He reached out and squeezed the back of my neck. His gaze darted over every inch of me. "What the fuck happened? Are you okay?"

My arms curled around his middle. "We are fine," I reassured him, even though it was taking everything in me to keep it together. I rested my head against his chest to keep my knees from giving out. I didn't realize how much I needed him until now.

He pinched his lips together and moved his gaze over to my wrecked car.

"What the hell!"

Will walked back over with Rex at his side. "Ava, I gave the deputy my statement. He has my number in case they need to reach me for any reason." He slipped his free hand in his pocket while holding on to the dog's leash with the other. "You must be the boyfriend."

Logan's grip along my back tightened. "I am. May I ask

who you are?" It was hard not to notice the edge in his tone.

Will cleared his throat. "William King. I met Ava and her daughter at the park. We were leaving at the same time, so I offered to walk her to her car."

"Really, do you always make a habit of walking women you just met to their cars?"

"Logan," I hissed.

"What?" he snapped at me. "I'm just trying to see if there is a connection somehow." He turned his frustration back to Will. "Were you at the park the entire time together? And if not, can you tell me where you were before that?"

"Logan." I pulled on his arm. He was in full interrogation mode. "That's enough."

"That's okay." Will gave me a polite smile and stuck his phone out to Logan. "I was on a conference call with work. They can verify it if you'd like."

"That's not necessary." I shot Logan a stern look to drop it.

"I gave the police everything they needed." Will pulled on his dog's leash. "Now that everything is under control, I just wanted to come over and say goodbye. It was nice meeting you both. I hope they find the person responsible for what happened today."

Logan had a scowl on his face as he watched Will and his dog walk to their car. Once he was out of view, I spun around and laid into him. "You were a being a jerk. He was nice enough to wait with us until the police came."

"Yeah, what a guy. I'm sure that was a real hardship for him. I saw the way he was looking at you."

My mouth hung open in shock. Was he serious right now?

"That's what you're choosing to focus on. Don't you think we have more important things to worry about?"

He shook his head, still looking pissed off at me for some reason. "Why didn't you park in the lot to begin with? Why did you park so far away?"

"Because it was packed. It was nice out, so I didn't mind walking a few extra feet. Jesus, Logan, really?"

Madison looked up at us. She was sitting on the ground, playing with my phone. She was being quiet and trying to act like she wasn't paying attention.

He closed his eyes and hung his head. "I'm sorry, please forgive me." He pulled me into his arms. "I was a nervous wreck after I got Madison's voicemail."

I melted into his embrace. "I know, but next time can you leave the attitude behind?"

He pulled back, brushing a piece of hair out of my eyes. "My mind went to every worst-case scenario on the way here. I didn't mean to come across as such a blockhead."

"You're not a blockhead." I stared into his eyes. "I'm sorry you were worried."

He let go and bent down, so he was at eye level with my daughter. "Thanks for calling me and telling me where you and your mom were. You were a big help today."

Her bottom lip trembled. "Why would someone do that to our car?"

"Come here, sweetheart." He opened his arms up, and she walked right into them. "I'm not sure, but I promise you I will find out who did."

Her lips tilted into a smile. "I know you won't let anything bad happen to us, right, Logan?"

"That's right, sweetheart. I'll always protect you." He ran a gentle hand up and down her back. "I know I wasn't very nice a few minutes ago, I was scared, but I shouldn't have acted like that. You and your mom mean the world to me. I just want you both safe."

She squeezed him tight. God, he was so good with her.

He straightened up and locked his eyes with me. "I'm going to talk to the sheriff for a minute. Why don't you and Madison wait in my truck. I won't be long. I'm sure you both want to get home."

I grabbed his arm and spoke low so only he could hear me. "I didn't give them Vanessa's name, but I think they know I have an idea of who it could be."

Something flickered across his features, something I couldn't quite figure out. He squeezed my hip and left me to talk to the sheriff.

I walked over to his truck and helped Madison inside. I called my insurance company to let them know what happened. By the time I was finished, I was mentally exhausted. A few minutes later, Logan jumped in and hit the locks.

"Are you going to get the bad guys who wrecked our car, Logan?" Madison asked from the back seat.

His jaw ticked. "I'm going to do everything I can, sweetheart."

Logan's body was tense as he looked in the rearview mirror and pulled out onto the street. He kept checking and rechecking the mirrors every time we switched lanes.

His phone rang, and he pulled it out of the cupholder. "What do you have for me, Marx?"

I looked over my shoulder to check on my daughter. Her gaze was trained out the window. She was being exceptionally quiet, which had me concerned.

Logan cursed under his breath and scrubbed a free hand across his jaw. It was hard to hear the other half of the conversation with all the road noise. From what little I could gather, it wasn't good news.

"Thanks for the update. Let's hope our tech guys get figure out who it's registered to." He hit *end* and shoved his phone back in the cupholder.

"How bad is it?"

"They found a tracker in your car."

I twisted in my seat. "What?"

He gritted his teeth. "In case you were wondering, this was not random."

"Would Vanessa really go this far?" I whispered, hoping my daughter wasn't listening. It was hard to believe that Logan could be married to someone capable of going to those extremes.

His mouth was tight, and he glanced in the rearview mirror. "Let's talk about this when we get back to the house."

I forced myself to relax, but I could feel the tension rolling off of him. It did nothing to soothe my own nerves, and honestly, I was freaked out. My head rested against the window, staring at the trees and buildings as they flew by in a blur.

As soon as we pulled into my garage, I gave Madison my iPad and sent her straight to her room.

"Do you want a beer?" I asked, already on my way to the kitchen.

"Actually, I could use something stronger."

My feet paused, and I glanced over my shoulder. "Whiskey, okay?"

"Yeah." He took a seat on my couch, bent forward, and dropped his head in his hands.

I searched through the cabinet, trying to find the bottle of Jack Daniels that I received as a gift from one of my clients last year at Christmas. I wasn't a fan of hard liquor unless it was mixed with something sweet or fruity. When I reached the unopened bottle, I was glad I never gave it away like I planned on. I added an ice cube, and poured a hefty amount into the glass. I left the bottle on the counter. I had a feeling he was going to want more than one drink. Hell, after the day I had, I might join him.

"Here." He looked up, and I placed the crystal tumbler in his hands.

"Thanks." He sighed and swallowed most of his drink back in one gulp.

I went to sit next to him, but he pulled me on his lap instead. "I hate her. I fucking hate her."

"We don't know for sure if it's even Vanessa." My fingers toyed with the hair on the back of his neck, trying to get him to relax. It was almost laughable how I was defending a woman who clearly hated me, but I could sense his struggle and wanted to approach this with a clear head. This would, no doubt, only complicate things further for us. But our relationship wasn't the only thing that would be affected, it could impact his job, and the fallout would not be good for Brina.

Fuck! Now I really hated the bitch. I picked up what was left of his drink and finished it off.

"I know it's her." He shook his head. "Who else do we know that's this fucking crazy?"

"Logan." I grabbed his arm, forcing him to look at me. "This is Brina's mother. Let's think about this. Let's be smart. Do you really think she would hurt me? Or do you think she's just trying to scare me?"

He turned his head away. "What I think doesn't matter. If she did this, who freaking knows how far she's willing to take things. This is beyond forgivable, and most importantly, it needs to stop."

I brushed my lips across his temple. I've never seen him so out of sorts. "We need to have proof before we confront her."

"I agree." He adjusted me on his lap. "I don't scare easily, but, Ava, I was fucking terrified." He was visibly shaking, and I was afraid there wasn't anything I could say or do to console him. "All Madison's voicemail said was someone smashed your car window, and the police were there, and she was afraid that a bad guy was after her."

I nuzzled my face into his neck. "Logan, we are both okay. Try to relax."

He ran a hand down my back. "This is my fault. I basically threw you right in her face. Marco warned me, she's the reason why he wanted me to stay away from you."

I placed my hand up to his stubbled cheek and forced him to look at me. "Were you the one who threw that brick through my windshield and slashed my tires?"

He scoffed. "Of course not."

"Then why the hell would you blame yourself?"

"Because I knew something like this could happen, but I couldn't stay away from you." His eyes slid shut and my heart hurt for him. "I don't want her to come between us. I don't want to lose you."

My eyes glistened with emotion, with how much this was tearing him apart. While today shook me to the core, my fear has slowly fading, turning to anger. The only thing I wanted to do was make things easier for him. My fingers dug into his shoulder, and I shifted my body sideways. "You won't lose me, but maybe we should slow down. If she's this unhinged, she's not going to stop until she gets what she wants."

His body stiffened. "No. We are not slowing down. I won't fucking allow her to come between us."

"Logan, this is getting really messy. I trust that you will deal with this, but she brought my daughter into this today. That is not okay with me." Tears sprung to my eyes. "As much as I want to be with you, if I have to choose between you and protecting my kid, I will choose my daughter. And I can't ask you to do what's best for mine at the sake of yours."

"Are you breaking up with me?"

I shook my head. "Absolutely not. I'm just trying to give you some space to sort through this. I'm also afraid of what the fallout will do to Brina."

He shook his head. His expression was a mixture of awe and disbelief. "I don't know if I want to shake you or kiss you right now." He pressed his lips together. "Thank you for thinking of Brina, but let me make something very clear. I give you my word that whatever actions I take, I will have both our daughters' best interest in mind. I think you have underestimated how much you and Madison mean to me." He bent down and took my mouth in a slow kiss.

I knew he meant those words. I just had a sinking feeling that things were going to get much worse before they got better.

TWENTY-FIVE

LOGAN

I sat at my desk, clicking my pen, going over the notes in front of me. I've reviewed the witness transcripts so many times that my eyes burned. There had to be a way to connect this asshole to the murder. I was just about to pull the gruesome crime scene photos out of the folder and lay them across my desk when a tall shadow appeared in front of me.

Mike Ramsey, my partner, slid into the metal chair opposite of me. He leaned forward and placed his elbows on the desk. "Fingerprints are in on Ava's car."

I lifted my eyes to meet his. "Okay." I tucked the photos back into the folder and set them aside.

"Prepare yourself." There was caution in his voice that I'd only heard him use a handful of times during the ten years we worked together.

He hesitated, linking his fingers together. "Vanessa's prints were all over your girl's SUV."

I blinked once. Twice. I knew it. I fucking knew it, even though I didn't want to believe it. Yet, who else could it be? Ava didn't have any enemies or ex-lovers with an unhealthy obsession, but I did. And now, she didn't just cross a line, but she stepped into a situation she would not be able to get out of. I would see to that.

His pudgy fingers rubbed at his mustache. "Listen, buddy. I know you are in a shit situation. Do you want my advice?"

I rubbed my eyes, exhausted from only getting three hours of sleep. "Not really, but you're going to give it to me anyway."

I wasn't trying to be a dick. I was just tired. So damned tired.

Mike sighed. "You've been different since you've been with Ava. Don't let Vanessa fuck it up. Do what you gotta do to protect the people you care about. You don't owe your ex-wife anything after the shit she's put you through."

"So, what are you saying?" I asked, spinning around in my chair to stare out the window. I've put up with a lot of crazy shit from Vanessa, but she took it too far this time.

"Your ex-wife ain't right in the head. We can arrest her." I looked away from the window, meeting his eyes. "There is enough evidence to bring her in."

I sat there for a few minutes, taking my time to process everything. If only I could turn back the clock. Put a stop to this somehow. I reached for the water bottle on my desk. My throat suddenly felt dry. "If I do that," I lowered my voice, "then I lose all control of the situation. Once she's charged, the DA will get to decide what happens."

He paused, looked around, and leaned forward in his chair. "Don't tell me you are thinking about protecting her?" he asked in disbelief.

I shook my head. "No, I'm trying to find a way to deal

with her and protect Ava and the girls at the same time. They are my priority."

"You shouldn't even be in this position."

I pinched my lips together. "Doesn't change my current situation though, does it?"

He tilted his head to the side. "There is an official police report filed. We ran prints. You can't cover this up."

"That's the last thing I plan to do."

"Care to explain?" he asked, trying to figure out where I was going with this, but I hadn't figured it out myself yet.

I hated that Vanessa had forced my hand, but I didn't have any other choice. I would not jeopardize my professional career and personal life for my ex-wife.

"I have a few ideas." I pointed my finger at him. "And don't worry, everything will be done by the book. I just need some time to figure a few things out. "

He rubbed his hands across his knuckles. "I wouldn't want to be in your shoes, brother."

I reached into my desk drawer to grab my keys. "Believe me, I wouldn't wish this shitshow on my worst enemy."

"Where are you going?"

"To fix this mess once and for all."

———

My hands tightened on the steering wheel as I sat in front of Vanessa's office building. I checked the time on my phone, knowing she would be leaving work at any second. I was doing my best to get my anger under control, but I was at my breaking point.

I spotted her long dark hair blowing in the breeze as

she chatted with one of her coworkers on their way out the door.

She came to a stop when she saw me leaning against her white Toyota. I had to force myself to stand still. To not react. I'd done everything in my power to avoid this moment, but now my hands were tied, and I had no choice.

"This is a surprise," she said, fetching her keys out of her purse. "What are you doing here?"

As usual, my ex-wife was stunning, but right now, I could barely stomach looking at her.

"I'm here to pay you a compliment."

Keep it cool. Keep it cool, I reminded myself.

She smiled, completely oblivious to what I was about to unleash on her. "What for?"

I stood to my full height and crossed my arms. "You have some really nice handwriting when you use a can a spray paint."

She smirked. Actually smirked.

"I don't know what you're talking about?"

"Really? Oh, that reminds me." I snapped my fingers, wishing I could snap something else instead. "The brick you wrote on was a nice touch. Next time though, you might want to go to Home Depot and buy one instead of using one off your back porch."

One of the very bricks I laid with my bare hands.

She looked at me, trying to act innocent. "Where is this coming from?"

"I'm glad you asked." I stepped toward her, unable to stop myself. "It came from Fairmount Park on States Drive. You know, where you smashed Ava's window and fucked up her car."

Her eyes skated across the parking lot. Probably

thinking of all the different ways she could spin this. She's certainly had plenty of time to come up with a list of excuses.

"What are you accusing me of exactly?" she asked with a hint of attitude in her tone.

I prepared myself for this on the drive over. I had a whole list of questions all planned out to ask her, but why waste words when all I'd get in return was lies.

"I'm not accusing you of anything." I gritted my teeth. "I'm telling you that your fingerprints were all over that fucking brick."

She sucked in a breath. "You ran my prints?"

No doubt, she never expected me to go that far. I noticed she didn't deny it either.

"How stupid are you? Do you have any idea what you've done? There is over a thousand dollars' worth of damage to Ava's car. That's a God damned felony." I roughed a hand through the top of my hair. "That little stunt could cost you your job. You can go to jail. You can lose your daughter. And for what?"

"I did you a favor. That's what! I did it for you!"

My eyes narrowed. "What the hell are you talking about?"

"Ava is not good enough for you. None of the women you've dated are good enough." She shook her head as if this all made perfect sense, and I was slow to catch on. "I've protected you, don't you see that?"

My mouth dropped open. Was she serious? I stared at the stranger in front of me, searching for a glimmer of the woman I married. I barely recognized her anymore.

"Vanessa, I don't know what fantasy land you're living in, but I'm officially jumping off this crazy train."

"You're just going to abandon me again? Like you did before."

Her tears were falling at a steady pace now, but all I could think about was the fear in Madison's voice when she left me that message. And I'll never forget the punch in the gut I felt when Ava suggested we slow things down.

I tilted my head up to the sky and dropped my gaze back to hers. "I did not abandon you. I left you. It's called a divorce."

This woman was so far removed from reality it was scary. I felt like a shitty cop. Shitty father. Shitty boyfriend. I should have picked up on her mental state before things spiraled so far out of control. But I tried to do what was best for my daughter. I tried to stay out of Vanessa's way. I figured life was easier that way. Oh, how fucking wrong I was.

"How can you treat me like this? I'm not crazy." I looked around, thankful that the parking lot was mostly empty. "I'm the mother of your child. Not someone you're trying to hunt down on the streets."

"You're out of control, that's what you are. And this stops today!"

She tensed, and I could see that my words had affected her. "I know you're angry, but once you calm down, you'll understand that I did this for the sake of our family. You love me and we belong together. Don't you see that? I've never given up on us."

I met her gaze, hoping she would hear what I was about to say. "Vanessa, I want you to get this through your thick head. There is no us. I do not love you. I question at times if I ever loved you. It's time you move the fuck on."

She gasped and started pounding on my chest. "Why are

you doing this? I'm losing my mind over here. I keep thinking you're going to wake up one day and realize you made a mistake. Why are you making me feel like this? Can't you see that I would do anything to get you back. Anything. Why do you think I've tried so hard to make you see that these other women all wrong for you? Tell me what I have to fucking do? Why can't we be together? Why? I don't understand? Because of her?" She started kicking and screaming. "She can't have you. Do you understand me?" She kept on swinging, but thankfully, I had good reflexes and was able to dodge her hits. "If you turn me in. If I lose my daughter…" She trailed off with a blank stare that chilled me to the bones.

"You'll what?" I asked cautiously. My body was frozen on the spot.

She hesitated, but I could tell by the emotions playing out on her face that something inside her had snapped. "I will kill myself and you will have no one to blame but yourself."

I staggered backward, taking in a deep breath and letting it out slowly. My ex-wife was farther gone than I imagined. How did I not see the signs? How could I not feel partly responsible for this?

"Don't talk like that." I tried to keep the panic out of my voice. "If you really feel that way, then I'm checking you into a hospital. You need help."

"Oh, now you want to help me." She wiped at the rivers that were flowing down her face. She was falling apart at the seams.

I grabbed her wrist, trying to calm her down. "I don't wish you any pain, Vanessa. I also can't allow things to continue like this."

She tried to kick me again, but I stepped back. "I

fucking hate her. If you want to help me then you will come back home, where you belong."

Her voice was filled with agony. Everything about this sucked.

"Vanessa, here is what's going to happen. You are going to turn yourself in. You will pay for the damages. You are going to hook yourself up with a therapist." Her eyes pleaded with me to stop, but I couldn't. "You will not come within ten feet of Ava or her daughter. If you don't do those things, I will have charges brought against you, issue a restraining order, and file for full custody of Brina."

"Oh my God." She fell against my chest and sobbed. I could feel her pain, and it gutted me to know that she was this sick. "How can you be so cold and heartless? How can you threaten me like this? Brina is all I have. You're really going to send me away and take her from me?"

I squeezed my eyes shut. "I don't want to do this, but you've left me with no choice. Get yourself some help and own up to what you did."

"All over a fucking car!"

"Let's not forget you've been stalking her. We found the tracker you put in her trunk." If she was this mentally unstable, who knows the extremes she would go to.

Her head whipped back. "What tracker? What on earth are you talking about?"

Something about her reaction gave me pause. I searched her face for any sign of a lie. Unlike earlier, when I knew for sure she was guilty, this felt different.

My brows creased. "They found the electronic tracking device you planted in her trunk," I said, holding my breath, waiting for that flicker of guilt to cross her face. Except it never came.

She wiped at her cheeks, shaking her head. "I can assure you that wasn't me."

I didn't know what made me believe her, but I did. Could the information in the report be a mistake? No, that was stupid. Vanessa's prints were on the brick, but Mike said they couldn't find anything on the tracking device. So, if it wasn't Vanessa, then who the hell could it be?

"Hello, are you listening to me?" she shouted, breaking through the static in my brain.

"I heard you." I cleared my throat and rested my hands on her arms. "Hear me out, okay? I don't want to see you locked up, because I don't think jail is the right place for you. But the things you're willing to do to get your revenge are escalating. This needs to stop."

She'd done unforgivable things in the past to drive the people away in my life. That's why I kept the women I dated at a distance. I should never have allowed things to get so out of control, and I won't be stupid enough to do it again. I had too much to lose this time.

"I'm not crazy," she pleaded with me. Did she not understand how wrong this was? No, I reminded myself. In her twisted mind, she felt justified.

"I'm going to be totally frank with you, Vanessa. You need help. You need to stop living in the past." A long stretch of silence passed between us. "It's not healthy. Brina needs her mother, so promise me, you'll do this for her and for yourself."

"I don't want to lose my daughter."

"I'll do whatever I can to make sure that doesn't happen," I promised her. I wanted to give her the assurance she needed. Encourage her in whatever way I could to seek help. "But you need to take that first step."

"Let me get this straight." She glowered at me but

seemed slightly calmer than a few minutes ago. "I have two options. I can either take my chances with the law and risk losing my daughter or commit myself to a crazy house. Do I have that right?"

"I know this seems drastic, but you've backed yourself into a corner here. The only chance you have of turning things around is to turn yourself in, pay the damages and get help. It's the only choice that makes sense."

It was also the only outcome I could live with. The thought of what this would do to my daughter gutted me. Brina needed a mother that was healthy. I wouldn't be able to sleep at night unless I knew my daughter was safe. If that meant sending Vanessa away to get treatment, then so be it.

Her shoulders fell on a defeated sigh. "You win, okay. I'll do what you want. I'll do it for Brina."

The conviction in her voice caught me off guard. If I was honest, I never expected her to cave. I thought for sure she would put up a fight to the bitter end. But as I stared at her more closely, she looked tired and broken down. It had to be exhausting trying to cling to a life that no longer existed.

"What happens now?" She folded her arms around her stomach and looked at me as if I had all the answers to her problems.

I held her gaze, hating everything about this. "First, you need to hire an attorney. Then you turn yourself in."

TWENTY-SIX

AVA

Logan's truck bounced along the uneven terrain as we turned into a long, winding driveway. It was so narrow I was afraid we'd end up in the creek below if he turned the steering wheel too hard. I let out a sigh of relief once we reached the bottom. And then my relief turned into amazement.

Holy shit! This place was gorgeous.

When he mentioned his family rented a camp in Lake Placid, this was not what I was expecting because this most certainly was not a camp.

He shifted the truck in park and smirked. "Let me guess, you were expecting a little run-down shack with an outdoor bathroom."

I ducked my head in my shoulder, feeling guilty. "Is it that obvious?"

He laughed. "Nah. I knew you had low expectations."

I swatted his leg. "Don't make me sound like a snob just because I like electricity and running water."

He held his hand up, drawing a box in the air with his

fingers. "No judgment zone here. How about a little tour of this place?"

After six hours in the car, I was ready to stretch my legs. "Sounds good." I glanced to the back seat where Madison and Brina were out like a light.

Logan hopped out and unloaded a few things from the back while I woke the girls up and followed him to the door.

"I think it's nice that your parents are giving us a few days to ourselves," I said, folding up all the charging cables so they wouldn't get tangled. After what happened with Vanessa, they thought we could use some time alone. The past few weeks have been taxing and very upsetting for Brina. All she knew was that her mom was sick, but I got the impression she understood more than she was letting on.

"Yeah, I agree." He pushed open the large rustic wood door.

"Wow," I said as soon as we stepped inside. There was a massive stone fireplace in the center of the room and a large flat screen TV mounted over the top. I walked over to the windows covering the back wall that overlooked Whiteface Mountain. The view was stunning. While it didn't come with an outdoor bathroom, it did have a seasonal outdoor shower I couldn't wait to try out.

This was not a camp. It was a huge house with a full wraparound porch, outdoor firepit, and sprawling yard. I glanced around at the state of-the-art stainless steel appliances and cozy décor. I was starting to see the appeal of country living.

The girls ran downstairs to the playroom to check out the pool table and skeet-ball machine while Logan carried in the rest of our things.

"Not a bad view, huh?" He rested his chin on my shoulder as I settled against him.

"It's stunning." I smiled when I felt his strong arms wrap around me. I closed my eyes briefly, breathing him in. I never wanted to move from this spot.

"I think the mountains are growing on you."

"I think you might be right. I could get used to this."

He kissed the back of my head and reached for my hand. "Come on, let's go out back."

We stepped onto the deck and leaned against the railing. The smell of fresh evergreen and clean open-air greeted us. I closed my eyes, surprised by how much I liked it here.

Logan smiled, but it lacked the usual sparkle that I was used to. The situation with Vanessa was wearing him down. I knew I should have just left him alone, but I couldn't help myself. I didn't want him to feel like he couldn't talk to me or share his thoughts.

"I was really worried about Brina," I said, hoping he wouldn't read more into my concern. "I'm glad she's doing better."

"This trip couldn't have come at a more perfect time. I think that's another reason why my folks insisted that we not cancel our plans. We needed this."

I hummed in agreement. After everything she put us through, we were both ready for a break. Things have been tense since she checked herself into a mental health facility. Logan has been torn up and riddled with guilt these couple of weeks. It was painful watching him walk around, feeling like he failed his daughter somehow. I was a fixer, so it was hard knowing there wasn't anything I could do to make him feel better.

Vanessa, as much as I disliked her, was finally owning

up to what she did. The district attorney cut her a deal. She paid for the damages to my car and was finally getting the help she needed. Regardless of how I felt, she was Brina's mother, and I just wanted her to get better. For all our sakes.

"So, what would you like to do first?" I reached for his hand, giving it a squeeze.

"Let's get the girls and go for a walk." We swung our hands back and forth as we made our way back to the house.

After putting the salads and burgers in the fridge, we strolled down along the shoreline. It was mostly rocks and shady trees, but it was the perfect place to clear my head.

Brina and Madison were off to the side in their own little world, and Logan, well, something was weighing on him.

"Hey, are you going to tell me what's wrong or are we going to pretend everything is hunky-dory?" I sat on the edge of the dock beside him.

His head slanted to the side. "You're very intuitive. You'd make a good cop."

"No, thanks. I'll just stick to dating one." His arms wrapped around my back. "I know this thing with Vanessa isn't easy, it's okay if you're worried about her."

He trained his gaze over my shoulder, looking out at the lake. "That's not it, I mean don't get me wrong, I want her to get better for Brina's sake…" He trailed off, and I waited for him to continue. "But there's something I haven't told you."

The wind blew, pushing my hair in front of my face. Logan tucked it back; his eyes watched mine. I could feel something chipping away at him. "Are you finally going to fill me in on what's been bothering you? Because if it's not Vanessa then I have no clue."

"That's exactly what I'm thinking," he muttered under his breath. I squinted my eyes and thought back to the past couple of weeks and how overprotective he's been. We got into an argument when he insisted on installing a security system in my house. At first, it seemed a little over the top to me, but I couldn't help feeling that there was more to the story.

"I've been avoiding telling you because I don't want you to worry."

"Keeping me in the dark and forcing me to draw my own conclusions doesn't seem like a good strategy. The truth is always best."

He released a sigh. "Vanessa didn't put the tracker in your car."

I twisted around to face him. "What are you talking about?"

I tried to remember every little detail that was listed in the police report, and wished I had paid better attention now. Honestly, I didn't think I needed to. Unless Vanessa had an accomplice, we didn't know about, nothing about that theory was even believable. She pleaded guilty. No one else was mentioned. I would remember if there was.

He shook his head. "It wasn't her, Ava."

My mind tried to put the pieces together, but nothing fit.

"This doesn't make any sense. She admitted to damaging my car and unless my memory is going, she didn't implicate anyone else. Other than Vanessa, I don't have any enemies."

"Maybe you have an admirer that you don't know about. Maybe it's the guy from the park."

I snorted out loud. This was crazy. "Logan, I never saw that man before that day and I haven't seen him since. It has to be her. I don't know why she's lying, but she is." He looked at me like he wanted to believe me, but something was holding him back. I don't care what she told him. I know it was her. It had to be. "Listen, I don't want you to worry, okay. Let's just enjoy this vacation and worry about the rest when we get back."

He cupped my cheek and pulled me into his arms. "I'll never stop worrying about you, Ava."

―――――

"Mom." Madison entered my room. "Brina and I are ready to go swimming." She groaned when she spotted me still in my pajamas.

"I'll be ready in a few minutes." I walked over to my suitcase sitting by the door. "We need to eat breakfast first. Go wait for me downstairs while I get dressed."

I slipped into my two-piece bathing suit and peeked in the mirror. My hand pressed against my stomach as if I could flatten it somehow. After being with Drew for so long, I never worried about how I looked, but I wanted Logan to like what he saw. Sure, he's seen me naked before, but this felt different. There would be no hiding under the covers, dimming the lights, and distracting him with my hands and mouth. The extra pounds around my hips would not be concealed with my body-shaping swim-suit that the saleslady said "would make me look ten pounds lighter."

I peeled my eyes away from the dimples on the back of my thighs and cursed myself for not joining the gym earlier in the summer. I slipped the coverup over my head, took a deep breath, and tiptoed down the stairs.

My heart melted into a puddle at my feet once I reached the kitchen. Logan's back was to me, and the girls were standing on either side of him, laughing over the griddle. "Ready for the next one?" he asked them both as they nodded their heads. "All right, what are we putting on this one? Blueberries or chocolate chips?"

"Chocolate chips," they both chanted.

"Morning." My smile was wide as I walked over to the coffee machine and poured a cup.

Logan turned and looked over his shoulder; his mouth curved into a lazy grin. His eyes zeroed in on my neck, where there was a small love bite left behind from last night. It made me think twice about putting my hair up today, so I decided to wear it down. The concealer I applied helped, but the coloring was a little off—not that the girls would notice.

Logan cleared his throat and looked down at Brina. "Why don't you girls grab your stuff and stay down by the shore. I'll bring the pancakes down and we can eat outside on the picnic table. And grab Madison a life vest out of the shed on your way down."

The girls sprinted out of the room, causing me to laugh a little because I knew where he was going with this. He set the spatula down and pushed the mixing bowl aside. His eyes held mine as he rested his hip against the counter.

"Do I get a good morning kiss?" He looked me up and down, seeming happy with what he saw.

"I suppose we could sneak one in."

He reached me in two quick strides, lifted me up, and set me on the counter. The surface was cool underneath my bottom. "Hi," I squeaked out as his fingers trailed down my back.

"Well?" he asked, stepping closer. My knees parted open as he moved between them. "Are you going to kiss me or not?"

I brought my hand up to his cheek and trailed my thumb along his chin. "Maybe you should ask nicely and start with the word *please*."

He ran his hands through my hair. "Oh, so I need permission to kiss you now?"

"Never, but maybe I should make you beg every once in a while." I drifted my hands along his chest, feeling his muscles ripple under my fingertips. The smell of his body-wash tickled my nose. "You smell so good." I breathed in his soapy scent. "Maybe you should invite me in the shower with you next time."

"I'm trying to be good here." His voice was strained, and I tried hard not to laugh. Honestly, I loved knowing that I could affect him this way. That these feelings weren't just one-sided.

"Where's the fun in that?" I whispered, watching his eyes turn heavy. He drove me crazy with need, so there was no way I would deny myself the opportunity to have his hands on me. I've missed having him in my bed these past couple of weeks, but he sure as hell made it up to me last night.

"Someone is feeling a little adventurous today." His hand slid underneath my coverup. "Were you hoping this little scrap of fabric would distract me? Or were you just trying to get me all hot and bothered?"

"If you can't handle the heat, maybe you should stay out of the kitchen." If he only knew how insecure I was and how much I wanted to please him.

He gave my nipple a light pinch and rolled it around his fingers. "Oh, I can handle it all right."

"Logan," I hissed and looked over my shoulder because the girls weren't too far away. It felt like we already pushed our luck enough last night. It was a good thing they were both sound sleepers and my room was on the other end of the house.

"Remember, you started this." He slipped his other hand behind my neck and took my mouth in his.

He kissed me hard and then soft, stroking and teasing until I could feel his erection growing thicker. The scrape of his jaw lit tiny sparks across my skin. He pulled me closer, and just like every other time, I lost myself in his touch. The passion I felt for him was unlike anything I've ever experienced before. I dragged my fingers along his swollen length, feeling it pulse against my palm. My hips pushed against his, silently begging him to make that ache between my legs disappear.

His hands shot down to my waist, halting my movements. "You need to stop doing that."

I sighed and looked up to the ceiling. I should have been happy that one of us was being sensible. "I know, but I wish we didn't have to."

"Trust me, baby, stopping is the last thing I want to do right now."

He snaked his arms around me and held me tight. Sometimes, I wondered if we were moving too fast and if it was normal to feel something this strong so quickly.

I dragged my eyes up to his to find him watching me with tenderness. He looked like he was considering saying something, but instead, he lifted his hand, resting it against my cheek.

"I'm crazy about you."

I sensed that he might be feeling things. Big things, and I didn't know what to make of it. I wanted to give him the parts of me he wanted. I just wasn't sure I was quite there yet. It wasn't the word love that scared me. It was the fear of what that would mean. I was terrified of losing another piece of my heart, even if he was healing what little was left of it.

"What a coincidence," I said, as he pressed a kiss against my neck. "I'm kinda crazy about you too."

I rested my cheek against his heart as his hand gently glided up and down my back. We stayed like that for a bit, neither one of is us in a hurry to move.

After a few minutes, he helped me off the counter, but kept his hands firmly on my waist like he didn't want to let go.

The pad of my fingertips traced the tiny white scar above his eyebrow. "I like this, it reminds me that you have flaws."

He barked out a laugh. "I'm far from perfect."

"I think I'll be the judge of that."

He brought my fingers up to his mouth and kissed my knuckles. "I should probably finish up with breakfast before they come looking for us. But I promise, we will finish what we started later."

I sighed until I remembered we had the place to ourselves for the next few days. There were plenty of things to keep the girls busy, and I planned to use them to my advantage. My mission was to make sure he found time to unwind and put his troubles behind him.

I would not let Vanessa ruin this trip. Regardless of what he believed, she had to be the one who put the tracker in my car. Nothing else made sense.

TWENTY-SEVEN

LOGAN

I LIFTED MY HEAD, TAKING IN THE VIEW IN FRONT OF ME. THE sun was already glistening on the lake, and there were already a few boats on the water. I took a sip of my coffee and breathed in the cool, crisp air.

I glanced at the message from my contact at the police station. After my conversation with Ava yesterday, I was second-guessing my theory on the tracker they found in her car. I read it one last time and fought the urge to chuck my phone in the water.

It was official; that tracking device did not come from Vanessa. Never in my life have I been so conflicted.

On the one hand, I was relieved it wasn't her. I just spoke with her doctor two days ago, they were adjusting her meds, and she was already showing signs of improvement. She was diagnosed with depression and bipolar disorder. She admitted experimenting with different medications when she was a teenager, but they made her gain weight, so she stopped taking them. Her mood swings and irritability now made sense, and I was glad that she was finally making progress.

On the other hand, someone had taken an unhealthy interest in my girlfriend. The dipshit from the park was the only person I could think of. What Ava didn't know was that I ran a background check, and he came up squeaky-clean. Which only irritated me even more because I would not rest until I found out who it was.

The sliding glass door to the deck opened. I turned to see a little head with dark hair moving toward me.

"Hi, Logan."

"Good morning, kiddo. Are you excited to go fishing today?"

Ava warned me that Madison would probably be up at the crack of dawn. She wouldn't stop talking about going fishing last night at dinner, so I wasn't the least bit surprised to see her smiling face. It was both comical and endearing how excited she was about today.

"I've got my pink fishing rod and tackle box all ready."

She slowly walked along the wobbly dock, wearing her blue and white polka dot bathing suit and her tie-dye towel with her name on it. I wrapped it around her shoulders, noticing a dusting of freckles across the bridge of her nose from the sun yesterday. I made a mental note to apply a little extra sunscreen on her face.

She leaned forward, pulling a hairbrush out of her bag along with a hair tie that matched her tackle box. "Can you help me with my hair?"

"Sure." I set my coffee down, and she settled herself in between my legs. "Are you ready to catch some fresh trout today?" I asked, running the brush through her tangles as softly as I could. Thank God I had a little girl of my own and knew how to do this.

"My mom starts from the bottom of my hair first and then moves her way up the top."

Or maybe not.

"Sorry." I winced and did as instructed.

"That's okay." She leaned her head back, giving me a view of the cute little dimples. "It doesn't hurt so bad when you do it that way."

"So, how many fish do you think we'll catch?"

"I don't know." She shrugged. "I just want to catch one biiiiggg fish."

"And what are we going to do with this big fish once we catch it?"

"We're going to gut it and cook it for dinner."

I cracked up at how animated she was. Madison was the exact opposite of Brina. If Brina caught a fish, she threw it back in the lake as quickly as she caught it. She was squeamish about handling live bait, so I bought her a box of artificial lures. Not many girls were fans of real earthworms, but my little friend here seemed pretty eager to get her hands muddy and dirty.

Once I smoothed out as many knots as best as I could, I pulled her hair back. "Do you want a high or low ponytail?"

"In the middle, please."

A smile split my cheeks. This little girl was slowly wrapping me around her finger. "What do you think? Should we get the boat ready and go wake the girls up?"

"I tried to wake Brina up, but she threw the covers back over her head. She snores pretty loud, you know."

I barked out another laugh. "She sure does." I tweaked her nose. "She snores so loud, I sometimes worry I might go deaf."

Her head tilted to the side in confusion. "Why would you go deaf?"

"It's a joke, but sometimes when you're exposed to loud noises all the time it can cause hearing loss."

"Is that why my mom always tells me to turn the TV down?"

"Yup. My mom used to tell my brother and me the same thing."

"My grandma tells me not to sit too close to the TV or it can ruin my eyes." She shook her head. "So I eat lots of carrots because I don't want to go blind. Did you know that carrots are good for your eyes?"

My lips twitched. "I've heard that before."

I spotted Ava making her way down to the foot of the dock. "Morning."

She looked beautiful with her hair pulled up on the top of her head, she probably put no effort into it, but she still took my breath away. If her daughter weren't practically sitting in my lap, I would pull her into me and kiss her senseless.

She averted her eyes as if she could read my mind.

Madison jumped to her feet and smiled. "Mom, Logan and I are going to get the boat ready."

"I'd like you to eat breakfast first." She set her coffee down and kissed Madison. "There are cinnamon rolls and yogurt on the counter. I'll be right up."

"Can I please get a good morning kiss too?" I teased, remembering our conversation yesterday.

She grinned as I pushed to my feet. "You already had your kiss right before you snuck out of my bed, but seeing that you asked so nicely, I think you deserve another one. "

"It was still technically dark outside, so that doesn't count."

She tilted her face up, and I couldn't help but draw her soft lips up to mine. I don't know how long the kiss went on for, but I knew I didn't want it to stop. Over the past few months, she's become the missing piece to my heart that I didn't even realize was lost. I never thought it was possible to be this happy.

The side door banged shut, and the girls came barreling across the lawn, running straight toward the water.

I pulled back, keeping Ava at arm's-length. "You ready to go catch some fish?"

She screwed her nose up and looked like she was about to use every excuse in the book to get out of it. "How about I stay back and let you and the girls bond over some boating and bass fishing?"

"Nope." I shook my head. "First, it's trout we are looking for and a deal is a deal."

"I don't remember making that deal."

"That's because," my voice was low as I leaned in, whispering into her ear so only she could hear me, "I had my mouth between your legs. You must have been preoccupied with other things."

I didn't even bother explaining when that conversation took place. She remembered it very clearly but still had every intention of pretending that she didn't. Ava had a habit of screwing up her nose and scratching the side of her head when she was lying like she was doing right now.

"That doesn't count." She pouted, but it only made her look more adorable. "Clearly, I'm not dressed for this type of outing." She gestured down to her pajamas. "Maybe you guys can come back and get me when you're done. The water should be a little warmer by then too."

"The water is going to be cold no matter what time of

the day it is, Ava. You're in the Adirondacks, not at some beach in Mexico."

"Well, if that's the case, then I'll just lounge in the chair, work on my tan, and read a book while you guys go and try to catch smelly fish."

She smiled smugly, looking too damned pleased with herself. I didn't have the heart to break it to her that she would be swimming with those smelly fish in about ten seconds.

I sighed. "I really don't want to have to do this." I looked at the water and then over to the girls, giving them the signal. We were prepared for this and came up with a plan last night. Ava was going in that lake whether she wanted to or not.

She followed my eyes and started to back up. "You wouldn't dare."

I picked her up in a flash and ran toward the dock. Ava was kicking and screaming, trying her best to escape my hold. Too bad for her, she was no match for my strength. I jumped off the dock, and the girls were right behind me. They all shrieked and yelled about how cold the water was. I had to admit, it was fucking freezing. For a minute, I thought my balls were going to turn to ice, but the sound of their laughter and the smile on their faces made it worth it.

The girls were eating s'mores, the sky was lit with stars, and the sound of nature was all around us. This place reminded me of how simple life could be once you unplugged and took a break from technology.

Ava slipped into the chair next to me, wearing a pair of

gray sweatpants and my green Eagles hoodie. "I thought the girls would have been worn out by now." My chest did a slight tilt as she pulled the sleeves to cover her hands to keep them warm. She looked like my sweatshirt brought her comfort. It was the same hoodie I let her borrow when we drove to the state park the night of her birthday. The one she never gave back to me.

I took a sip of my beer and inhaled the smell of burning wood from the campfire. "Hopefully, they'll sleep good tonight."

We spent the entire day on the water. I took the girls tubing, and Ava sat on the back of the boat, taking picture after picture. Their squeals were loud every time they bounced in the air and flipped over into waves.

When we got back, they did cannonballs off the dock, not minding the chilly water one bit, while I grilled the chicken and the tiny rainbow trout we caught for dinner. They even begged us to take the kayaks up and down along the shore once we finished eating.

The sunset was beautiful, and the memories were unforgettable. I wanted to hit a pause button and make time stand still.

"Don't forget, we promised them we would watch a movie tonight." She set her glass down on the table and climbed into my lap.

I reclined back in the chair and closed my eyes. "I'm not sure I'll make it through a movie tonight. I'm beat. I'll probably pass out in the recliner."

Ava drew small little circles on my chest. "If you pass out in the recliner then I can't sneak into your room later."

"Babe, I'm not sure I have the energy to get it up tonight."

"Are you turning down an opportunity to have sex with me?"

I rubbed my eyes as the smoke from the fire made its way up to us. "Ava, while your ass was resting in a lounge chair, sipping on White Claws, mine was setting up lawn games, hiking in the woods, and chasing after these two little energizer bunnies who have more energy than a nuclear power plant."

"Oh, my God, you are so dramatic."

"Tell that to my aching muscles."

She arched an eyebrow. "Are you slowing down, Detective? I've heard once men reach their thirties, they start losing their stamina."

I pinched her ass. "My stamina is just fine."

"You need to tell them no sometimes. Stop being such a pushover."

I pulled her back against his chest. "I love spoiling both of them. I never thought I'd have this. This feeling of peace in the middle of chaos." She turned her head to meet my eyes. "My life before was hard, it was nothing like it is now. I hear the guys at work complain about their marriage, I used to be that guy. I was miserable, and top that off with all the ugliness I see every day when I'm on the job, it's not easy, Ava. So, when I get to experience this." I moved closer and looked over at Madison and Brina, who were giggling over the campfire. "It adds a little light in my dark world."

A world I had every intention on keeping.

TWENTY-EIGHT

AVA

"THANKS FOR YOUR HELP WITH THE YARDWORK," I SAID, wiping a bead of sweat off my forehead. We just got back from our trip last night and I wanted to get as many projects done as I could before I went back to work tomorrow.

Logan picked up his water bottle and narrowed his eyes. "Stop thanking me, Ava."

I watched as he guzzled almost the entire water bottle in one gulp. "Are you sure you still want to cut the grass? We don't have to get everything done today."

The man was obsessed with yardwork, something I didn't understand. He was the only person I knew who did this stuff for fun.

"Yes, I'm sure. Don't worry, you can float in the pool now that we're done pulling the weeds and power washing the house."

"I still don't understand why the rain can't just wash away the dirt." I was reaching for a towel to wipe off the mud on my arm when my cell phone started ringing.

Glancing down at the caller ID, I frowned. My mother's next-door neighbor, Maria, never called me, especially on a Sunday morning when they were supposed to be at their weekly breakfast.

"Hi, Maria."

"Ava, I'm so sorry to bother you. Your mom didn't want me to call," she paused for a minute before continuing, "but it's bad and it's been happening more than you know."

"What's been happening?" I asked, even though I already had a pretty good idea.

Logan lifted his head from where he was lacing his sneakers up.

"She was supposed to pick me up for our morning breakfast and when she didn't answer her phone..." she sobbed. "I walked over to the house and found her at the bottom of the stairs."

I gasped. "Is she..."

Logan pushed to his feet at the panic in my voice. He was watching me with concern.

"She's alive and conscious. She's a little banged up, but she's okay. She said she fell but I don't think that's what really happened."

Maria had every right to question my mother. Richard has been drinking more, and my mother's "accidents" were happening more frequently. I was going to kill that son of a bitch.

"How bad is it? Is anything broken?" I felt Logan's hand on my shoulder.

"I think her ankle might be sprained. She's sore, but I don't think anything's broken. I offered to drive her to the hospital to get it checked out, but you know how headstrong your mom can be."

"Thank you for calling. I'm on my way."

I hung up, grabbed my tennis shoes off the mat, and quickly slid them on my feet. I didn't even realize that Logan was talking to someone on the phone.

He was finishing his call and slid his phone into the pocket of his shorts. "My parents will watch Madison and Brina. I know you want to get to your mom, but you're in no condition to drive."

"I'll be fine. Can you stay with the girls until they get here?"

"No way. You're a wreck, and I'm coming with you. Plus, if your stepfather did assault her, there isn't a chance in hell I'm letting you go over there alone. I don't want you or Madison stepping foot in that house unless I'm with you, understood?" He placed his hands on my shoulders and looked me in the eyes. "Ava, listen to me. My parents are already on their way. I'm sending a couple of officers to the house now."

I let out a sigh of relief. She was going to be pissed at me, but I was past caring at this point.

When we pulled onto her street, I immediately spotted two police cruisers at the end of the driveway. Logan squeezed my hand and gave me a reassuring nod. It was comforting having him with me.

Walking inside, I wasn't sure what I would find, but there was no broken glass or tipped-over furniture. There wasn't a thing out of place.

"Mom," I called out, looking over at the bottom of the stairs where Maria said she had fallen.

"I'm in the kitchen."

When I rounded the corner and saw her sitting at the table in one piece, I sighed with relief. Maria was next to her, giving the female officer her statement.

I bent down in front of her, looking her over for injuries. She winced when my hand landed on her ankle. "It's just sprained, not broken."

"What about these?" I asked, trailing my hand along the blue and purple bruises dotting her arm.

"They don't hurt. It's just my ankle, and my hip is a little sore."

"I think you need to get checked out by a doctor."

The male officer came over and shook Logan's hand. "We offered to call an ambulance but she declined."

My mother shook her head. "I'm okay. I don't need to go to the hospital. Maria gave me some Advil. I'm feeling better already."

She wanted everyone to think things were fine. A lump grew in my throat at the thought of her resigning herself to this life. I wish I had done something sooner to stop this.

Logan cleared his throat and held out his hand. "I don't know if you remember me, but we've met before. Logan Blake."

She looked at me briefly and back to him. I could see the questions in her eyes. "Yes, of course I do."

"I'm going to grab a first aid kit." Needing a minute to calm down, I excused myself and made my way into the bathroom. Never in my life had I been so angry and filled with so much hatred. I needed to get myself under control before I went back out there.

My hands shook as I opened the medicine cabinet. I swore on Drew's grave I would find a way to convince her to leave him, because if I didn't, there was a good chance I'd be burying her in a grave right next to his.

After locating the swabs and bandages, I grabbed a washcloth and a hand towel and walked back out to the kitchen.

I could hear voices as I got closer. My mom was shaking her head, sticking to her story about falling down the stairs. I was disappointed that they were just taking notes without questioning her. They had to know she was lying.

I clutched the box tightly in my hands. "Mom, it's going to be okay. Just tell them the truth."

Her head lifted at my words. She looked slightly worried that I called her out. "I am telling the truth. My bruises are from falling."

I took her wrist in my hand and turned it over. "You are not doing yourself any favors by protecting him."

"Ava, you don't know what you're talking about."

Was she serious?

"I know you're scared, but you don't need to lie for him." My eyes filled with tears while dabbing the cuts along her hand and arm. "Just tell them what really happened."

She turned in her seat and pleaded with them to believe her. "He's just having a little bit of money issues. He was having a bad day. He didn't mean to hurt me."

I was careful not to lash out, but this was getting beyond ridiculous. She had to know that this would only continue unless she did something about it. How many times has this happened, and I didn't know about it?

The officers standing around the table didn't seem the least bit surprised by this. They regarded me with pity. Unless she gave them an official statement, there wasn't anything they could do. Their hands were tied.

I gritted my teeth. "You need to stop defending him." The frustration in my voice could not be concealed. "You and I both know this isn't the first time he's hurt you."

"He only gets like that when he's drinking." Her eyes darted to the floor. "He doesn't know what he's doing."

"He left you at the bottom of the stairs. Did he even stay long enough to know if you were conscious or not?" I looked around the house, struggling to come to terms with the fact that he left her in that condition. "Where is that son of a bitch?"

She shifted in her seat. "He's at the casino."

Of course he was.

"When do you think he'll be back?" She couldn't be here when he got home. God only knows what he would do once he found out the police were called.

She reached for a tissue and wiped her eyes. "It depends on if he's winning or losing."

My gaze bounced to Logan's. "We've got to get her out of here before he returns."

She shook her head. "I'm not going anywhere. It's not as bad as you think. He's just got a little bit of a temper on him. Gets mad sometimes."

"Getting mad for stupid things like forgetting something at the store and not having supper ready on time is not normal." I caught sight of her ankle that looked like it needed an ice pack for swelling. I walked over to the freezer and wrapped up a few ice cubes in a towel. I bent down on my knees and pressed it up against the swelling. "You don't deserve to live your life this way. No one does."

"Ava." Her eyes looked up at the officer as he was reviewing his notes before looking back at me. "Everything isn't always so black and white."

"I can't stand to see you like this." I closed my eyes, praying and hoping I could get through to her. "You are still young enough to move on with your life. You don't need him."

She looked like she didn't believe me. "Where am I going? I'm fifty-six with no job, no money, and no real work experience. The only thing I know how to do is cook and clean."

She had relied on him for so long. She didn't know how to do anything on her own. My heart twisted in my chest at how much self-doubt she carried. And I hated feeling like if I said the wrong thing, it would only make things worse.

"It is never too late to start over, and you won't have to do it on your own." I reached for her hand. "I know you feel trapped, but imagine how much better you'll feel once you're finally free of this life."

"Leaving him isn't that simple."

I could tell she was at war with herself and feeling uneasy. I had to find a way to get her away from him. There had to be a way because I was afraid if I didn't, there might come a day where it would be too late.

I squeezed my eyes shut and rubbed my temples. "So, you would rather endure the abuse, is that what you're saying? I can't sit by and continue to let him hurt you." My chest was tight with anger and frustration on her behalf. "How many more beatings are you willing to endure?"

"I can't just quit on my marriage. I'm not made that way." She looked away, unable to meet my gaze.

"He's not worth it!"

I wanted to hug her, shake her, fight for her, but she would never allow it. She didn't want this life, no one did, but she didn't know any other way.

"I made a promise to God. For better or for worse. I told you before. He's not a perfect man, he's sick. When he's sober, he's a completely different person. He can't control what happens when he's drinking."

"I know you love him, but, Mom, you have to leave him. I'm afraid if you don't there will be a day where I'll be calling the morgue instead of the police. I need you. Your granddaughter needs you. Please. Let me help you." She turned her head to the side and wiped her eyes. She knew what I was saying made sense; she just didn't want to hear the truth.

Logan walked over and settled into the seat next to me. He placed his arms on the table. "I know this is uncomfortable, but Ava wouldn't be pushing you so hard if she didn't believe in you. I've seen this play out many times during my career." He looked at her with sad eyes. "You're a victim and regardless of what he says and does, you still love him. No one is judging you for that," he explained gently. "But he's an abuser, and he's never going to stop hurting you, no matter how much you believe you can change him. You can't."

"But he loves me. I do things I know will set him off, so it's my fault sometimes." She dabbed at her eyes as Maria set a glass of water in front of her. "He told me no else will ever love me."

Logan pursed his lips. "He wants you to believe that, because that's his way of staying in control. He's only manipulating you and taking advantage of your trust." He floated his gaze to mine in silent warning. He had so much more experience dealing with this than I did. "Ava just wants to help you, but the choice to leave has to be yours. If you want, I can get you in touch with people who specialize in domestic violence. I know things look bleak and you're scared, but there are a lot of great resources out there today."

My mother looked around the room in a panic. "Where would I go?"

"You could stay with me," I offered. I had a guest bedroom and plenty of room. She could stay with us as long as she needed to.

"No." She shook her head. "He would find me and convince me to come back. It's not safe for you to get in the middle of this."

Logan looked at me. "I could set her up in a safe shelter."

"She's not going to a shelter," I snapped. I knew he was trying to help, but she would be safe with me. I watched enough TV shows to know that those places weren't always safe. Sometimes they could be worse. "There has to be another option."

Logan flattened his lips together in irritation and sighed. "She needs to go somewhere that has the resources to help her. She has been psychologically and physically abused." He turned back to my mother. "But the first step is pressing charges. You are not helping him by staying silent. You are only enabling him."

"If I do press charges, he'll only come looking for me." She sat up straight and shot her gaze to mine. "It wouldn't be safe for you and Madison. He already knows how you feel about him."

My shoulders slumped forward. I understood what they were both saying. My house would be the first place he would check.

Logan peered at her from across the table. "I'm glad you're thinking that far ahead, but we can't do anything until you tell us what really happened."

She shook her head, and my heart hurt for her when tears started running down her face. "You can't arrest him unless I give a statement, correct?" She tried to sound strong, but I think she was just scared because she knew it was the right thing to do.

"You're right. I can't," he confirmed, looking calm and composed. I appreciated his level-headed approach to ensure her safety. "I know you're nervous, and that's okay. But I give you my word, I will do everything in my power to make sure he never lays another hand on you again. However, I can't do that if you don't cooperate."

A moment of silence passed. I could feel her mind shifting. Maybe the reality of her situation was finally catching up to her.

I wrung my hands in front of me, praying and hoping that this would be the last time we would be sitting in this kitchen. I wanted her away from this house, and as far away from Richard as she could get.

After what felt like forever, she finally looked up at me. "I'm sorry, Ava. I shouldn't have waited this long. It's not that I haven't wanted to leave him before, but every time I've tried, he would do something to make me stay. He would buy me gifts and tell me he was sorry." Her tears were flowing freely now. Maybe she would feel better once she got it all out. "If I do this, I'll need to go someplace where he'll never find me."

Maria leaned forward in her chair and rested her arm on my mother's leg. "You could stay with my sister, Angela, the one who lives in Orlando. Her husband just passed away a few months ago, so I know she would love the company."

"Does Richard know about this sister?" I had to ask because we couldn't take any chances.

Maria shook her head and smiled. "She loves living in Florida. She never comes to visit up north."

I blew out a breath. Okay. This was a good start.

Logan turned to face my mother fully. "We are going to do everything we can to get you through this." He weighed his next words carefully. "You've been dealing with a lot. A little time and space to heal will do you some good."

She looked over to the officers standing off to the side and touched her face. "I'd like to give my statement now."

A huge burst of relief left my lungs. "I'm so proud of you."

Her eyes were glossy. "I never wanted to be a burden to you. I never wanted you to see me like this. I'm your mother. It's my job to protect you. You shouldn't have to worry about me."

"You're my family. You could never be a burden."

Logan stood up from his chair and pulled the officers out of the room. My mother watched them for a minute before turning to me. "He's a good man, Ava. You better hold on to that one."

I dabbed at my eyes and shook my head. "Don't worry, Mom. I promise, I have no intention of letting him go."

My mother packed a bag and went to the police station to give them her official statement. Logan booked us a flight to Orlando, where my mother would be staying temporarily with Maria's sister.

Madison and I were going to help her get settled and wait for things to cool down. When Logan dropped us off at the airport, he hugged my mom and told her he was proud of her. He said goodbye to Madison and made her promise to catch a lizard and bring it home, so Splish and Splash would have company.

He saw me roll my eyes and drew me in for a long, slow kiss. What I wouldn't know until a few days later was that it would be the last kiss we would share. And I would be breaking that promise I made to my mother, along with my heart.

TWENTY-NINE

LOGAN

I USED TO GET A THRILL WORKING UNDERCOVER BACK WHEN I was young and fearless. Pushing my luck and putting myself in dangerous situations was as much as a turn-on as hooking up with a beautiful woman. I've seen and done it all. I've signed up for every assignment. But spending the last two nights looking through surveillance videos and sitting in a seedy strip club wasn't as exciting as I remembered it to be.

Mike and I sat on our barstools, nursing our draft beers. The pounding bass speakers shook the walls as the topless dancers pressed their bodies and ran their hands along the men who dished out dollar bills for their attention. While I always admired a beautiful woman, it sucked that this was how some of them had to make a living.

I spotted the red hair and black-framed glasses through the mirror over the bar. We've spent the last month learning his routines. We learned his gym schedule, his eating habits, and even the brand of cigarettes he liked to smoke when no one was looking. Ironically, it was one of those cigarette butts found at the crime scene that led us to him. We also had a physical description from a witness that saw him harassing the victim the night she was killed. Yet, it still wasn't enough evidence for us to charge him. We needed something more concrete. He's been under heavy surveillance twenty-four seven, walking around living his double life as a dentist in Valley Forge. I'm sure he thought he got away with ending the life of that young woman, which was why I couldn't figure out why he would risk coming back to the scene of the crime.

Without saying a word, my partner, Mike, gave me a nod as we both caught sight of him.

I gulped down a good portion of my beer, edged out of my seat, and kept a close eye on Kevin Wilson as he strutted through the club. He acted like he didn't have a care in the world. When he reached the back door that led to the alley, he looked over his shoulder and caught my gaze. His eyebrows knitted together as if he were trying to place me.

He slipped out the door, and I moved in that direction, keeping a slow pace. I didn't want any unwanted attention, and the last thing I needed was to have my cover blown.

As soon as we stepped outside, I did my best to ignore the smell of urine and the dirty dumpster that filled the air. There were all kinds of questionable activities that took place in these alleys at night. I didn't even want to think about what I'd find in broad daylight.

We walked quickly and quietly, and I spotted the new camera in the corner that the owner had finally installed. The cheap bastard was reluctant to fork over the cash, but I guess a dead woman found in the alley behind his establishment wasn't all that good for business.

I kept my hand on my Glock, ready to pull it out at a

second's notice. My eyes swept across the narrow passage-way, trying to stay as quiet as possible. Why the hell didn't he leave through the front entrance? Was he looking for something? Was he waiting for someone? He looked over his shoulder, spotting us—again.

Fuck! I turned my head to the right, trying to keep my face hidden. He ducked across the street and beeped the locks to a car sitting at the curb. We were so focused on catching up to him; we didn't notice the dark shadow until it was too late.

The cold tip of the knife pressed against my side. "Empty your pockets now."

You've got to be fucking shitting me.

"You don't want to do this, man." I raised my hands in the air and met Mike's eyes. He gave me a look that said exactly what I was thinking. *What a fucking idiot.*

Everything in me wanted to pull my gun out and show this shithead who he was dealing with. But that would only lead to more paperwork, and it wouldn't look good for me professionally. Sure, it was self-defense, but I was trained not to use my weapon unless I absolutely had to.

The guy's pupils were dilated, and the knife shook in his hands as he swayed to the left a little bit. Great, a druggie who was looking to score his next hit.

"I know exactly what I want, so stop fucking talking and hand it over." He licked his lips a little too eagerly as his eyes darted to my pockets. Did he think we were just going to hand over our money and walk away? I counted in my head how many steps it would take to get out of this alley, all the while keeping my eyes locked on the skinny fuck with the knife pointed in my side.

The cop in me took one long look at him. Trying to remember every little detail about his weathered face, just in case things went south. He had a birthmark on his right cheekbone, eyes as black as his worn T-shirt, and three bottom teeth, chipped and yellow. A jagged scar ran down the right side of his neck. I could pick him out of an over-sold crowd at an Eagles game if I had to.

"Listen, pal." Mike stepped forward, trying to distract him. "We don't have anything you want, so let my friend go."

"Shut up, and empty your damn pockets." Spit flew from his mouth as the blade pressed deeper into my side. "Or I'll slice his ribs in half."

"All right." Mike held his hands out. "Calm down."

We weren't prepared for this, but we were trained to deal with these types of situations. Mike patted his side, feeling for the butt of his gun. The poor fucker had no idea what was coming.

I gave Mike a signal to keep distracting him so I could knock him off his feet. He was smaller than me but high as a kite and probably felt like he had a good chance of getting away. He was going to be very disappointed.

"Stop right there," he yelled at Mike, and moved the point of the knife up toward my chest. I felt the tip of the blade cut through my clothing and the point pierce through my skin. A burning sensation spread through my insides. I didn't even hesitate. I whirled around and twisted his arm. The blade fell from his hands, and he screamed out in pain. I slammed my good elbow into his stomach, watching the knife skid across the pavement. When he went to reach for it, I slammed my entire weight into his side.

I don't fucking think so, shithead.

I bent at the waist and tackled him to the ground. My shoulder ached as we rolled around on the filthy, piss-stained concrete. I had to give the guy credit; he was putting up a damn good fight for a skinny bastard. A tingling pain shot through me as we both smacked up against the green dumpster. There was a small amount of blood soaking through my shirt. It wasn't horrible, but it still fucking hurt like hell.

Mike advanced on him, ripping his hands off of me. He yanked him back and lifted him up, grabbing him by the shirt. The guy didn't look like he gave a fuck that he was about to get his ass kicked.

He threw a sloppy punch and missed. Mike shoved him down hard on the cement, keeping his knee pressed down on his back.

I slumped down to the ground, trying to get my breathing under control. I brought my hand up to my chest. Blood started to drip through my shirt and leak down onto my hand. I forced myself to my feet and bent over, trying to calm my racing heart.

My eyes peeled open, and I gave Mike a nod, letting him know I was fine.

The idiot was still trying to wrestle his body away as Mike pulled his cuffs out. "Police. You're under arrest."

"I'm going to sue you mother fucking pigs," he screamed out in pain, trying to cover up his bloody nose.

"Oh, yeah." Mike bent forward, gathering his hands behind his back, and snapped the cuffs around his wrists. "What are you going to sue us for, dipshit?"

"Police brutality, and you guys were discriminating against me because I'm homeless."

"Is that so?" Mike pushed harder on his back as he struggled against the restraints. "Maybe we should add resisting arrest to your list of charges."

I winced as I moved up in front of him. I balled my

hand into a fist, thinking how this fucker just screwed up a month's worth of work. Mike pulled out his cell and called for backup. We didn't drive patrol cars, and I didn't want his smelly ass stinking up my car.

"You hang out here often?" I asked as a thought popped into my head. Mike met my stare, knowing where I was going with this. "What can you tell us about the guy who walked out the back door before us?"

"The ginger?" His gaze darted to the side. Oh, he knew something all right. "Look, I like the guys in blue, I don't want any trouble."

Given that this is probably his nightly hangout, my guess was he saw or heard something the night that woman was killed. I decided I needed to approach this differently. I could make him think we suspected it was him, and have a little fun doing it, or take him downtown, book him and throw him in a cell for the night. But then I'd have to wait until morning to interrogate him. The aching stab wound right next to my heart made the first option sound much better.

"Where did you get the knife?" I asked, staring him down and ignoring the pain in my chest.

His head jerked back, eyes wide. "It's mine," he lied. He was nervous, good. Maybe now he would start talking. When people got scared, they got desperate.

"Interesting." I wiped my hand along my flexing jaw. "There was a dancer left stabbed to death, right in this very alley with a knife just like the one you're holding in your hands. Pretty strange coincidence, don't you think?"

"Whoa, dude, what the fuck? You seriously think it was me?"

I tilted my head to the side and eyed him carefully. "Let's see, what do you think, Mike?" I glanced at my partner. "First degree murder, assaulting a police officer with a deadly weapon, oh, and resisting arrest. How much time do you think he'd get?"

"At least twenty-five years, possibly life." He smirked, playing along.

The dude started crying, and I saw piss running down his pant leg. "I won't make it in prison, man. Look at me. I'm skinny and I ain't got no tattoos. I'll be someone's bitch within the first week."

"Well, today is your lucky day." I pressed my fist to his chest. The pain in mine was getting worse, and I wanted to return the favor. "All you have to do is tell me if you've seen that man before."

He looked down at the ground and hesitated. He couldn't possibly be stupid enough to think he'd get out of this.

"Is he a friend of yours?" Mike asked.

"Does it look like we travel in the same social circles? Dude drives an Audi."

Ahh…so he was familiar with his car. I think we might have found another witness.

"How do you know what kind of car he drives?" Mike said, glancing my way briefly and back to him. "And before you answer that. Consider this your last warning."

"What's going to happen to me?" His eyes started to shift all around us, looking for a way to escape. Good luck, dumbass.

"What's your name?" I asked. I was running out of patience, and still pissed at myself for being distracted earlier.

"Barry."

"All right, Barry." I started pacing in front of him in slow steps. "Here's the deal. As you can see, I'm in a little bit of pain here from the knife you rammed in my chest. I don't have time to play games, so I'm going to give it to you straight. You're going to jail for attempted murder of a police officer. Now, how long you stay there is up to you."

"I didn't know you guys were cops, I swear."

"You need to calm down and start talking. Your ride is on its way to take you to jail. There is only one way to save your ass right now. Tell us where you got the knife and what you know about that guy. If you don't tell us before that patrol car pulls up, the deal is off the table."

"Don't you have to offer me an attorney first?" He looked two seconds away from freaking out again.

"I'm just simply asking where you got the knife. If you think you're going to implicate yourself in the murder that took place in this alley a few months ago, then we'd be happy to read you your rights, book you, and call for a defense attorney."

"I didn't kill her, I swear. I bumped into him that night as he was rounding the corner of the alley. I spotted Tammy on the ground and the bloody knife in his hand. He chased me, but I know the streets better than him, so I was able to get away. He's been driving around in his Audi asking about me. A guy like that don't come down to the south side of Philly unless he wants something, or someone." He swallowed nervously. "My brother knows I'm always getting myself in trouble. He bought me a switchblade so I could protect myself. He'd be pissed at me if he knew I was robbing people."

We were getting off topic here.

"You sure the guy you just saw was him?" It sounded like my suspect was coming back to the scene of the crime, trying to tie up a loose end. Barry didn't know it yet, but we might have just saved his life tonight.

"I'm sure. I always liked Tammy." He blinked and looked over to the small crowd that had gathered around. "She was always nice to me. She would give me snacks and soda." He smiled at the memory and frowned. "I was mad when I saw what he did to her."

"All right, Barry." Mike patted his chest. "I'm going to have you stop there." Two Philly PD cars, flashing their red and blue lights, pulled up. Barry still seemed like he was trying to figure out if he had any other options.

I looked over Mike's shoulder at the sound of more sirens getting closer. Only it wasn't another cop car that just rolled up.

"I don't need an ambulance, Mike." I knew it was policy, but fuck that. It was unnecessary.

He pointed to my chest. "You need to get that checked out." There was a warning in his tone, and I knew well enough not to argue. I grumbled as the paramedics raced over. "I can take it from here," he said and swiftly walked away. "Call me with an update once they get you patched up," he yelled over his shoulder as I watched Barry get shoved into the back of the police cruiser.

At least now we had a witness. Too bad I had to get stabbed to get that information. My skin burned like it was on fire. All I could think about was how pissed Ava would be when she found out what had happened.

THIRTY

AVA

MY KNEES BOUNCED WITH NERVES AS MY UBER PULLED AWAY from the airport. I tapped on the last message and reread it for the umpteenth time to ensure I didn't miss anything.

Luke: We just left the hospital. We are headed to Logan's house now. Text us when you land.

When Luke called last night and told me Logan had been stabbed, I booked the first flight out in the morning. My mom insisted on Madison staying with her in Florida for a few extra days, which worked out better because I wasn't sure what I'd have on my hands, and I wanted to give Logan all my attention.

My head rested against the back of the seat, and I did my best to tune out the driver, who was trying to make small talk during the twenty-five-minute drive. My thoughts were racing, and regardless of how hard Luke tried to reassure me that Logan was fine, my panic would not go away until I saw him with my own eyes.

The second my Uber pulled up in front of his house, I bolted from my seat. My driver gave me the stink eye, not liking that I hopped out of the car before he had a chance to put it in park.

I sprinted up the driveway and was completely out of breath when I reached his front door and pushed it open. His entire family was there, but all I could focus on was him. My knees almost gave out when I confirmed he was in one piece.

He was resting on the couch, surrounded by a mountain of pillows and covered in blankets. I wasn't sure what to expect, but he looked normal, so I took that as a good sign.

He opened his arms once he saw me. I rushed over and palmed his cheeks. "I was so worried." Tears clouded my vision as I looked over his injury. "I got here as fast as I could."

He grabbed my hands and pulled my mouth to his. "You really didn't need to cut your trip short." He brushed his lips softly against mine. "I'm fine, but I'm glad you're here."

"There is no place else I'd rather be." I melted into his embrace and buried my face into his neck. After taking a few minutes to soak him in, I lifted my head and waved to his mother. She was sipping her coffee while her head rested on Patrick's shoulder. Luke sat in a chair in the corner, smiling warmly at us.

"Thank you for calling me, Luke."

"Of course." He crossed his legs and leaned back. His eyes shifted to his brother. "I wanted to make sure to keep you in the loop. My little brother has a habit of downplaying his injuries."

I shook my head. "Not surprising."

Logan squeezed my hip. "I'm right here, you know.

You guys don't need to talk about me like I'm not in the room."

I rested my cheek against his chest, and he winced. "Shit, I'm sorry." There was a white gauze bandage peeking up through the neckline of his T-shirt. I ran my hand lightly over the top of his injury and nestled myself into his good side.

He wiped the moisture from under my eyes and kissed me on the lips. "I'm fine, sweetheart."

"See what I mean." Luke rose from the chair and brought Logan an extra pillow to help support his arm.

"Your brother is right." I adjusted the blanket over his lap. "It has to hurt."

"Trust me, I've had a punch to the chest that's hurt worse than this."

"I'm more concerned about your heart," his mother said, and he cut his gaze to hers. "You need to follow up with your cardiologist."

"Mom." His eyes narrowed in warning. I tilted my head to the side, trying to figure out what was going on.

She sighed like she was losing patience with him. "You can't take chances like that, you know better."

I turned my attention to Logan, my brows pinched in confusion. "What's wrong with your heart?"

He picked up the TV remote to pause whatever show they'd been watching. "There is nothing wrong with my heart. My mom is just being paranoid."

"I'm sorry. You know how I worry." Kelly wiped her eyes as Luke stood off to the side, curling his hands around the back of the loveseat. The expression on his face made no sense.

"Am I missing something here?" There was obviously something they weren't telling me. I was trying to read between the lines, but I was so exhausted from the lack of sleep that I couldn't get my brain to function properly.

Logan dragged a hand over his face. He took a deep breath and closed his eyes. "Luke is a heart transplant recipient. My mom is extra cautious and freaks out about every little thing that happens to us."

It took me a minute to register what he said. "I'm sorry. I did not know that." I looked over to Luke. "Is everything okay? Are you having complications?"

"I'm fine." He patted his chest. "The new ticker is doing great, actually." While I appreciated his attempt at humor, I was still baffled as to why everyone in this room still seemed worried about Logan.

Patrick stood up, looking at his watch. "Why don't we go home and get some rest. We'll check in with you in a few hours."

Kelly grabbed her purse and handed me a piece of paper. "Here are the instructions on his wound care and medications. His antibiotics and pain pills are on the table. Please call us if either of you need anything." She squeezed my arm and flicked a glance over to her son. The guilt in her features threw me off.

Luke glanced at his brother and gave him a nod. I watched them all bolt toward the door like they couldn't get out of here fast enough. I didn't know that the hell was going on but it couldn't have been good.

A thick layer of silence filled the room. "Is there a reason why you never mentioned your brother's heart transplant?"

Logan brought his hand up to his jaw and scratched it aggressively. "I didn't want you to worry."

"Why would I need to worry?"

He was taking his sweet time answering me, and I was

running out of patience. "Logan, I'm going to ask you one more time. Why would I need to worry?"

He hung his head and closed his eyes. "We share the same genetic heart issue. The only difference is, he has symptoms and I don't."

My world tilted to the side, yet somehow my body remained still. "What was wrong with his heart?"

"He was diagnosed with cardiomyopathy. It's a disease that can cause thickening of the heart muscle, which can lead to other complications. After his transplant, his doctor suggested we all get tested. We found out that the disease runs on my mom's side of the family."

"What about you?" My breathing was heavy, and I tried to slow it down so I could focus. "And what about Brina? Please tell me she's okay."

Logan was an adult, but Brina was so young. I couldn't imagine if that were Madison.

He gave me a small smile. "She tested negative. She's fine."

I blew out a sigh of relief, but it quickly disappeared. "But you're not fine, are you? That's why your mom was so worried?"

He closed his eyes. "I have the gene, but I don't have any physical symptoms. My heart function is completely normal."

"Logan, I'm not a doctor. I have no idea what any of this means."

"It means I can have the gene but never develop symptoms. I see a specialist once a year and have a cardio workup done to make sure there is no thickening of the heart muscle. Really, it's not a big deal."

"Not a big deal? Your brother had a heart transplant. How can you say that? Just because you don't have symptoms now, that doesn't mean they won't develop later in life."

He released a heavy breath, seeming frustrated with me. "Ava, my grandmother lived to be eighty-five without any heart issues until the last four years of her life. It's not a death sentence."

I jerked back, caught off by his tone. How dare he act like he had a right to snap at me? I was the one who should be angry. This was not something he should have kept from me. He's had plenty of opportunities to bring this up, but he intentionally kept me in the dark. I was planning a future with him, all the while he knew there was a chance he might not have one.

My fear was turning into panic, and that wasn't a good thing. "You didn't think this is something I should know?"

"It's not something I like to talk about. Until the doctors tell me I have something to worry about, I'm going to live my life. Because guess what, Ava? There's not a damn thing I can do about it except address the symptoms as they arise. If I ever go into heart failure, there are things they can do to treat it." His tone sharpened to match his eyes. "But what good is it going to do me to worry about something that I can't control and may never happen?"

"You should have told me!" I shouted. "You should have been more upfront with me."

"Why? So you can fixate on all the things that could go wrong? Why do you think I didn't tell you right away about the accident? Because I knew you would focus on every worst-case scenario." He yanked on the ends of his hair in frustration. "I know how twitchy you get about death, so I didn't want to spook you."

"Twitchy?" Could he be any more insulting? "You've got to be fucking kidding me. You had a front row seat and witnessed firsthand how well I handled the death of my husband. You didn't think I had a right to know what I might be facing in the future?"

"It always comes back to *your husband*, doesn't it?" I narrowed my eyes, feeling like everything was spiraling out of control. "He's always going to be your husband and I'm what?"

"We are not doing this right now." I stared at him, feeling the frustration building. "You need to stop comparing yourself to Drew. I have never once, since we started dating, made you feel like a substitute for him."

He pressed his lips together and stared at me. "It doesn't help the way I feel, though, does it?"

"I guess it doesn't," I said, feeling pissed off that he didn't recognize the effort I'd put into this relationship or how far we've come. "Tell me the truth. Were you ever planning on telling me?"

"I told you, I was afraid of how you would react. I wanted to make sure we were solid before I put that burden on you."

To think that I was ready to give him everything and now…God, how could I give my heart away again knowing that there was a good chance I could lose him. How could I knowingly sign myself up for that type of pain again? I wanted to scream and punch something at the unfairness of it all.

I stood up and ran a hand over my face. "I need a minute."

"No, you don't get a minute," he fired back. The raw panic in his voice almost did me in. "I need you to look at me. Really look at me. I'm fine. Don't let this news get inside your head. It will probably end up being nothing."

I blinked away the tears, making no attempt to hide

them. The pain was a familiar feeling, and as fucked up as it was, I needed it because it felt like I'd just gotten the wind knocked out of me. I needed strength in any form I could get it.

"I don't know if I can do this." Tears slid down my cheeks because I knew in order to save my own heart, I might have to break his.

"Wow! I guess I know where I stand, huh?" He looked at the clock on the wall. "Less than ten minutes ago, you were crying in my arms, thankful I was alive. But the thought of me being sick in the future is enough for you to leave me. The reason why I didn't say anything was because I was afraid you couldn't handle the truth, looks like I was right. I thought if I could get you to love me, that would be enough to keep you. I guess I had it all wrong. You were never meant to be mine, because you'll always be *his*. I'll never be the one you really want. Just fucking admit it, Ava." His eyes filled with anger. "This was never going to last and I was a fool to think that it would."

I wanted to speak, to tell him how wrong he was, but I couldn't get myself to talk.

"I'm such a fool." He shook his head. "Here you are ready to push me away, and I want to get down on my knees and beg you to stay. Do you have any idea how much I love you? I love you so goddamned much that I would trade places with Drew in a heartbeat if I could. Yes, I would trade my life for his because I know he is and always will be your entire world."

I choked back a sob, overwhelmed with guilt. His insecurities about Drew ran much deeper than I realized. "Please stop."

His eyes grew hard. "Just be honest with me and own up to it. Because I sure as fuck know that if Drew was the one with the genetic heart issue, the last thing you would do was think about leaving him because of it."

"That's not fair," I sobbed. "He was my husband!"

"Exactly, and I'm just a guy you're fucking around with."

My tears were flowing at a relentless pace. "How can you think that?"

I wish I could bring myself to tell him how untrue that statement was. My feelings for Logan ran so much deeper than I ever thought they could. But he was being so stubborn right now, and I had a feeling anything I said would get thrown back in my face.

Anger that I had no right to took over. The back of my eyelids burned with emotion that I couldn't quite get a grip on. He didn't fully understand what he was asking of me.

"Do you have any idea how it feels to have your whole world ripped apart?" My entire body shook as the truth I'd been holding in came tumbling from my lips. "No, you don't know. You don't know what it's like to hold your daughter at night while she screams for her father." I swiped at my cheeks. "Or how much energy it takes to get out of bed every morning when all you want to do is sleep all day." He went to grab my arm, but I pulled away. I wasn't looking for pity or trying to make him feel guilty. I wanted him to understand my reasoning. "Can you imagine how embarrassing it is to rely on your best friend to help you shower and dress just so you can go through the motions to please everybody else? To feel like a failure because you're fucking up at every turn because you went from being part of a team to have to do it all on your own?" His eyes filled with unshed tears as I struggled to get the rest out. "You become so terrified of losing everyone you love that you push them away because it's easier than waiting for them to leave you? How can you ask me to put myself and Madison through that again?"

I turned away from him, unable to look him in the eyes. How could I? No matter how much I wanted to be with him, I was afraid I would lose everything all over again.

"You don't need to do this," he pleaded with me. "Don't let your fears take away our future."

"Our future? You mean the one we might not have." His eyes widened, and I hated myself for hurting him. It was unfair to blame him for something he couldn't control. But the funny thing about fear, it unleashed at the slightest hint of a threat. "I'm sorry, I know I'm acting selfish right now, but investing in a future with you and having it taken away would destroy me. I couldn't handle going through that again."

"So, you're just going to leave me because I might get sick one day. That's good to know."

"This is not easy for me. I need to think of my daughter. I need to do what's best for her. For us. Even though I l-lo…."

His eyes seared into mine, silently begging me to say the words, but I couldn't get them out.

What the hell was wrong with me?

"You love me. I know you do." I could feel the pain in his voice, making that guilt I felt in my gut settle in deeper. "I feel it in every kiss, every touch, every moment we're together. You might not love me as much as you love him, but I know you do."

"You have no idea what you're talking about it."

"Then tell me what part I'm wrong about?"

I could end this right now and tell him he is who I

want. That he was the man I was in love with, but that would only complicate things because maybe he was right. Maybe this wasn't meant to last.

"This isn't just about you and me," I reminded him. "I need to do what's best for Madison."

"I have a daughter too. You're not the only one who puts their kid first. But I would never, ever give up on you like you are on me right now."

"I never said I was giving up on you!" I closed my eyes, wishing I could admit to him how much his love terrified me. But instead, I forced those steel walls up around my heart. It was the only thing keeping me from falling into that deep, dark place I left months ago. The last thing I wanted to do was go back there. "Can you please just give me some time to wrap my head around this?"

"It doesn't sound like I have any other choice, do I?"

"Why are you so angry with me?"

"Why can't you just tell me you love me?"

"Because it feels like you're giving me an ultimatum here, and that's not fair." Not to mention he was angry. So damn angry. There was too much at stake here, and I was feeling overwhelmed. But at the same time, it was crazy how well he understood me.

"If you can't say the words, then I don't know what the fuck we're doing here. I've laid it all on the line for you, Ava. You said that you're scared that we might not have a future, but clearly what you really aren't saying is that you don't want one with me. If you're not sure you can be with me, then maybe that's a sign that this will never work."

I stared at him, not knowing how to respond. It felt like I was in flight-or-fight mode and everything in me told me to run. Maybe I was overreacting, but he was asking, no commanding, and I refused to be put on the spot.

"Listen, emotions are running high right now, and I don't want to throw away what we have in the heat of the moment."

"But that's exactly what it feels like." He looked away, swallowing hard. "If you love someone, your first thought isn't about leaving them the day they get home from the hospital after getting stabbed. Instead of giving me comfort, you're making this all about you. You should be in my arms, telling me everything is going to be okay. Instead, some of the first words out of your mouth are, 'I don't think I can do this.'"

"You're right. I'm so sorry." I took a step forward, but he held his hand out.

"I don't want your pity. You want time? You got it. Take all the time you need to figure out if you love me enough." How I managed to keep it together, I had no idea. "If you decide that you can't handle any type of future with me, and you want to spend the rest of your life guarding your heart, then no hard feelings. But what you're offering me right now isn't enough anymore."

I took a step back. "I want to give you more, but I'm not sure I can." The thought of losing him only fueled my fear, because once you experienced that level of pain, you did everything you could to avoid it from ever happening again.

"Then maybe you already have your answer." A lone tear slipped down his cheek. He tried to brush it away, but another one fell right after. "Marco is going to be here any minute. You can go now."

A painful cry fell from my lips. Never in my life have I felt so torn. I wanted to run back into his arms and pretend that this wasn't happening. I wanted to take back every-thing I said, but I couldn't bring myself to do it.

I looked at him one last time as I walked to the door, trying to memorize every little detail about him. "I wish I wasn't such a coward, because you deserve so much more."

"Goodbye, Ava." His voice was final, and I couldn't blame him. My chest constricted, and my eyes burned with tears. The regret and the remorse almost had me turning around, but instead, I walked away even if it was the last thing I wanted to do.

THIRTY-ONE

AVA

With a deep breath, I stared at Madison's back-to-school list. I had a few small items to check off, but I was saving them for when she got home from her trip. She was spending a few extra days with my mom, and I was taking advantage of my time alone. It was hard to believe that summer was coming to an end, and she would be starting fourth grade in a little over a week.

I picked up my Kindle and went to grab my lunch when I heard the microwave beep. Getting lost in a good book while stuffing my face with a frozen pizza seemed to be the extent of my life.

Studying the books I downloaded was actually kind of humorous. They were all thrillers and mysteries. Usually, I would read romance, but the last thing I was in the mood for was someone else's happily ever after.

I was trying to decide which book I wanted to start next when my phone buzzed on the counter. Amelia's name flashed across the screen. I've been dodging her calls, keeping our communication strictly to text messages.

I couldn't keep avoiding her, and putting this conversation off.

The serial killer book I was about to start would have to wait.

"Hello."

"Hallelujah! She finally picks up the phone."

It was surprising that she hadn't driven over and beaten down my door by now.

"You know why I haven't been able to return your calls."

"Yeah, because you knew I'd talk some sense into you."

This is what I got for getting involved with Marco's best friend. I closed my eyes, wishing it didn't have to be like this because my life would be a hell of a lot easier right now.

"Amelia…"

"I was calling to tell you that Marco took Logan for his follow-up appointment today. Just in case you were wondering how he was doing. You know, after being stabbed in the chest."

I sighed and slumped down on the barstool. The Kindle was pushed aside. "What did the doctor say?"

"He removed the stitches. Everything is healing. No complications. He cleared him to go back to work as long as he stays out of dark alleys for now."

"Thanks for letting me know."

"He also got checked over by a cardiologist and everything looks fine. Luckily, the length of the knife and the angle of the blade just missed his left ventricle, otherwise we would be having a different conversation."

"I can't tell how relieved I am to hear that."

"You could call him yourself and let him know that you care."

"Amelia." My eyes closed. "Of course, I care, but that doesn't change the fact that he should have told me about his heart condition," I said, feeling the need to defend myself. How could she expect me to be okay with him keeping something like that from me?

"If he did, then you wouldn't have given him a chance. I've been in his shoes before, remember? So, I can sympathize with him on this one. I kept the agreement I made with my grandfather from Marco, and it blew up in my face. It took him getting shot for me to realize that I had made a mistake."

I exhaled a breath, knowing what she said was true. "It doesn't change anything and I'm not sure what you want me to say."

Did she think that this was what I wanted?

"Ava, I won't pretend to know what's best for you. Just ask yourself one thing."

"What?"

"You said you didn't want to get hurt again and couldn't suffer through another broken heart. How does your heart feel right now?"

"My heart fucking hurts. Is that what you want to hear?" Amelia was my best friend. She was usually on my side. She was just trying to prove a point, she wasn't trying to upset me, or maybe she was, I didn't know anymore.

"Listen, I'm not judging you. We all say things when we're scared and angry. But Ava," she sighed, "you love him. Really love him. You, out of everyone, should know there are no guarantees in this life. No one can promise or predict the future. If you want my opinion, you're wasting time. Precious time you will never get back again. And I don't need to remind you that Logan is a catch. He won't be single forever."

"Why are you telling me this?" She couldn't possibly think this was helping. "And he's not fucking perfect. He has flaws just like everyone else." I started pacing around my kitchen, my eyes narrowing on the damn fish tank. "He leaves the cap off the toothpaste and doesn't rinse the sink out after brushing his teeth. He listens to the TV way too loud. He has a gross habit of cleaning the hair from his electric razor in the toilet and leaving beard trimmings all over the rim," I informed her, ticking everything off the list. "And speaking of the toilet, he sometimes misses his target when he goes in the middle of the night. He can be moody, especially after he's had a long workday."

My mind began to spin with everything he did wrong, but then I remembered how he loved to tangle his fingers in my hair when we kissed. How he would always make sure I had my dinner plate before he ate his. He would insist on holding me whenever we slept together. I normally liked my space, but with him, I could never get close enough. Whenever we were around other people, he would make a point to keep his hand on my knee or around my shoulders. It was like he needed to touch me, even if his focus was on other people. He was attentive, caring, funny, and always the first to say he was sorry, even when he had no reason to apologize.

Doubt started to creep its way inside my head. The pain in his eyes. The fear in his voice. It was a continuous loop. Did I overreact? Did I handle it all wrong? Of course, I fucking did.

"I know he's not perfect. No one is, but that man loves you."

"I know you mean well," I said, feeling like I was being

split in two. Part of me wanted to beg him for forgiveness. The other half was intent on protecting what was left of my heart.

"I'm just trying to help you see what is right in front of you. Logan is a good guy." She wasn't wrong, but I really wish she would stop reminding me. "He would do anything for you and Madison. I know you're terrified of losing another person you love, but pushing him away because he could potentially get sick one day is bullshit. That man brought a smile back to your face. He helped fill in some of those gaps that Drew left behind. But you got so wrapped up in your own fears you couldn't see straight." I didn't know how to defend myself against her words. Everything she said was true. "You lost your first love and survived. You don't need to throw away your second just because you're afraid of losing it."

"I didn't expect to feel this way."

"What way?"

"So weak and hollow."

"If you didn't love him then you wouldn't feel that way. You can deny it all you want but it's true."

I rolled my eyes, knowing she couldn't see me. There was no way I could deny it. I did love him, and the regret was killing me. I was ashamed at how I handled things, making his situation all about me. I had no idea why I acted that way, but I've had a lot of time to process what I said. And with each passing day, I hated myself more and more.

"I made a mistake," I admitted, wiping away the tears.

"It's not too late to fix it." Her voice was hopeful and full of conviction.

I hoped she was right because I needed to tell him the

truth. That I did love him, and I didn't mean all those mean, hurtful things that came out of my mouth.

There was a knock on my door. I scooted my chair back and squinted out the window.

Panic set in when I saw who was standing there.

"Oh my God! Richard's here," I whispered into the phone, hoping he couldn't hear me.

"What the hell! Don't you dare answer that door." Another loud knock sounded through the house as soon as she said that.

"What the fuck do I do?" A wave of nausea hit me. "I thought he was still in jail."

"I'm calling Marco."

"Amelia, don't be ridiculous. Just give me a minute to get rid of him."

"Ava," she yelled into the phone as I set it down and hurried through the house. If he came here thinking I would tell him where my mother was, he was going to be very disappointed.

I took in a deep breath and swung the door open. "Richard, what are you doing here?"

"Hello, Ava." His face twisted into something I didn't like. "Aren't you going to invite me in?"

My hand tightened around the doorframe. "If you're looking for my mother, she isn't here."

"That's interesting. She's not at home either." He sneered. "No thanks to you."

I swallowed deeply and stared at the man my mother had spent the last fifteen years with. She married him, thinking he would give her comfort and security. Instead, he robbed years from her that she would never get back.

"No, Richard. My mother isn't home because you allowed your rage to get the better of you. Maybe if you didn't become so unhinged and addicted to alcohol, you'd still have a wife."

I nervously glanced over at my phone, hoping that Amelia was still on the line listening.

His laugh was dark, just like his eyes. "You really think I give a shit what you think? You're only pissing me off and I'm not going anywhere until you tell me where she is."

"That's not going to happen." I tried to hide the tremor in my voice along with my fear.

"Don't play games with me or I'll make it ten times worse for her."

"Do I need to remind you about the restraining order she filed against you?"

"Do you really think I won't find her?" He tilted his head and stepped forward. "That I give a shit about a fucking piece of paper."

"You need to leave right now." I attempted to slam the door in his face, but he kicked his boot out to stop it from closing.

"This is your last chance. Tell me where she is? I'm done fucking around." I winced at his breath. He smelled like alcohol and stale cigars.

My eyes frantically scanned the room, looking for anything that could be used as a weapon. The kitchen drawer where I kept my sharp knives was too far out of my reach. There was a pair of scissors on the coffee table nearby, but I had to move backward to get to them.

I backed away in that direction when all six foot two of the deranged-looking man moved directly into my personal space. Feeling trapped, I wondered if this was the paralyzing fear my mother felt at being completely at his mercy. My feet slipped against the floor, and my eyes flew to the door, wondering if my neighbors would be able to hear me if I screamed.

"You're nothing but a little bitch, you know that!"

I barely had time to register the smack before it hit my cheek. "You think because you're sleeping with a cop now that you can one up me?" His face reddened. "He might have found that tracker I put in your car, but I'll find your mother if it's the last thing I ever do." My eyes widened. Logan was right, it wasn't Vanessa.

"It was you," I said, bringing my fingers up to my stinging cheek.

"You think I'm fucking stupid? I knew you would eventually take her from me." He shouted and then landed another smack against my temple. Pain like I'd never felt before seared through me as I struggled to stay on my feet. "You turned her against me, and it's time you pay the fucking price for running your filthy mouth." He grabbed the back of my hair; pain ripped through my scalp. "It's time I teach you a real lesson like I should have when you were a punk-ass teenager." His fist struck the side of my head before I knew it was coming.

It felt like I had the wind knocked out of me. He gripped my shirt and shoved me against the wall. His fist came toward my face again. I tried to duck my head, but his knuckles made contact with my cheekbone. The radiating pain was enough to send my body to the floor.

Tears burned the back of my eyes as his steel-toed boot connected with my ribs. "Fuck," I screamed out in pain. My entire body throbbed in agony. I tried to roll around and move away, but it only made the pain worse. My limbs felt heavy, and I made the mistake of letting out a cough. I wanted to run and get away from this fucking lunatic, but my body wouldn't cooperate.

"Scream all you want, you little cunt." His laugh was maniacal and showed no mercy. I tried to curl up in a ball to protect myself. I felt another kick, and I could hear the snap and pop of my bones crack. The sharp pain made my vision blur.

"Why are you doing this?" Everything spun around me, making it hard to concentrate as he leaned over me.

"Tell. Me. Where. She. Is." His hand came down to my throat, and he squeezed so hard, I had no doubt he was trying to kill me. The hatred in his voice, along with the pressure against my skin, had me fearing that I was at the end of my life.

"I told you, I don't know," I said, struggling to breathe.

"Liar!" He released his hold and spat in my face. "Your mother never would have left me if you didn't poison her with your lies."

"She left because she was sick of getting beaten, you bastard." I squinted toward the door. If only I had the energy to make a run for it.

"I'm warning you." He grabbed my throat again. My body thrashed against his, but all the oxygen was being squeezed out of me, making my attempts useless.

He released his hold on me and left me gasping for air. He started rummaging through my kitchen drawers, pulling them out completely, and throwing them across the room in frustration. "I'm going to find her and make her sorry she ever left me."

I could see blood on the floor—my blood. Everything ached, but I slowly dragged my body toward the door while he was distracted with tearing my house upside down. What he was hoping to find, I had no fucking clue. I just knew I had to get out of there before he killed me.

I brought my hand up to my throat and focused on breathing. I wasn't going down without a fight.

As soundlessly as I could, I inched my way toward freedom. My body felt weak as I lifted my arms enough to reach the doorknob. The sound of sirens in the distance had Richard turning around. I tried not to panic when he withdrew a pistol from his coat pocket and pointed it at me. I knew at that moment that I had taken things too far. I should never have provoked him.

"Where do you think you're going?" His heavy footsteps pounded against the floor. I slid my eyes shut, knowing I was completely out of options.

"Amelia called for help," I croaked out as the sound of sirens got closer. "You don't need to do this, Richard. You can turn yourself in, you don't have to kill me."

"I should end your life right now and send you to the grave, right next to Drew, but you're not fucking worth sitting in a prison cell."

I blinked up at him; fear like I'd never felt before raced through me. He took his foot and jammed it into my shoulder one last time before he flung the door open. The second he hit the concrete steps, a police cruiser skidded to a halt, sending the two front wheels onto the curb. My eyes squinted at their flashing lights.

"Stop right there. Drop the gun. Lie down on your stomach and keep your hands where I can see them," the cop commanded.

I placed my hand over my brow and peeked outside. Everything was blurry, but I could still make out the two police officers who were crouched behind the open car doors. Their service weapons were aimed directly at my stepfather.

Without any warning, Richard fired two shots directly

at the officers. I heard the shatter of a windshield and flung my arms over my head and tried to roll away from the door. Richard jumped off the porch and tried to use my landscaping as a cover. I heard the sound of gunfire and looked across my yard in time to see Richard fall to his knees and clutch his chest. One officer ran over to the lifeless body on my grass. The other approached me slowly. He took one look at me and paused.

"You okay, miss?"

I nodded my head, unable to speak.

"You better call for an ambulance," he called out to his partner, who was checking Richard's body for a pulse.

"I will." He stood up and tucked his gun away. "I'll make sure to tell the one coming for this one that they don't need to hurry." He pulled out his phone, and I winced at all the blood oozing out of Richard's chest. "The suspect is dead. You're safe now, miss."

Those were the last words I heard before everything went black. My final thought was that I never got to tell Logan that I loved him.

THIRTY-TWO

LOGAN

I scrubbed a hand along my face and read through each report for the umpteenth time. I'd been sitting around my house going stir crazy for the past two weeks. I thought coming into the office and cleaning out some case files I'd been working on before I got injured would be a good distraction. No matter how much I stared at the evidence in front of me, I still couldn't concentrate. For the first time in my career, my heart wasn't in the job.

"Blake, what the fuck are you doing here?" The booming voice of Captain Macholl scared the hell out of me. "You're still on leave."

"Well, nice to see you too, Captain," I said, turning around to greet him in person.

I was just about ready to explain myself when my cell phone vibrated on my desk. "Hold on one second." I held my hand up and frowned when I saw Marco's name on the screen. I just talked to him earlier today. "What's up, Marco. Did you forget something?"

"Logan, it's Ava." He paused; something about his tone sent a chill down my spine. "She's been assaulted. I'm at the hospital right now with Amelia. You need to get here as soon as you can."

"What the fuck did you just say?" I shot out of my rolling chair, sending it flying across the bullpen. "Assaulted how?"

"Not that. A physical assault." He rushed out to say, and I felt the tightness in my chest loosen slightly. "I'll explain when you get here."

"The hell you will." Was he crazy? "You'll tell me now!"

"Look, Logan, we are wasting time. Now get to your truck and get down to HUP as fast as you can. You can call me when you're here."

I started flying through my desk drawer in search of my keys. "Captain, I have an emergency. I'll explain later." I almost tripped over the rubber mat underneath my feet.

He pushed his glasses up to the bridge of his nose. "Drive safe, Blake." He squinted his eyes in concern. "I just got a report that we had two officers involved in a fatal shooting. We don't need any more tragedies to share with the eleven o'clock news."

I started running through the office, ignoring all the stares from my fellow officers. I didn't even bother with the elevator. Instead, I took the stairs two at a time until I reached the lobby of the building. I scrambled through the revolving door and raced through the employee parking lot.

I clicked the remote starter on my key fob as I sprinted toward my truck. By the time I reached the driver's seat, I was out of breath. The engine roared to life; rain smacked against my windshield as I spun out of the parking lot. My foot wasted no time before slamming down on the accelerator once I hit the street.

I picked up my phone and called Marco back. "Tell me what happened," I barked out as soon as he picked up.

"She was on the phone with Amelia when her stepfather showed up. He was all boozed up and looking for trouble. Amelia stayed on the line with her the entire time. She could hear them shouting, and when she heard Ava scream out in pain, she hung up and called nine-one-one. Two officers arrived on the scene. The idiot tried to escape and fired on our guys. They returned fire, killing him instantly. By the time I pulled up, Ava was already being loaded into an ambulance."

Her fucking stepfather. She never liked that son of a bitch. As far as I was concerned, those two officers did us a huge favor. I should have felt relief that he was no longer a threat, but man, I was pissed that I didn't get a go at him before they took him out.

"What kind of injuries is Ava dealing with?" I held my breath as a burning sensation took over my chest.

"The doctors are still looking her over as we speak. She was black and blue when I saw her. Maybe a few broken bones. That's all I know as of right now."

I gripped my phone. "Thanks for calling me."

"Of course. Drive safe. I'll see you soon."

I ended the call and let out a long exhale, feeling a little tension ease from my body. Every conceivable scenario spun through my head, and none of them were any good. I couldn't let my mind go to the dark places it was trying to go to. All I knew was she was injured, and I had no idea how bad it was. I needed to see her with my own eyes. Touch her with my hands and make sure she was okay. She was alive, and I needed to focus on that.

I weaved through traffic and broke every traffic rule known to mankind with zero fucks to give. I tried my best to remain fixated on the road in front of me while driving as fast as possible. No matter how hard I tried, I couldn't get there quick enough.

My truck skidded to a stop in a valet parking spot at the front of the emergency room. I threw my keys to the attendant, not even waiting for them to hand me a claim ticket.

My heart rate picked up as I squeezed through the revolving doors to the hospital. Once I made it to her floor, I ran over to the nurse's station, passing by a few officers I recognized and pulled out my badge.

"Ava Donavon." My hands shook as I held my shield in my hands.

The middle-aged nurse looked up from her screen. "They are bringing her to imaging now for an MRI." She clicked a few keys on her computer. "There is a waiting room down the hall. You can wait there, and I'll have someone let you know when we have a room ready for her."

I nodded my head and followed her instructions. I walked down the bright hallway that was buzzing with activity. Nurses and doctors passed me by with their rolling carts. I spotted Marco and Amelia as soon as I entered the waiting room. Amelia leaped from her chair as soon as she saw me.

"Oh, God, Logan." I caught her by the waist as she fell apart against my chest. "Thank God you're here." Her voice was shaky and filled with anguish. The last time I saw her so distraught was when Marco got shot. No doubt this was stirring up memories from the last time we were in a tiny little waiting room like this.

I eased her back down carefully into the chair and crouched in front of her. I placed my arms on her shoulders. "I need you to walk me through what happened. Marco said you were on the phone with her when Richard showed up."

"We were talking about you. I was really hard on her." She sobbed and buried her head on my shoulder. "I was just trying to help."

"Shh…" I pulled her tight against me. "You did help. You called nine-one-one. If you weren't on the phone with her when that bastard showed up, he probably would have killed her."

My jaw locked up tight at the thought.

She lifted her head and wiped her tears away. "I just wanted you guys to work things out." She hiccupped a sob. "She felt terrible for the things she said. She didn't mean a word of it. Please tell me you believe me."

"I'm not worried about that right now." I was too worried about Ava and focused on staying calm.

"She loves you so much, Logan. I know what she had with Drew was real, but what she feels for you means everything to her. She felt terrible for the things she said. She was scared of her feelings, afraid of letting go of Drew. She was going to beg for your forgiveness."

Amelia was rambling, probably in shock. I wanted to console her, but all I could think about was the attack and what Ava must have gone through. I was on pins and needles about the extent of her injuries. I wasn't concerned with the status of our relationship because I decided on the way here, we were going to be together and make things work. I wouldn't stop fighting for us until I took my last breath.

I slid onto the cold metal chair between Marco and Amelia, feeling like I was going out of my mind. I scrolled through my phone, looking for any updates as my knees nervously bounced. I had no idea how long I'd been here. It could have been five minutes or five hours. My focus had turned to shit, so I stood from my chair and started to pace. Marco handed me a water bottle.

"What's taking so long?" I asked, running my hand through my hair. I haven't stopped since I got here. I knew the hospital expected you to sit still and patiently wait for updates, but I was ready to lose my shit.

Finally, a doctor in blue scrubs appeared in the doorway. "Family of Ava Donavon?"

I stood and met her halfway across the room.

"Everything went well. I popped her shoulder back in place and bandaged up her ribs. The damage to her ribs did not require surgery but her shoulder will. She is going to need to follow up with an orthopedic surgeon to reattach a small piece of her scapula bone that broke away. I'm going to write up a referral so she can get seen this week." She stuffed her hands in the pockets of her white lab coat. "I gave her a sedative so she could her rest. We did see a small skull fracture, which is common with head trauma. We expect it will heal on its own, but we'd like to keep her here for a day or two to watch for any swelling in the brain. Do you have any questions for me?"

"When can I see her?"

"You can see her now." Her eyes scanned the waiting room. "Only one person at a time."

I looked over my shoulder at Amelia. She waved me off. "Don't be an idiot. You know your face is the one she'll be looking for when she opens her eyes."

The doctor gave me a kind smile and held her hand out. "Right this way."

She was talking as she led me down the hall, but I

honestly had no idea what she was saying. The only thing I could focus on was getting to Ava.

"Now, I just want to warn you," she said as we approached the door. "Ava sustained a few facial injuries, so her face will look bruised and puffy. It's going to take some time for the swelling to go down. We had a plastic surgeon look over her wounds, and the doctor was confident that there won't be any permanent damage."

"I understand." I swallowed thickly. She gave me a sympathetic look that did nothing to calm my fears.

"Very well. I'll give you some privacy."

Taking a deep breath, I stepped into the quiet, sterile room. I'd just been warned, but the sight in front of me halted me in my tracks. I took in every line, every cut, every bruise. I've seen my fair share of unimaginable things during my police career, but nothing could have prepared me for this.

I dragged the chair closer to the bed and slumped into it. I grabbed Ava's hand and winced once I got a closer look. Tears gathered in my eyes as they raked over her bruises. It was a good thing that fucker was dead, or I would have killed him myself. It almost did me in just thinking about what she had to go through. The pain she had to endure. What he fucking put her through.

I wanted to break something, or better yet, I wanted to haul my ass down to the morgue and tear that dead bastard apart from limb to limb.

I raised my hand to her purple and red cheek. "God, Ava, how the hell could he do this to you?" I clenched my jaw and focused on breathing through my nose. "I hope you realize that when you wake up, things are going to change. I am never ever letting you out of my sight again." I glanced at the two IV poles and all the tubes running out of her arm. "As long as I have breath in my lungs, no one will ever lay a hand on you again. You are mine, Ava Donavon, and pretty soon that last name is going to change too. I swear to you, as God as my witness, we are going to move past all the bullshit and find a way to make things work. Because this heart of mine, regardless of what condition it's in, is yours forever. You, Brina, and Madison are my entire world." I rested my head in her lap to the sound of the monitors beeping in the background.

As the minutes passed, I sat there in silence and thought about everything that led to our breakup. There was so much that needed to be said, but I wasn't sure where we would even start. All I could do was sit and think while she slept. I would give anything to trade places with her.

A small moan caused me to snap to attention. "Logan."

I gathered her hand in mine and scrambled forward. "Oh, thank God. How do you feel, babe?"

"Water." Her voice was hoarse. "I need water."

I picked up the paper cup and brought it to her mouth. "Here, just a couple sips." I lined the straw up to her lips as she bent her head forward to reach it.

"Thank you." She looked around the room and down at the IV in her arm. Her gaze started to dart around the room. "Richard," she croaked, but I placed a hand to her lips.

"He's not ever going to hurt you again," I said as if I needed the confirmation myself.

She tried to lift her head off the pillow but groaned. "Everything hurts."

"Damn it, Ava." I pressed the call button for the nurse. "You have to lie still. You have a concussion and a few broken bones."

Her face winced. "I'm okay." She licked her dry lips. "Just a little sore."

My knuckles skimmed over her cheeks. "I think I had ten years taken off my life when I got the call from Marco."

She brought my hand to her lips and pressed her mouth against my skin. "I'm sorry." Her touch helped calm the rage flowing inside me. "I'm sorry about what I said to you, and more importantly, what I didn't say."

"Ava." I paused, trying not to show how angry I was, not at her, but at what happened. That was the last thing she needed to deal with. "We can talk about all that later."

The same nurse from earlier came in. "Hello, it's good to see you are awake." She rounded the foot of the bed so she could push a few buttons on the monitor. "Your vitals look great. How do you feel?"

"I feel fine." I glared at her, and she winced. "My shoulder and my neck are just a little sore."

My eyes went to the handprint on her neck, and I clenched my fists a couple times. I had to look away to get a hold of myself.

She handed Ava a little paper cup with pills in it. "Here, these should help." The nurse wrote a few things down on the whiteboard on the wall while another nurse replaced an IV bag. "Dr. Fatime will be in shortly." She gathered up a few supplies, and they both walked out of the room.

I pushed her hair back off her shoulder. "I can't even imagine how scared you must have been. I should have been there. I should have protected you."

She reached out, placing her hand over my wrist. "I need to tell you something before these pain meds kick in. I don't ever want you to feel like you are second best. I don't ever want you to question my feelings for you again.

I love you, Logan Blake. I'm sorry that this is the first time you are hearing these words." Tears welled in her eyes. "I know you've been waiting to hear me say them, but they don't seem like enough right now." She shook her head. "When I thought I was going to die, my last thought was that I never got to tell you that I loved you. If you give me another chance, I'll never give you another reason to doubt my feelings for you again."

"You don't need to even ask me for another chance, because I'm already yours." I cupped her face and pressed my lips to hers. "I love you too, and I should have been honest with you from the start."

"A life with you is the only one I want, but you have to promise me something."

Her eyes slid shut as I ran my finger along her jawline. "Anything."

She linked her fingers with mine. "If you develop symptoms or if the doctor sees something that causes concern, you'll tell me."

This woman was just waking up in a hospital bed after being beaten by her stepfather, and she was worried about me. If I had a ring in my pocket, I'd slip it on her finger right now.

"You can come to every appointment," I promised her. "I'll give you access to all my medical files. I'll give you *whatever you want.*"

"I only want you, and I know you'll do whatever you can to stay healthy."

"Damn straight. Especially when I have you and the girls to live for."

"Do my mom and Madison know what happened?"

I folded the thin blanket around her. "Amelia spoke to your mom a little while ago." I cleared my throat. "She booked them a flight out of Orlando for tomorrow after-noon. Madison doesn't know that you're in the hospital."

"Thank God." She sighed. "Although I'm not sure how I'm going to cover up these bruises. I must look awful."

I planted a kiss on her temple. "You look beautiful."

"I need to call my mom. Regardless of what happened with Richard, he was her husband."

I rubbed the back of my neck. "She was a little emotional, but she was more worried about you."

"You talked to her?"

"Briefly." My eyes watched hers. "She's in shock, and feeling a little guilty."

"She can't possibly think this is her fault?"

"Ava," I reached for her hand, "you need to stop worrying about everyone else. Just focus on getting better."

"Logan." Her eyes softened as she brought her hand up to my face. "Are you okay?"

I rubbed the back of her hand. "You're in a hospital bed and you're asking me if I'm okay?"

"You must have been so worried." Her eyes filled with tears, and it was taking every bit of strength I had to keep it together.

My chin trembled. "Honestly, I'm still feeling a little unsettled. I'm trying to come to terms with what happened to you, but I need you to understand something."

She ran her thumb over my cheek. "What is it?"

"When you're released from the hospital, I'm going wherever you are. Either I move in with you or you and Madison move in with me. Completely your choice, but I can't go another day without you."

"Is that your way of saying you want to live together?"

She looked at my shoulder. "And can you even take care of me right now? Aren't you still recovering yourself?"

I could see the reluctance on her face, but thank God she wasn't fighting me on this. "We can recover together."

"I like that idea."

Taking her face in my hands, I brought my lips down to hers, tasting the salty tears. I needed this just as bad as she did.

Her eyelids fluttered closed, and she let out a yawn. "I think my pain meds are starting to kick in." She shifted to the side, inviting me to come closer. "Lay with me."

Ava lifted her head so I could slide my arm underneath. Very slowly, she tucked herself into my side. I laid completely still on the edge of the mattress, trying not to touch any of the wires connected to her body. She rested her head on my chest, and I closed my eyes and held her. I just wanted to block out the past few hours and never leave this bed. I wanted to shelter her and shield her from the hurt and the pain that would follow her once she left this hospital. I would use whatever strength I had to get her through these next few weeks. She had a long recovery ahead, but she was safe, and she was in my arms, where she would always stay. And for the first time in weeks, I was finally able to drift off to sleep.

THIRTY-THREE

AVA

It's been three months since the incident with Richard. My physical scars were almost gone, and my shoulder was healing nicely, thanks to some intense physical therapy. After finishing my last session this morning, I was ready to blow off some steam.

My mother, Amelia, and I spent the day at the spa and hit the mall for a little Christmas shopping. We pretty much wiped out a few stores, not caring one bit that we went a little overboard.

"Well, your house is still standing, so that's a good sign," Amelia joked as we walked up my snow-covered driveway. Our hands were loaded with packages. Now I remember why I preferred online shopping. One click and they were boxed up and delivered to your doorstep the next day.

"Don't jinx us. We haven't seen the inside yet," I reminded her, trying to balance all the bags in one hand. They were heavy and straining my fingers.

The guys wanted no part of this shopping trip, so we left them home with the kids. The only thing we could do was pray that everyone was in one piece when we returned.

"Are you sure you don't want me to store all these gifts for you?" my mom asked as I typed the code into the garage door panel. "I have plenty of space in the spare bedroom at my condo."

I smiled while ducking my head under the door as it went up. "Don't you have a guest visiting this weekend? Or is he not using the spare bedroom?"

Her face turned beet red as she turned it away from me. Amelia bumped my shoulder. "Be nice now."

My mother had recently met someone online. I thought she would struggle after Richard's death, but she admitted that she only felt relief that he couldn't hurt either one of us again. Greg was good for her. They had a lot of things in common, wanted to travel to the same places, and best of all, he doted on my mother. The only thing I didn't like was that he lived in Montana. At the speed at which these two were falling for each other, I wouldn't be surprised if they got engaged before I did.

"Did you and Logan work out a plan with Vanessa yet?" Amelia asked as we stuffed the bags into the trunk of my car and covered them with a blanket so the girls wouldn't see them. They already found a couple of small packages in my closet, so I had to get creative and find a new hiding spot. "Yes, Brina's going to spend Christmas Eve with us and Logan's family. We'll bring her home after dinner and pick her up after breakfast the next day."

"Sounds like Vanessa is being accommodating."

"I think Bryce has something to do with that." I made sure the bags were completely hidden and closed the trunk.

Vanessa met Bryce at the facility where she received

her treatment. He was one of the attending doctors on staff, although not hers. They started dating after she was released. I wasn't sure how serious they were because she and I still weren't the best of friends. But she wasn't slashing my tires, or throwing bricks through my window anymore, so that was progress.

I walked around Logan's truck, sitting on his side of the garage, and took my wet boots off on the mat. Sometimes, I still couldn't believe we lived together, but after the attack, I was grateful to have him here. The last thing I wanted was to be alone in the same house I was attacked in.

When we reached my kitchen, I groaned at all the candy, pizza boxes, and beer bottles taking up space on my countertop. We followed the sounds of raised voices into the dining room, where three grown men, along with their young daughters, sat at my table with a huge pile of poker chips in the middle.

"Are they teaching them to play poker?" I asked, glancing around at the men who at least had the decency to look guilty.

"They asked if we could teach them how to play," Marco said defensively.

"Really?" Amelia came up behind me. "Is this what you do when you're home watching Gia all day while I'm at the office?"

"C'mon." He took a sip of his beer and shot her that grin that usually got him out of trouble. "You're making me look bad. You know how hard I work during the day while you're off being a badass, running your own company."

Marco recently resigned from the police force so he could stay home with Gia. He wanted Amelia to focus on her career, and it wasn't like they needed the extra income. Amelia came from money, so they could be flexible with certain things. He still worked part-time doing private security, but at his own pace. The unconventional arrangement worked for them, and I had to admit, Marco was a really good dad.

"Whatever. It's obvious you're deflecting." She glanced over at the heaping pile of chips in front of Emery. "Apparently, I'm in the wrong profession." Her attention turned to Quinn. "Does your wife know your daughter is a card shark?"

He swung his arm along the back of her chair. "You know what they say. What happens at the poker table, stays at the poker table. Isn't that right, peanut?" He slanted his head to the side and winked at Emery.

"Dad said I'm his lucky charm and whatever we win, we'll split fifty-fifty."

"Aren't you just Dad of the Year." I folded my hands along the back of Brina's chair and leaned forward to glance at her cards.

"You're home early." Logan shot me a wink and stood up. "You must have kicked ass today at physical therapy."

I crossed my arms. "Don't even think about using that charm on me."

He strode toward me, cards in his hands and a grin on his stupid, handsome face. "Relax, we're helping the girls with their math skills."

My mother parked her hands on her hips. "Tell me how teaching them the difference between a flush and full house helps with their addition and subtraction?"

Marco threw his cards in the middle of the table. "I tried to tell him *Yahtzee* would have been a better choice."

"What were you thinking?" I asked the men at the table

while the girls scooped up the chips when their fathers weren't looking.

Logan cupped my face in his hands and gave me a soft kiss. "We were just having a little fun. How was your shopping day?"

"Fine, but judging by your nonexistent pile of chips, I'm worried we won't be able to pay the credit card bill next month."

He pulled me into his arms, and instinctively, I laid my head against his chest. "We could always ask the girls for a loan."

Amelia shook her head and lifted Gia out of her bouncy seat. "Playtime is over. We have to be at your mom's for dinner in an hour."

Quinn cleared his throat. "We should probably get going too."

We said our goodbyes and sent the girls up to their room. I started cleaning up the kitchen when the doorbell rang. Someone must have forgotten something. I raced over to answer it, surprised to see Luke.

"Hey, I didn't know you were stopping by. Come on in." I started to walk away but stopped when I noticed he was frozen in the doorway.

"I got your letter." Luke's eyes were trained on me. They were brimming with unshed tears.

I blinked in confusion. "What letter?"

He grabbed a white envelope out of his back pocket. I recognized the hospital logo right away. "Oh, my God." I sucked in a breath. "It was you?"

My shoulders started to shake, and a sob broke through my chest at that sudden realization.

Logan caught me before I hit the ground. His brows knitted together like he was trying to work out a puzzle piece in his head. "Would one of you mind filling me in?"

Luke took a cautious step forward. "I received a letter today from my donor family." A tear dripped down my cheek, and another one soon followed. "His wife sent me a letter. She wanted to stay anonymous, but wanted me to know her husband's name. His name was Drew, and they met in college." My mouth parted on a whimper. "She told me about his family and how much he loved his little girl. She mentioned his hobbies, even listed his favorite foods." He smiled gently and moved his gaze to his brother. "She told me that she was finally strong enough to reach out to me and share her story. She had found love again with a great man that Drew would have approved of. She wanted to move on and let go of the past. It was her way of finally saying goodbye."

I felt an overwhelming sense of guilt and closure when I handed the letter over to the transplant coordinator at the hospital. I thought I was finally putting that piece of my past behind me. Never in a million years did I think Luke was the recipient who received my husband's heart. Looking at him now felt like I was seeing him for the first time.

"Ava." Luke hesitated before reaching for my hand. "I am just as shocked as you are."

I moved quickly, gathering him in my arms, and sobbed. Relief, gratitude, and loss all swirled inside me. I clutched on to Luke, feeling my throat swell with affection. There was always this strange connection I felt toward him. Now I understood why.

Luke brushed the hair off of my face and wiped my eyes. "You are a brave, strong woman." His own tears started to fall. "My family and I will be forever grateful for your sacrifice. I will honor this heart. I will cherish this gift until it no longer beats. There will never be a day where I won't remember Drew."

I placed my trembling hand on his chest and closed my eyes. His heart was pounding, and for the first time since Drew's death, it felt like he was here with me. I didn't feel the familiar pain or loss. Instead, my soul felt at peace.

"I can never thank you enough." His voice sounded so small as he shook his head, overcome with emotion.

Slowly, I lifted my gaze to Logan's. The expression on his face broke something inside of me. His eyes were cast down to the ground; I couldn't quite read him, but it didn't look good. His shoulders looked deflated, like he was worried this would somehow change things between us. My stomach pinched with worry. Did he think that this would somehow make me love him any less? It only made me love him even more. If this wasn't a sign that fate put us together, I don't know what was.

I swiped a hand across my cheek and rested it against Luke's beating heart. My husband's heart. This was my chance to say goodbye. "Thank you for loving me." I closed my eyes and smiled. "You gave me a good life, but now it's time to say goodbye." A new wave of tears sprung free, but they weren't sad. There was solace in the fact that there was a part of him that would live on. His big, beautiful heart was giving life and breath to someone else. It saved a son, a brother, a friend, and so much more. Now, it was time for that heart to go on and beat for someone else.

Logan's gaze was turned away. He was still unable to meet my eyes.

I moved my hand up to Luke's cheek. "You're right, you have a gift. That's what they call it, the gift of life." I allowed myself a minute to get my emotions under control. "Don't waste it. Find the right person to share this with."

He nodded and brushed his lips to my forehead. "I'm going to give you both some privacy." He turned and placed a hand on Logan's shoulder. "I know this is a lot to wrap your head around. This doesn't have to change anything. Things don't have to be weird."

There was a thick, heavy silence filling the room as we watched his brother leave. I squeezed my eyes shut, allowing myself a minute to collect my thoughts.

The door clicked shut, and I turned my focus to Logan. I approached him with slow steps, never taking my eyes off of him. I studied his face carefully, trying to figure out how to calm his fears.

"I need you to understand something." I reached for his hand and closed my eyes when his thumb rubbed over the top of it. "I loved Drew, I really did, but I'm no longer in love with him. I haven't been for a long time." I inhaled slowly. "Our love was sweet and steady, but our ending was cut short. There will always be a hole in my heart that he left behind, but you fill up the parts that matter." His eyes locked on mine. "I might have been his forever, but he wasn't mine." He brushed a lock of hair away from my face. "Writing that letter was my way of saying goodbye. Your brother may have Drew's heart inside his chest, but yours is the only one I want."

He pressed his forehead to mine, and I could feel his sense of relief. "I'm sorry that you feel the need to reassure me. This news is a lot to take in. I freaked out for a moment. Only because you hold so much power over me, Ava. I don't think you realize how deep my love for you flows." He shook his head. "For a split second I felt you slipping away from me, and I just wanted to pull you back." His voice was strained and conflicted. "I was afraid that this would somehow come between us. I know it's stupid, but it seemed like we had finally moved forward and I love you too much, the thought of going backward…"

"Shh…" I placed a finger over his lips. "We are not going backward."

He dropped his face into my neck. "Now I feel like an asshole. Luke has wanted to meet his donor family since the second he opened his eyes after the surgery. I took that joy away from him."

I played with the hair on the back of his neck. "I'm glad it was him. I can't think of anyone more deserving."

"You can trust him to take care of that heart." He placed a tender kiss on my forehead. "I promise."

I let out a sigh of relief. "Taking Drew off the ventilator was the hardest thing I've ever done, but knowing I saved your brother's life takes some of that pain away."

He leaned back and studied me. "So, we're good?"

"One hundred percent." I smiled up at him. "I want this to officially be the end of this chapter. It's time to start a new one. Together."

EPILOGUE
LOGAN

EIGHT MONTHS LATER

"AVA, WHAT DO YOU THINK YOU'RE DOING?" I ASKED, standing over the top of her as she lay splayed across the back of the boat.

Her hand flew to her chest, which caused her phone to fall on the floor. "Jesus. You scared me."

I bent down and noticed the Kindle app open. Holding it up out of reach, I gave her a stern look. "I am so disappointed in you right now."

She rolled her eyes and tried to snatch the phone out of my hands, but I wasn't having it. "I don't think so, sweetheart. We had a deal."

Ava pushed herself up to a sitting position. My eyes landed on the fishing pole that was resting along the back of the seat. "That's supposed to be in the water," I pointed out, trying to act like I don't find this whole thing amusing.

"You fell asleep. I was bored, because news flash"—she threw her hands out to the side—"this is boring!"

"I thought I could trust you, but clearly I can't. I rested my eyes for ten minutes."

"Right." She batted her eyelashes. "You looked so peaceful, I didn't want to disturb you."

I tucked her phone in the pocket of my swim trunks—another boat whipped by, causing ours to rock slightly. I held out my hand. "How about we take a break and have some lunch."

She placed her palm in mine so I could pull her up. "That's the best idea you had all day." She looked relieved as she glanced around Mirror Lake. My parents rented the same camp as they did last summer. Ava and I made a compromise. We each got to pick one trip a year. So, in February, we took the girls to Disney World and then spent a couple of days on the beach. And this trip was mine, although it would be a lot more enjoyable if she weren't so grumpy about fishing.

"What is all this?" she asked as I lifted the lid off the cooler. I laid the cheese, nuts, crackers, and olives carefully along the small white table. My hands shook as I reached for the bottle of champagne under the ice.

"I have something for you." My heart pounded in my chest as I reached into my pocket. I handed her the fishing lure I had personalized.

Her eyes traced over every word, and then she slowly looked up to me. The lure was in the shape of a heart. On the front, it read, *I'm ready to be one less fish in the sea,* and on the back, it said, *Will you marry me?*

Tears blurred her vision. "Logan," she whispered but stayed utterly still.

"Ava, I wasn't fishing for love, but I'm so glad you swam to me. Will you to take bait and be my hook of a life-time? Be my biggest catch?"

Her eyes widened. "Is this seriously my proposal?"

I reached into my back pocket and pulled out a black box. "Well, when you put it like that." I got down on one knee.

Her breath caught as tears rolled down her cheeks. I took the ring out of the box and held it up.

"Ava Donavon. I've loved you from the moment I first laid eyes on you. You weren't mine at the time, so I waited. Honestly, I would wait a lifetime for you." I blew out a breath. "I've grown to love everything about you. I love how you cheat at game night, and I love how you constantly remind me to put my dirty clothes in the hamper. I love how you steal my pillow every night and fight with me over the temperature on the thermostat." We both laughed, but she cupped my face, urging me to continue. "If you say yes, I promise to always let you win so you'll never have to cheat at *Yahtzee* again. I promise to never leave another dirty sock on the floor. I promise to buy you your own pillow so you won't have to take mine. I promise to cover you with extra blankets on the nights when you complain it's too cold."

I gave her a crooked smile, trying to fight the tears that stung my eyes. "If you say yes, I promise that you'll never feel alone. I promise to fill your days with laughter. I promise to reach for your hand every night before we drift off to sleep. I promise to be patient and understanding, especially when you need it the most. I promise to always put your needs above my own." I swallowed deeply. "I promise to love you until I take my last breath. Will you please say yes to spending a lifetime together as my wife? Will you marry me?"

Her smile was blinding, but it was hard not to notice the love shining in her warm brown eyes. "Yes, Logan. My answer is yes." She placed her hand in mine. "I would be honored to be your wife."

My hands were shaking as I slipped the ring onto her finger. I wanted to remember this moment for the rest of my life. It felt like everything I'd been searching for was standing right in front of me. Every missing piece of my soul was finally in its place. She threw her arms around my neck and planted her lips on mine. I cradled her face in my hands and poured all my love into our kiss. My heart was full, and I knew right then and there that I would spend the rest of my days loving her.

She brought her hand up to my chest and held my eyes. "I convinced myself that I would never find happiness again. I would have been fine on my own, but I'm glad I don't have to be just fine. I'm glad I get to share this life with you. You are the best thing that's ever happened to me." She closed her eyes and brushed her nose against mine. When she opened them, the tears kept coming. "For the rest of my life, I will spend every day loving you. I will love you harder than anyone ever has."

Our mouths met in a kiss. It was soft and slow and filled with so much promise.

"I can't believe you're going to be mine, forever." I reached for the champagne and started to pour it into the plastic flute glasses. Her hand shot out, and I paused.

"No champagne for me."

She looked nervous. Very nervous. She bit down on her bottom lip, and I set the bottle aside.

"Is there something you want to tell me?" I swallowed hard and tried not to get my hopes up.

"I'm pregnant."

My eyes fell to her stomach. "You're sure?"

I noticed that she seemed a little off lately, but I assumed she was just preoccupied with making sure we had everything we needed for this trip.

She shook her head. "I went to the doctor this week to confirm, and they did an ultrasound." Her fingers toyed with the collar on my shirt. "I know this is unexpected, but I'm happy about it."

I lifted her up and spun her around, peppering kisses along her face. "God, I love you. I can't believe this." I laughed. "This the best day of my life." I took a moment and just held her. I never wanted to let her go. "So, what do we do now?" I slid her down my chest and looked around, still trying to process this. "Do we eat lunch, or bring the boat back and tell my parents and the girls first?"

"It's up to you, Daddy."

I shook my head. "I can't believe we're having a kid. Do you think it's a boy? I mean, I don't care, but it would be nice to not feel outnumbered all the time."

"Oh, I'm pretty sure there is a good chance at least one of them is a boy."

"Good, I just want a healthy baby, and I'll be happy either way, but a boy would be..." I stopped, stared, and blinked. "What do you mean *one* of them?"

"Surprise! We're having twins."

"Holy shit!"

I hope you enjoyed reading Logan and Ava's story. I know you have many other books to choose from. Thanks for taking the time to read mine. If you could kindly leave a brief review, it would greatly appreciate.

I'd love to stay in touch and invite you to visit my website.

sjonesauthor.com

Or Scan:

ALSO BY S. JONES

THE HARD SERIES

Hard to Love (Chase & Emily)

Hard to Stay (Brad & Lexi)

Hard to Leave (Jack & Chloe)

THE PROTECTIVE SERIES

Whatever It Takes (Quinn & Charlotte)

Whatever You Need (Marco &Amelia)

Whatever You Want (Logan & Ava)

THE ATLANTA ARROWS SERIES

Fumbled Love (Maverick & Kinley)

Fumbled Beginning (JP & Rylee)

Fumbled Arrangement (Rhett and Natalie)

ABOUT THE AUTHOR

S. Jones is a contemporary romance author from Upstate New York. She has a strong passion for writing and reading stories that will rip your heart out before it's put back together again.

If she's not buried in her writing cave, she's usually reading or planning out her next vacation.

She loves to travel to different places and spends all her free with her husband, and two college age children.

When the weather permits, you can find her outside walking her golden retriever, or enjoying a nice cocktail by the pool. She loves cooking and entertaining for her family and friends.

When she's not holding a glass of wine in one hand and her kindle in the other, she loves to hear from her readers at:

authorsjoneswrites@gmail.com

THANK YOU

A quick thank you to Carolina Leon, the best PA (or should I say Boss Lady) around. I appreciate all you do for me. To the authors and bloggers that I've met along the way, thank you for answering all my questions and for always being there. Virginia and Marla, you both polish up the mess I send to you and make it readable. You both rock! To my Sassy Readers, I love you guys so hard. You guys make me smile, and my favorite part of the day is hanging out with you. Thank you for your support and your encouragement.

Finally, thanks to my husband, who is my biggest supporter and never complains when the house is a mess or when there's nothing to eat in the house. To my children, I love you more than words could ever say.

9 781737 088769